THE SINNER

MICHAEL BRAY

Copyright © 2025 by Michael Bray
All rights reserved.

No part of this publication may be reproduced, distributed, or transmitted in any form or by any means, including photocopying, recording, or other electronic or mechanical methods, without the prior written permission of the publisher, except as permitted by U.S. copyright law.

The story, all names, characters, and incidents portrayed in this production are fictitious. No identification with actual persons (living or deceased), places, buildings, and products is intended or should be inferred.

First edition 2025

CONNECT WITH THE AUTHOR AT:

f MICHAELBRAYAUTHOR   @ MICHAELBRAYAUTHOR
X @MICHAELBRAUAUTH   d @MICHAEL_BRAY_AUTHOR
◉ @MICHAELBRAYAUTHOR   ✉ DARKCORNERSBOOK@GMAIL.COM

WWW.MICHAELBRAYAUTHOR.NET

October 9th, 2017

THE END OF A LIFE

It isn't true that a person's life flashes before their eyes before they die.

There was time for Mary Jordan to register the thought as the car snapped away from her and lost grip on the road surface. There had been warnings on the radio of black ice, but so far, she had experienced none of it as she snaked the car through the Cumbrian hills, and as her confidence had grown, so had her speed.

During daylight hours, the hills would be a spectacular display of natural dips and valleys of green, untouched by man and breathtaking in their beauty. Now, at night, they were inky masses on either side of a road illuminated only by her car headlights. The snap happened without warning, her stomach plunging as she felt the rear of the car slide away from her. Mary was an experienced driver and knew what to do.

Turn into the slide, ease off the brakes and try to get back in control.

The first part she did, turning the car in the same direction the rear wanted to go, and as expected, the car gripped the road, the brief second of relief gone as fast as it had arrived.

The Truck.

It was coming around the blind bend, the white glow of headlights foretelling its arrival.

There was no blame on the driver. He was minding his own

business, delivering canned goods to a local depot, his mind already turning towards heading home to catch the second half of the football game.

Headlights on her now and blinding, putting a spotlight on the consequences of her stupid mistake.

The tires had bitten at the wrong time and she was pointing towards oblivion, the black husks of countryside like the maw of some immense beast waiting for her.

The Truck loomed large, chrome blocking out the opaque night, headlights causing a kaleidoscope of colour against the rain-streaked windscreen.

Impact.

The truck obliterated her Mazda, windows imploding, sleet and glass slamming into her face.

Two tastes in quick succession. Sweet fear, followed by bitter blood.

A weightless moment before gravity dragged the car back towards earth, tumbling and spinning to rest seventy feet down the drop. There was no white light. Just a final pulse from a dying brain.

She thought of her children, and the awful truth she had always planned to tell them and now would never get the chance.

An inferno ignited the dark as the frantic truck driver looked on from the hole in the barrier, hands shaking as he fished out his phone to call for help.

This is the story of the end of a life.

October 18th 2017

A FUNERAL

Dan Jordan had received over a dozen commiserations so far. Distant relative was taking on a whole new meaning as he looked at the room full of strangers who had converged at the family home. He sat in the corner, trying to blend into the large bookcase at his back, swilling a double bourbon as the clock ticked on. He wondered when they'd finally go. They would probably stay until all the food and drinks were gone. Looking at his glass, he realised he could assist them with that, at the very least, and took another sip.

As he watched the mourners pick at the spread of dips and sandwiches as they discussed the life of the deceased like wretched buzzards, he tried to think of a time any of them had visited the house when his mother had been alive. He couldn't place a single one of them, which was sending him towards that dangerous place where alcohol and anger combust into something unpleasant.

His plan to stay inconspicuous looked like it might work until his Uncle Herbert – who he had last seen when he was seven years old - made eye contact and crossed the room, expression a carefully constructed mask of sympathy. He held out his arms, pulling Dan into an embrace he didn't want and giving him a nose full of overpowering aftershave. Herbert was a big man with huge jowls and thinning black hair. Dan could see the hair dye stains on his scalp. Beneath the cheap aftershave, Dan could smell the faint aroma of old sweat.

'Dan, I'm so sorry. Your mother was a good person. To die like that was...' he trailed off and shook his head, taking a drink instead of finishing the thought as he dipped into the book of mourner clichés.

Dan heard himself respond, his mouth working on autopilot as he went through the motions of the things he had been saying all afternoon.

Yes, Uncle Herbert, I'm fine.

No, we didn't expect it either.

Yes, I'm sure she would be proud of the turnout.

No, I don't suppose she would want us to dwell on it.

Small talk exhausted. An awkward silence fell between the two. Herbert made a point of noticing his glass was empty, and disappeared back into the throng to find a refill. Dan watched him go, then looked at his own glass, no longer thirsty. He wondered why it took a death to bring the hangers on creeping out of the woodwork to see what they could get.

Dan spotted his Great Aunt Sheila making a beeline for him, all cheap jewellery and makeup applied with a trowel. Like Herbert before her, she too was wearing the insincere expression of sympathy. Before Dan could brace himself for another similar conversation, a stranger intercepted Sheila. The two knew each other, though, as they shared a laugh which earned them enough disapproving glances to talk in more hushed tones.

'Weird, isn't it?'

'It's a load of bollocks,' he said, as his sister perched on the sofa beside him. 'None of these people care. They're here to see what they can get. It's a joke.'

Rebecca nodded and sipped her wine as they watched the congregation. 'It's how people mourn, I suppose. Everyone is different.'

'I want them to leave us alone. Today has been hard enough.'

Rebecca was tall and slender, eyes a deep blue to his dull

brown, her hair golden and hip length to his shapeless crew cut. Where Dan had a prominent jaw and hooked nose, Rebecca had sharp cheekbones and the delicate features of a pixie. Where she was fiery and impulsive, he was calm and considered. They were so different, yet so alike. 'How are you coping?' She asked.

'I hate this.'

'That's not what I asked. I wanted to know how you're coping.'

'Not good. I could understand if she had been ill or something. To go out like this feels unfair.'

'That's the worst part of it. I went into her room the other day and couldn't stay. It's like she was due back any second. Her empty coffee cup was by the bed, her clothes for work hung on the wardrobe door. It's so surreal.'

Dan stared into his glass. 'You know what I keep doing?'

'What?'

He glanced at her, then looked back at his drink. 'I keep looking at the last text I sent her. It's all so normal. I was asking her if she had any ideas for your birthday and she replied she'd talk to me about it when she got back. I didn't even reply to her.'

He wiped his eyes and turned away so she couldn't see him crying.

'I get where you're coming from. A couple of weeks ago we were a family, now it's just us. It will take time to adapt.'

'Look at them, Becks, eating and drinking like locusts. What are the odds we never see or hear from them again once their bellies are full?'

'They have every right to mourn their own way.'

'They're parasites.' He said, loud enough to draw a few glances from the room.

'They're upset.'

Dan swallowed what remained in his glass and set it down on the side. 'I'm sorry. I'm not handling this too well, am I?'

'There's no wrong way to grieve. I know one thing. She'd give you hell for sitting here feeling sorry for yourself. I can see it now. Her giving you *the look*.'

That raised a smile, followed by a laugh. 'Yeah, you're right. God, I remember *the look* well. You knew you'd fucked up if you got that glare. Remember when we went to get those tattoos, and we'd been gone all day and hadn't let her know?'

Rebecca grinned as she recalled the memory. 'Oh yeah. We were so worried that she would go crazy with us, but she shrugged it off and told us they were our bodies to do what we wanted with.'

'Yeah, I remember. God, was that only two years ago?' Dan said, the laugh fading away.

Rebecca nodded. 'Yeah. It's like a different lifetime now.'

'Thanks for this,' Dan said.

'For what?'

'Having a normal conversation.'

Rebecca leaned over, nudging his shoulder with hers. 'We've got to stick together. We only have each other.'

Dan nodded. 'It feels like so many things are still unanswered. What do we do about the house? Are there still things we need to do or arrange? Do we try to track down Dad again?'

'No, we don't. It's obvious he doesn't want to be found.'

'Yeah, but-'

'Remember last time? We tracked him down to that little town outside Manchester? He said we had too much baggage, the prick. We don't owe him a fucking thing.'

Dan nodded. 'I'll give you that, but he has a right to know Mum died.'

'No. He lost all rights to that when he walked out on us. Besides, nobody even knows where he is. Forget about him. It's about the two of us now.'

Rebecca looked at the man who was standing beside them, waiting for a gap in the conversation so he could interject.

'Hi, can I help you?'

The man's cheek twitched, as if he had considered smiling, then realised the setting wasn't appropriate. 'I'm looking for Daniel and Rebecca Jordan.'

'That's us,' Rebecca said.

'My name is Barnes. I was hoping to speak to you regarding your mother's estate.'

Barnes had no real distinguishable features. He had one of those neutral faces that would be hard to pick out in a crowd. The only slight distinction was the bulbous quality to his nose, and, much like uncle Herbert, a comb over designed to hide the fact that the hair that once lived underneath was gone for good.

'Robert Goldman is looking after that side of things. I don't think this is the time to discuss it. We only got back from the funeral a couple of hours ago.' Rebecca said.

'My apologies. I'm more than aware that Goldman and Goldman are overseeing the bulk of the proceedings. This is an unrelated matter and one of some urgency.'

Rebecca glanced at her brother, who was struggling to keep his temper under control. 'Still, this isn't a good time. Can I ask who sent you?'

This time, Barnes did smile, a slight gesture as if he had remembered a private joke intended for him. 'Actually, I'm here under instruction from Mrs Jordan to contact you in the event of her demise.'

Barnes held out a white card with his number embossed on the front in gold. 'I wonder if the two of you might come to my office when convenient?'

Dan looked at the card. The paper grade felt expensive. 'There's no address on here.'

Barnes shifted position and cleared this throat. 'No, we have moved to a new office and are waiting for new cards.' Realising this was irrelevant, he cleared this throat again. 'Please, call the number when you are free. It's a direct line for my secretary. She will give you directions to the office and book an appointment.'

Rebecca took the card from Dan and ran her fingers across the surface. 'Can you tell us what this is about?'

'Sadly not. Your mother left very specific instructions. Please schedule a meeting at your convenience. This isn't a time sensitive matter, but is important.'

'Okay, Mr Barnes, thank you. We'll call you in a few days.' Rebecca said, shaking his hand. Barnes extended the handshake to Dan, but he refused the offering. Point made; he withdrew his hand.

'I look forward to hearing from you. My sincere condolences for your loss.'

They watched Barnes leave, weaving through the milling crowd towards the exit.

'What do you suppose that was about?' Dan said.

'I don't know, but he seemed keen to speak to us.'

'Great, just when this day was already the drizzling shits.'

Rebecca slapped him on the leg and stood.

'All right. Come on, let's mingle with the relatives. We won't likely see them ever again after this.'

Without letting him argue his way out, Rebecca dragged him by the arm into the crowd where Aunt Sheila, who he had avoided earlier, got them both this time.

A WASHED-UP OLD BASTARD

Robbins picked at the bland ready meal with his fork, unable to muster the desire to finish eating. The packaging said it was some kind of casserole, but the brown soupy mess looked more how it should be on the way out rather than the way in. With that thought killing the little appetite he had, he set the plate aside on the small table beside his chair. One thing he was aware of more than anything in the years since he had retired is that television, the stuff on during the day, at least, was awful. He flicked through a few channels hoping to find something worth watching then gave up, turning off the TV and tossing the remote next to the uneaten ready meal. He scratched his head, fingers gliding between what little wisps of hair remained and wondered what he was going to do with the rest of his day.

Four decades of climbing the ranks to detective had afforded him a comfortable home and financial security, but ironically, the sacrifices along the way had cost him what he now valued most. His wife found being married to a detective frustrating, lonely, and ultimately, it destroyed their marriage. It had never occurred to him when he was in the job, on that relentless climb to the next rung of the ladder – there was no time for that. His days bled into nights, a constant cycle of chasing leads and awaiting crucial information that might finally solve the case, long after his shift ended. Being immersed in police work made it hard to grasp what was happening elsewhere. Now, on the other side of it, there had been plenty of time to reflect on the idea that he had been a shitty husband. When he sat and thought about things - the number of missed dinners and broken promises he had subjected his now ex-wife to over the years - the only shock to him was why she didn't leave him sooner than she did. It had been the realisation and guilt of this revelation which caused him not to put up a fight when she filed for divorce. He tried his best to make it easy for her. In his eyes, she had already suffered enough over the years. The worst part about it was that he still loved her, not that he could ever say that now. The situation was beyond repair. It was right to let her go.

As the crushing pain of reminiscing gnawed deep in his gut, he looked around the room at the mantle full of photographs. Him and Sandy in happier times, his hair thick and black instead of the wispy scatter it had become. Blue eyes sharp as opposed to dull from a lifetime of stress and seeing horrors no man should see.

The vibration of his mobile phone broke his morbid train of thought. Only one person ever called him (apart from the handful of calls a week from strangers trying to sell him things he had no use for). He answered, lifting the outdated Samsung to his ear.

'Sandy. I was thinking about you.'

'Nothing bad, I hope.'

'No, not at all, thinking about the past. I sometimes wonder where the damn time goes.' She was silent for a second, and he wished he had led with something less on the nose.

'You need to get out more. Moping around that place isn't good for you.'

As if it were that easy. How could he tell her he had nowhere to go and nobody to go with? The friends he had when he was a detective were still active and too busy to be available. It was the ultimate irony he had become to them the same thing he had been to his wife, a lonely ghost wandering around the house, hoping for something to break the boredom.

'Alexander? Are you there?'

'Yeah, sorry.' He muttered. She was the only one who called him Alexander. To everyone else, he was Alex or Al. Never to her, though. To her, he was Alexander and always had been.

'Well, I'm calling to tell you I won't be around for a couple of weeks and I didn't want you to worry.'

'Why won't you be around?' There it was. That brief flash of the detective instinct, the curiosity that even age couldn't take from him.

'Bill is taking me on a cruise. Mediterranean.'

'Another one? Didn't you go on a cruise a few months back?' It was hard to hide the bitterness. Harder still to hide the hint of jealousy. Not only was he miserable, he hated how easily she had moved on to better things. Bill with his successful business and thick head of hair. Bill who would never have to drag the corpse of a half-frozen prostitute with her brains caved in out of the gutter at three in the morning in the dead of winter. Fucking Bill, who didn't know how lucky he was.

'We did. Now we're going again.' she was pissed off. He could hear it in her voice. You don't spend almost thirty years with someone, even if things didn't work out, without knowing the signs.

'I meant nothing by it. I'm just saying it wasn't too long since the last one.'

Silence. That meant he had *really* fucked it up. 'Sorry, Sandy. It's one of those days, that's all.'

Just like that, the situation diffused, and both of them lost their anger.

'Take care of yourself, okay? I worry about you. It's not healthy to spend so much time alone.'

He thought about that. Him with his misery and ready meals. Sandy and Bill, soaking up the sun under blue skies.

'I'm fine, don't worry.'

When Sandy next spoke, it was cautious and probing.

'I was speaking to Jill last week. Perhaps you two could reconnect.'

Pain and shame caught in his throat.

'It's been so long now, I wouldn't know what to say.'

He could imagine Sandy's reaction, the image clear in his mind. She would be at the kitchen counter in the extravagant house Bill owned, a cigarette hanging from her fingers, phone nestled in the crook of her shoulder as she drank her coffee with her free hand.

'Alexander, are you there?' Sandy asked.

'Sorry, yeah, I'm here.'

'I was saying the two of you need to put this aside and reconnect. You're as stubborn as each other.'

'You know how things ended between us. She made her feelings clear.'

'And so did you. One of you needs to make the first move.'

'She knows where I am if she wants to talk.'

'Still, I think-'

'Damn it, Sandy, can you drop it?' He knew he had messed up, as there was the silence again. The sound of disappointment. 'Look, Sandy, I'm sorry. This is a sore subject, that's all. I didn't mean to snap.'

'It's fine. It's none of my business, anyway.'

There it is. The note of frustration he remembered from the past when she was unhappy with something he had said or done, or when he'd call to say he wouldn't be able to make another meal or to break plans because work had got in the way.

'Sandy…'

'No. You've made your point. All I was going to say was you have a grandchild you've never met. Surely that's enough to set your stubbornness aside and reach out.'

'And like I said, she knows where I am if she wants to talk.'

Sandy sighed. 'Fine. Like I said, I'm keeping out of it. I wanted to tell you I'd be away for a few weeks, so you didn't worry. I'll call you when I get back.'

There was no time to plan an answer. The line was dead in his ear. Robbins put his phone on the table beside his chair and listened to the silence of the house.

He had never felt so alone.

October 24th 2017

THE REVELATION

His office didn't reflect the lavishness implied by Barnes's expensive business cards. It was a nondescript glass fronted building sandwiched between a Chinese takeaway and a chemist. The location wasn't good, almost lower class, the street front littered with swirling, discarded crisp packets and food wrappers. When they arrived, dour off-white walls, fake potted plants in need of a run over with a duster had greeted Dan and Rebecca. It didn't look like somewhere their mother would do business with, which added to the mystery.

As bland and uninviting as it was outside and waiting area were, Barnes's office screamed high end. All plush leather and expensive oak. There was a faint smell of age and polish which, even if artificial, matched the aesthetic in the most perfect way possible. Dan and Rebecca sat on one side of the desk with Barnes on the other. Here in his natural habitat, Barnes appeared much more comfortable. He cut something of an imposing figure, hands folded on the desk, nails manicured. 'Thank you both for coming. I appreciate this is a troublesome time for you.'

'What is this about?' Rebecca asked.

Barnes took two envelopes from his drawer and slid them across the desk.

'Your Mother left instructions that, in the untimely event of her death, I should disclose certain information to the two of you.'

'What kind of information?' Dan asked as he scanned the envelope.

'This matter relates to your father.'

Rebecca glanced at Dan, then back to Barnes. 'There must be a mistake. We have no contact with our father, at least not since he and my mother divorced fifteen years ago. The split wasn't amicable, and I'd be surprised if she wanted anything to do with—'

Barnes raised a hand to stop her.

'Please, let me explain. This is a complicated situation.'

'Whatever it is, just tell us, Mr Barnes. Mum always said it was best to rip the plaster straight off rather than peel it away slowly.' Dan said.

'Very well. Derek Jordan is not your father.'

Silence swallowed the room, the only sound coming from the ornate clock behind Barnes's desk. Brother and sister glance at each other with identical expressions of confusion.

Rebecca was the first to break the silence. 'I don't understand. What do you mean, he's not our father? He's not in our lives now, but we have memories. Days out at the beach, opening gifts on Christmas Day. There are photos. What you're saying makes no sense.'

Dan was taking this all in. He was opening and closing his fists as he listened.

Barnes shifted position. 'Yes, well, this is where things become more complicated. Your mother believed that keeping this information from you was in your best interests. It was to be made clear to you if this day ever came that her decision not to disclose this information was to protect you.'

'Protect us from what?' Dan said.

'Derek Jordan raised you as his own, but you are not his biological children.'

That blanket of silence enveloped the room again. The clock

was ticking, but neither Dan nor Rebecca could hear it. They were too busy trying to process. Barnes, it seemed, wanted this portion of the meeting to be over, and so he went on, determined to get everything out and on the table rather than drip feed.

'Prior to meeting Derek, your mother had a relationship with another man that ended in difficult circumstances. To protect you, they hid your father's identity after the relationship ended because of safety concerns.'

'Protect us from what?' Rebecca said, glancing at her brother, who was stone faced as he watched Barnes.

'Think of my involvement as a contingency plan put in place by your mother so that, if anything should happen to her, the two of you would be told the truth. The trigger to initiate contact was, unfortunately, the passing of Mrs Jordan.'

'What could have been so bad for our mother to go to these lengths to hide it?' Rebecca asked.

'Stop stalling, Mr Barnes. Who is he? Who is our father?' Dan said, his patience razor thin, eyes bulging.

Barnes opened his desk drawer and took out a photograph, which he placed on the desk so they could see it. The photograph was of a man, bald with a greying beard down to his chest, skin tanned and cracked like old leather. From within, cold dark eyes stared out.

Dan snorted a laugh. Not because it was funny. It wasn't a million miles away from being a scream. 'Is this a joke?' he managed, looking from Barnes to the photo and back.

Rebecca remained silent. She had yet to take her eyes off the photograph.

Barnes folded his hands on the tabletop. 'I appreciate this is difficult. Can I assume by your reactions you know who this man is?'

It was a photo they had seen before. An image used for countless true crime documentaries and books, even for a twisted adult colouring book, converted into white spaces with thick black lines.

That was the thought that tipped Dan over the edge. He let out a sound, something between scream and laugh.

'Your birth father is James Warwick.'

'Fuck,' Dan muttered. If Barnes heard it, he didn't acknowledge it. He was in full flow now and showed no sign of stopping.

'I understand this is difficult to hear, however your mother's wishes were that you would be told the truth. As you can see, there was no easy way to deliver this to you. I apologise for the distress.'

Dan and Rebecca looked at each other, both knowing what the other was thinking in that mysterious way close siblings sometimes did.

'How did our mother become involved with this? It not her character at all.' Rebecca asked. She had composed herself now, and other than the slight tremble in her voice, she was refusing to show any emotion.

'I'm afraid she didn't provide that information.'

Dan shook his head. 'You're saying you don't know? It's not like we can fucking ask her about it now.'

'Hey, calm down,' Rebecca said, putting a hand on his arm. Dan pulled away.

Barnes, for his part, remained calm. It seemed this process – delivering tough news – was something he had done for a long time and he was good at it.

Dan leaned back in his seat and ran his hands through his hair. 'What do we do now, Becks?' he said, anger giving way to sorrow. She squeezed his forearm. He hadn't called her Becks for years, not since they were kids. It was clear he was struggling with this.

Barnes cleared his throat. 'Your mother limited the information she provided, as she had no wish for you to pursue this any further. She didn't want you to contact him. That was something she wanted to be made clear to you both.'

Silence swallowed the room again.

'So, what do we do now?' Rebecca asked.

'My advice, Miss Jordan, is that you and your brother go back to your lives. This information need not change your future. The full detailing of Mrs Jordan's wishes is in the envelopes I provided. My role is now at an end.'

Barnes folded his hands on his desk, his face becoming solemn. 'If I can give you both one last piece of advice. As tempting as it may be, as much as curiosity may eat away at you, under no circumstances should you consider making contact, for reasons which should be obvious, knowing what he did. Go home and forget if you can.'

The first part, they would do. The second would be more difficult to manage.

JUST ANOTHER DRIFTER

Amarillo, Texas, June 18th 1972

Glowing brilliant orange in the black summer night, the fire had dwindled to embers. Most of those present were drunk, high, or both. The enticing smell of weed, a gentle strum of a guitar. A joint was making its way around, each person taking a hit and passing it on. A blonde girl with bright eyes offered the man beside her a half-smoked joint, but he refused.

'You sure you don't want some? It's good stuff.' She said, slurring her words.

'No, not for me.' The man replied, taking the joint and passing it on around the line. The girl continued to look at him, his chiselled features and shoulder length hair lit by the glow of the fire.

'You look like Jim Morrison.' She blurted.

The man glanced at her and shrugged. 'I get that a lot. It's the hair.'

'It's the cheekbones.'

She laughed at herself, throwing her head back. The man stared into the glowing embers of the fire, declining to engage further.

'Hey, what's your name?' the girl asked.

This time, he turned his attention from the fire, eyes burning into hers instead. 'Would you believe it if I said it was Jim?'

The girl sipped her beer. 'I'd say you were full of shit. To look like him *and* have the same name is too weird.'

'Coincidence or not, it's true.' Jim said. He turned his attention back to the flames. 'This is how I look. I'm not changing because some famous guy looks the same.'

'Okay, take it easy.' She grabbed one of the beer bottles half buried in the sand beside her, popped off the cap and held it out towards him. 'Drink?'

The man held her gaze, taking the beer and sipping it without breaking eye contact.

'Gloria, if you wanted to know,' she said as he handed the beer back. Gloria was a popular girl, and had grown accustomed to brushing off advances of would-be suitors. The idea there was someone she was interested in and he wasn't playing the game made her all the more intrigued.

'So, what brings you here? This hardly seems like your kind of crowd.'

'Oh yeah? And what kind of crowd do you think I'd better fit?'

Gloria looked around the at the stoned and drunk teens. 'I'm unsure, but not this.'

'Buddy of mine talked me into coming. Figured I had nothing else to do, so here I am.'

'Here you are,' Gloria repeated, unable to figure him out. 'You know, you don't have to stay. Nobody would mind if you left.'

'Bored with my company already?'

'No, it's not that,' she blurted, knowing it was too forceful, too desperate. She felt the rush of embarrassment and tried her best to ride the wave and play it cool.

'I like the fire,' Jim said, staring into the hot embers.

Gloria sipped her beer. 'Stands to reason, looking like Morrison.' She sang a few warbled bars from the Doors classic, Light my Fire, then stopped when he didn't find it funny.

'You can lose yourself in the flames and see things if you look for long enough.'

'What things?'

'Depends what you are looking for. The past. The future. Life. Death. Love. Lust. Change.'

'Yeah, well, if there's one thing this world needs, it's change. It's a mess.'

He turned to face her. 'You're right, this world needs change. It needs to be awoken.'

Gloria shifted position, the world outside of Jim falling away. 'It's never going to happen. The government tells us what they want us to think and nobody ever questions it.'

Jim nodded. 'We need a revolution. A rebellion.'

Gloria laughed, then seeing Jim was serious, stopped. 'Alright, for argument's sake, what kind of rebellion do you think people like us could start? We've got no power. Who would listen to us?'

'You would have to force them to listen. Do something extreme to get their attention.'

Gloria shuffled, digging her bare feet into the sand. 'Oh yeah, like what?'

He stared into the flames, hair tousled by the breeze as he sought his answer amid the embers. Gloria was sure he would not answer at all when he turned to her, eyes alive with the flickering flames. 'I'd do what Hitler did.'

Gloria stifled her laugh when she realised he was serious. 'You'd start a war?'

'No, of course not. What I mean is, I would create something. An idea. Something people could get behind, something that would revolutionise the world.'

'Yeah, well, I'm not sure Hitler is the best role model.'

'I don't justify what he did, but the idea he had, the plan to make, in his mind, at least, the world a better place, has to be commended, doesn't it?'

Gloria shook her head. 'He was a lunatic who oversaw the murder of millions of people. Nothing about that was right or a good idea. Anyway, this is all getting a bit too political for me. It's bringing my mood down. Can we talk about something else?'

Jim sighed and turned back to the fire, losing interest in the conversation. 'You don't understand. Just forget it.'

She could sense the loss of interest, and even as the popular girl, she didn't like it, because for a reason she couldn't understand, this stranger captivated her, and she wanted to see where things might go.

'So, explain it,' she said, shuffling around to face him. 'Come on, I'm interested.' It was true, she was interested. She was also angry at his viewpoint and wanted to see how fiercely he was filling to fight for it. Jim sat for a moment, wondering if it was worth trying to explain. Eventually, he too shifted position, so that they were sitting pointing towards each other, the rest of the group forgotten.

'Hear me out,' he said, looking her in the eye, not wavering. 'History perceives Hitler to be the villain. Perpetrator of murder, ruthless in the slaughter of innocents as he took territory after territory through the world, right?'

Gloria nodded.

'When the war ended, and Hitler put a bullet in his own head, it was the victors wrote the history books.'

'What does that have to do with anything?'

'It means that those who won dictated how the story will be told. Have you ever heard the story of the War from a German perspective? Or a Japanese point of view?'

'No, I can't say I have.'

'You should look it up. Rather than a hate figure, his people loved Hitler, and he had unanimous support from the public. He reduced unemployment, and even when he expanded the German territory, his idea was to bring a more prosperous and safer world to his people. No other world leader had the guts to do it.'

'Wait, are you one of those Nazi supporters? If you are, I don't think we have anything else to talk about.'

Jim laughed, shaking his head.

'Of course not. What they did was horrific. What I'm getting at is the idea, not the execution. The concept is to make the world better by doing something so extreme that it will always be remembered. Hitler did it wrong. I would do it the right way.'

'And that's what you want? To dictate how people should live? What race is acceptable? Sounds pretty similar to me.'

'What I want is for the world to adopt a different way of thinking. To use their own minds, instead of following what they're told to do.'

'So do it. There is nothing to stop you. If you want that, then do it.'

Jim shook his head. 'Something like that needs a leader, a speaker who can get people to buy in. That's not me. I'm not good with people.'

'I wouldn't say that. We just met and I'm prepared to listen to anything you have to say.'

'I don't have the confidence.'

'Then you're no better than anyone else. If you want change, you better make it happen. If not, you may as well stay here brooding.'

Jim grinned then, a real grin. It was such a complete shift in character it caught her off guard. 'You say what you think, don't you?'

'Always have and always will. Now enough talk. Come on.'

'Where are we going?'

'Somewhere quiet.'

She grabbed him by the hand and dragged him to his feet, leading him away from the campfire to the darkness of the surrounding sand dunes.

AGAINST BETTER JUDGEMENT

Weeks passed, but the house felt empty and hopeless without their mother. The mourners and well-wishers had gone back to their lives, and the death of Mary Jordan was forgotten. For Dan and Rebecca, the wounds of her death were still raw and open, made worse by what they had learned from Barnes.

Sorting their mother's belongings—a simple chore—uncovered a wealth of memories; every item, even the most commonplace, held profound significance.

Rebecca had sorted Mary's clothes into boxes to give to charity, apart from a red scarf which she kept for herself. Dan couldn't face doing anything so personal. To him, those items were still hers, and he felt wrong preparing them for disposal. He was finding the burden of death harder to bear than his sister, and so was instead sitting at the kitchen table going through another box of letters and paperwork from her office, trying to put together a list of places which still needed to be notified of her passing. Other items were being discarded. As Dan stuffed an old yellowed Christmas card from Uncle Jimmy into the black bag of things to be thrown away, he found it odd by how easily the contents of a person's life could be reduced down to such small amounts of inconsequential matter. The things that needed to be settled, such as outstanding bills were his responsibility. It was easier to deal with these less personal items. He had fallen into a rhythm of sorting the material into piles for either storage, to be dealt with (those bills will need to be paid, even if the payee was a pile of ashes in an urn) or disposal. His stomach grumbled, demanding sustenance. He was about to call through to the other room to ask

Rebecca if she wanted a sandwich when something in the box caught his eye. It was a diary. It had a burgundy velvet like covering which over the years had worn away, leaving black clumps of bare card underneath. What looked like water damage stained one corner, and he could see that the pages were yellow with age. He ran his fingers over the rough texture of the cover, not liking the way it felt. He flicked it open. The pages were disappointing in how bland they were. A list of telephone numbers scrawled in blue pen of various family members. Aunts and uncles, cousins and nieces, some dead, others long out of touch. He turned a few pages of random things, such as shopping lists and appointments. It was nothing more than an old diary she had forgotten to throw away. He skimmed to December, to the month he and Rebecca had been born, curious if there was anything written in there about them, but it was blank. He was about to add it to the throw away stack when he noticed something in the back of the book. It was a sealed envelope, faded with age. On the front, written in their mother's handwriting, were his and his sisters' names.

II

'You're sure?' Rebecca had that questioning look on her face that bugged him. Eyebrows raised, mouth in a semi-pout.

'I'm sure. Read it for yourself if you don't believe me.' He pushed the diary and letter across the table towards her.

She stared at him for a few seconds, picked up the letter and read it.

'Looks like it was a draft of the letter we got from Barnes, but filled with more details.' Dan said as his sister read on.

When she had finished, Rebecca set the letter on the table. 'What do we do about this?'

Dan shrugged. 'I don't know. The details in here, it's different from the ones we got from Barnes. His was so matter of fact and clinical. This one, though, there's passion in there. Emotion. It's clear what happened between mum and Warwick was more than a fling. There was a relationship there. A real one.'

Rebecca nodded in agreement.

'So, what do we do? Ignore it as she wanted us to? Or do we dig a little? And if we do, where does it end? A phone call? A visit? Is this something we want to dig up if we don't need to?' She stood and paced the kitchen. Somewhere in the distance, there was the steady drone of a lawnmower, as life went on as normal.

'I get what you're saying, and I've had the same thoughts. I don't see what good it would do to get involved. This isn't an ordinary situation with an ordinary man, Becks. Everyone knows what he did and why he's in prison. I'll admit, I'm curious, but nothing good would come from getting any more involved with this. I'm thinking we should get on with our lives as Mum wanted. She went to a lot of trouble to keep this from us.'

Rebecca picked up the letter again, skimming over the words. 'I don't disagree with you. Maybe we should leave it alone. This other voice in my head says we might get answers to all these questions we have. *How* this happened. *Why* this happened, *why* him? I don't know what to do.' She said, dabbing the corners of her eyes with the sleeve of her sweater. 'I'm sorry, this is a lot to take in.'

He stared at his fingernails, then at the old scar on the back of his hand from when he fell off his bike as a child. He wasn't used to seeing his sister this way. 'What do you want to do?' he asked, hoping she had the answers he didn't.

'I can't decide if I'm angry or upset, or if I even understand. It's like someone pulled the rug from under us and everything we used to know is different now.'

'The only thing I keep going back to is this idea that it was always her intention to tell us about this. I think in an ideal world, she'd have done it herself.'

'But I don't understand why she wouldn't tell us as soon as we were old enough to understand.' She was pacing again as she spoke.

'I do. It's obvious she wanted to protect us. A man like that who did those terrible things... No mother would want her children anywhere near it.'

'I want to know what happened between them, how they came to be close enough to have children. This guy is a fucking murderer and here we are, part of that same genetic line. You must be curious how it could happen?'

'I'm not arguing that. Believe me, it's messing with my head, too. Part of me wants to file this away and forget it ever happened. Then, when I think about it more, I feel like we deserve... something.'

'We deserve to know the truth.' She said, sitting down again. It grew quiet. Even the buzzing lawnmower had silenced.

Dan could see how upset she was getting. 'We don't need to chase this, Becks. We can forget it and move on. It's unlikely this guy even knows who we are, or if we even exist. My point is, we won't like what we find.'

She shook her head, tucking a lock of hair behind her ear. 'I don't think I can ignore this.'

'You don't know that. It's because it's so raw right now.'

'It will eat away at us, Dan. Can you imagine how it will be in six months? A year? How can we live knowing we are the son and daughter of a monster? Worse, how long could you stand not knowing the truth? How they met? How we came to be?' she was getting heated.

'Getting upset won't help. We need to take some time to work out what is best.' Dan replied.

'I get that, I do. But we can't wait forever. He's on Death Row, you know.'

'Of course I know that.'

'So, what if they execute him before we have time to talk to him? He might be the only one around who can give us answers.'

'And you think he would? Come on, you've read the articles. What makes you think he'll even speak to us if he's as bad as the reports say?' Dan was getting angry too now. It was all too much.

Rebecca chewed on her sweater sleeve. Dan hadn't seen her do that since they were children. 'I want to know.' She said.

'About what?'

'About everything. I feel like we need to do something other than bury this and hope it goes away.'

His sister was stubborn, much more than he was, and once she had her mind set on an idea, it was almost impossible to change it. 'If this is what you want to do, we can at least look into it. He's in Huntsville, I think. So, we would need to see what the rules are. It's another country. I have no idea if you're even allowed to visit people on death row.'

'I'm sure we could find out what the procedure is,' Rebecca

seemed calmer now her brother was coming around to the idea.

'I'll make some enquiries, but if they say no, I won't fight it. Agreed?'

Rebecca nodded.

'Then let me make some calls and see what the next steps are. Even if he made us, this guy isn't our father. You need to remember that, Becks. Remember the things he did. Can you do that?'

She nodded.

'Alright, let me see what I can find out.'

GLORIA

January, 1973

Elaine and George Pennington owned a mid-size ranch outside of Amarillo. Their daughter Gloria had for the last four months been living there with Jim, much to the frustration of her parents, who, although disapproving, knew their daughter was old enough to make her own decisions. Elaine stood at the kitchen sink, staring out of the window at the pair, unable to shake the feeling that something was wrong.

'Stop staring. You're making it obvious.'

Elaine turned to George, who sat at the table, peering at her over his newspaper.

'I don't like it, George. I don't like *him*.'

George pushed his black-rimmed glasses up his nose and lowered the paper. He was a thin man with a bulbous nose and greying hair parted to the left. His cheeks pocked with old scars - shrapnel wounds from the war - a time he refused to discuss even with Elaine. 'I don't like it either, but you were the one who told her he could stay. Remember that.'

'What else could I do? See the boy homeless? You know he has nowhere to go.'

'He's a grown man. We don't owe him anything.'

Elaine turned back to the window.

'Gloria would never forgive us. The boy has done nothing wrong, it's just... I get a bad feeling about him.'

'It's your daughter. Any man would make you feel uneasy,' George said, disappearing back behind his newspaper as his interest in the conversation waned.

'She's your daughter too.'

George lowered the paper, rolling his eyes. 'I'm not saying I approve. I worry about her, of course I do, but I was raised to make my own decisions. The *right* decisions. She's a good girl, Elaine. We should trust her to do the right thing.'

'And what if she doesn't? What if he turns out to be trouble?'

'Then we'll intervene and ask him to leave.'

'And the rest? His so-called friends? They're here all the time, too. When will this stop, George?'

This time, he didn't bother to lower the paper. 'Just stop fretting and leave them be. They'll move on soon enough and things will go back to normal. You'll see.'

Elaine hoped her husband was right. For her part, she couldn't shake the feeling he had misjudged the situation.

II

'Is she still watching?' Gloria said. They were sitting on the grass overlooking the rolling greens and yellows of the nearby fields. Jim looked past Gloria to the house, where Mary's silhouette lurked at the edge of the kitchen window.

'As always. I told you she doesn't like me.'

'She's overprotective.'

Jim grinned and turned his attention back to Gloria. 'I don't blame her. I wouldn't want my daughter mixing with someone like me.'

'Stop it. I know what's best for me.' She held his hands. 'I know what I want.'

She leaned in to kiss him, but Jim pulled away.

'What's wrong?'

Jim flicked his eyes towards the house, then pulled his hands away. 'Not when she's watching. It will only make it worse.'

Gloria glared at the window, which was enough to make her mother's silhouette duck out of sight. Satisfied, she turned back to Jim. 'It's weird.'

'What is?'

She nodded to the people they'd recruited over the past few months, who were sitting in small clusters nearby. Gloria's parents thought they were just friends, but Gloria had told them they could camp as long as they did it beyond the scrub of trees bordering the property and out of sight of the main house. 'Them. How they follow you and trust you.'

'Trust *us*,' Jim said. He looked at the three men and four women sitting in a rough circle twenty feet away. One man had an acoustic guitar and was strumming not quite perfect renditions of various hit songs as the others sang along. 'This is your place. You've given them somewhere to be. Me too. None of this could have happened without you, Gloria. Never forget that.'

'You don't see it, do you?'

'See what?'

'It feels like we're on the edge of something. Something exciting.'

Jim glanced at the house, where Mary's curious shadow had

reappeared at the kitchen window. 'I hope you're right. No, I think you are, now I think about it. We're a small group, granted, but it's encouraging, isn't it? That there are others who think the same way?'

'They're looking to you to lead them into this. Whatever it is.'

Jim shuffled, flicking a glance at the silhouette at the kitchen window. 'Yeah, well, the problem is, I don't see myself as a leader. I'm not a people person.'

'That's bullshit.'

Jim grinned. 'See? *That's* the confidence of a leader. So, tell me, why is it bullshit?'

She grabbed his hands again, staring into his eyes. 'Remember when we first met that night on the beach?'

'Yeah.'

'We talked about this idea. About change. You and me, one on one.' Gloria leaned closer; her eyes filled with excitement. 'You convinced me right there, even without specifics of what it might look like.'

'We were just talking.'

'It was the *way* you spoke. The way everything you said made sense. How it sounded so right. Even though we'd just met, I was ready to do anything you asked. Anything you wanted.' She paused, considering her words. 'Only someone who is a natural leader could do that. Those words coming from someone else wouldn't have made any difference to my life. Coming from you, they did.'

Jim looked past Gloria to the shadow at the window. He waved, causing it to duck out of the way. 'Let's say you're right. What if others don't buy into this?'

'They're here with us now, aren't they?'

'Because of you and the things you said to bring them here. Plus, you've given them a place to stay. A lot of these kids were homeless. Drifting around looking for a purpose. That is a big part of it.'

She stared into his eyes, trying to figure out what was going on behind them, but they gave nothing away.

'I wish you could see yourself the way I do. How special you are.'

Jim stroked her cheek. 'Whatever happens with this, wherever it goes from here, we do it together as equals. Got it?'

They sat for a moment, the smell of dry grass and sound of not quite right guitar notes filling the air.

'I'm worried about the rest of the group. Right now, they're happy enough to camp in the fields, but they can't do that forever. Not when winter rolls in. They will need a permanent place to stay if we intend to build something here.'

'They can stay in the house.'

Jim laughed. 'I'm sure your family would allow that. We'd have to kill them before they agreed to that, I think.'

'I'd do it if you wanted me to. I'd give them the option to leave first. But if it came to it, I'd do it for you.'

Jim was silent for a moment. An insect buzzed past his face.

'I'm not asking for that. I don't want you to kill your parents, Gloria. It seems a little extreme, don't you think? Remember when we talked about Hitler and how he went too far?' He added a smile, trying to lighten the mood.

Gloria's eyes were like dark voids without empathy. 'If you believe enough in something, you'll do anything to make it happen.

You could start something here. Something *real*, something to make a difference, but you have to believe, because if you don't, nobody else will.'

Gloria took his hands. 'I know it isn't a false dawn. You and me together, we can make it happen no matter what.'

'And if someone tries to stop it?'

'Then we eliminate it. The time for sitting around and talking about this is over. We either do it or we forget it. No middle ground.'

Jim stared at the window, leaned in, and kissed Gloria hard.

THE WARDEN

Huntsville Penitentiary, Texas
November 18th 2017

Dust swirled in the hot Texas air. The flight from England had been long, and the combination of heat and jet lag was taking its toll. Dan had expected his enquiries to lead to nothing. A seemingly endless barrage of phone calls and emails, coupled with the constant redirection from one person to another, ultimately guided him in the right direction. Securing their travel plans, they booked flights and arranged for time off work, and now they had arrived halfway around the world and staring into the abyss of the unknown. The entire process has felt like a nausea inducing rollercoaster, one which was at coming to a stop ahead of the next dizzying climb. They pulled to a halt outside the prison. To Dan, the red brick building looked more like a courthouse than the high-security jail he had expected, its architecture somehow at odds with its purpose. A quick look at his sister revealed nothing—she was texting, AirPods firmly in place.

'You sure you want to do this?' he asked.

She didn't hear him, lost in her music.

'Hey, Becks,' He nudged her arm, and she snapped away from what she was doing, removing one earphone.

'Sorry, what was that?'

'I said, are you sure you want to do this?'

Rebecca stared at the building, as if trying to see through it to what waited inside.

'As ready as I will be, I think.'

They got out of the car. The heat was unlike anything they had ever experienced. Dan couldn't understand how the residents lived with it. It was almost oppressive. He glanced again at his sister. She had shoved her phone and AirPods in her bag, and was staring at the building entrance.

'Okay,' he said. 'Let's go.'

The pair walked towards the entrance, unsure of what was awaiting them inside.

II

Warden Beadle's office was small, cluttered with files and folders. The man himself, in his forties, was the opposite of his surroundings. Immaculate, not a sandy hair out of place, the line of his parting arrow straight. As they entered, he stood to greet them, flashing a perfect smile and shaking each of them by the hand, gold bracelet jangling on his wrist.

'I'm so sorry about the delay in seeing you. I had to take a call that I couldn't postpone. Please, take a seat.'

Beadle gestured to the two chairs on the opposite side of his desk as he too sat, folding his hands on the mahogany tabletop, manicured nailed fingers interlocked.

'It's good to see you both. I hope the journey wasn't too taxing.'

'No, it was fine. We're tired, but that's to be expected.'

Beadle nodded. 'You should have slept on the plane. Try to stave off the jet lag.'

'My sister isn't a good flyer. She gets anxious.'

'Ah, I see,' Beadle said, grin widening. 'I have a cousin who is the same way. Watched too many of those air crash programs, I think. Still, at least you're here now.'

'Thank you for agreeing to see us, Warden Beadle.'

Beadle waved a dismissive hand, causing his overpriced bracelet to jingle in response. 'Please, call me Mike. To the inmates, I'm Warden Beadle. We don't have to be so formal here. How are you finding Texas so far?'

'Hot,' Dan said. He was already clammy with sweat.

Beadle laughed. 'I imagine it's a world away from what you're used to over in England.'

Dan and Rebecca exchanged looks. Beadle took the cue and dispatched with the pleasantries, growing serious.

'I'm familiar with the tragic circumstances which have caused this scenario of your visit here today to unfold. Commiserations to you both it must have come as quite the shock.'

'It did.' Dan tugged at the neck of his T-shirt, which was clammy against his back.

Beadle saw. 'You'll get used to that. Texas heat. Of course, it's not what we would call a scorcher yet. You should see this place in July. You can fry an egg on the hood of a car. Let me switch on the air. This isn't the biggest of offices and with three of us in here, it could get uncomfortable.'

Rather than get up, Beadle used one of his manicured fingernails to push the intercom button and speak to his secretary.

'Janine, switch the air conditioning on, would you? Also, wait a second,'

He turned to Dan and Rebecca, finger still on the button. 'Can I get either of you a drink? Tea? Coffee?'

'Nothing for me, thanks.' Dan said.

'How about you?' Beadle said, turning to Rebecca.

'Could I have water?'

'Water, got it.'

He turned back to the intercom even though it was clear Janine must have heard the entire conversation unfold. 'Could you also grab a bottle of water from the fridge? Make sure it's cold. And I'll take a coffee. Remember, no sugar. I'm trying to cut down.'

Releasing both secretary and finger from the intercom, he turned back to Dan and Rebecca, and his expression changed, the smile fading.

'Now, I suppose we ought to talk about your reason for this visit. I understand the two of you will have lots of questions. However, I have to reconfirm what I've said during our phone conversations. I still don't feel a personal visit is the correct course of action. I have to put that on record so you are aware of my professional stance. There is so much you don't know about that man.'

'We've done some research on him online.' 'Becks - Rebecca has been all over the research side. Books, websites, news reports. She's done a lot to prepare us for this. We know what we're getting into.'

'With all due respect, you don't,' Beadle fired back. 'I appreciate you may well have done your research and the like, but that can only paint part of the picture. Have you ever seen that image of an iceberg where only a small portion of the overall bulk is showing above the water? Well, that's James Warwick.'

Beadle stopped speaking as Janine entered the office. She handed the bottle of water to Rebecca and set the coffee on the desk. Beadle picked it up, sipped it, winced at the temperature, and set it back on the desk. With Janine gone as quickly as she had arrived, the conversation resumed.

'Are you saying now we're here that you won't let us see him?' Rebecca asked.

Beadle shook his head. 'Please, I think you misunderstand. I can't stop you from visiting your father. I have no legal right to deny your visitation. As you say, there would have been no point in having you come all this way to deny you.'

'Then why the resistance?' Dan asked.

Beadle shifted position as the air conditioning whirred to life. 'This is a case of making sure you understand what is the best course of action for everyone involved.'

'I don't understand.' Rebecca said.

Beadle sat up straight, his face serious.

Rebecca thought this must be how he was when having to speak to unruly inmates or deal with a squabble with his staff. 'Think of it like this. A prison environment is, despite the best efforts of the staff, a volatile one. There is a fine balance between chaos and calm. It is my job to maintain that balance for the safety and security of everyone. I have concerns about the impact this visit might have.'

Dan turned to the Warden. 'Sorry if we seem a little confused by all this. I don't see how one visit would affect the whole of the prison.'

Beadle tried to smile, but it came out as an uncomfortable grimace, as if he had forgotten how to perform that simple gesture. He gave up and sipped his coffee.

'It's like this,' he said, setting the cup down. 'James Warwick has been with us now for almost twenty years on our death row block. True enough, he gets regular correspondence. Fan mail, letters from crazies offering to marry him, that kind of thing. The point being, he has a way of existing that he is used to. This situation, because of its unusual nature, is likely to cause disruption. Someone like him, with his history and notoriety, over time, becomes something of a figure of status within the prison. Call it a warped sense of respect from the other inmates. His reaction when you meet him to break the news of who you are is something I have strong concerns about.'

'He doesn't know about us?' Rebecca said, unable to hide her surprise.

'No. Why would he?'

'I thought someone from the prison would have told him by now.' Dan said.

Beadle shook his head and took another sip of his coffee. 'Who you are and why you are here is something you will have to share with him during the visit.'

'So, what do you suggest, Mr Beadle? As you can tell, this is all new to us and, if we're honest, it's quite overwhelming.' Rebecca said.

Beadle sat back in his seat, deep in thought. 'How about this? You could walk in there today and reveal who you are. However, that would be the worst possible way to present this to him. I would have concerns about his reaction. How long are you here in Texas?'

'Two weeks. We wanted to take some time to look around where our mother grew up. Try to get a feel for how her life was before we were born.' Dan said.

'Then can I make a suggestion? Take a couple of days to think everything through. Faced with the reality of what was once a seed of an idea, it may be a good idea to take a little more time to decide your approach.'

Dan thought of that rollercoaster again, wheels clacking, racing along as he clung on to the safety bar by his fingertips. Slowing down felt like a good idea. 'In the meantime, if it would make things easier, and with your permission, my staff and I can take steps to inform Warwick of the situation. We couldn't do so without your authorisation. If you would prefer us to break the news who you are, it would be easier if we were to control the how and why to cause minimal disruption to the prison population. Is this something you would consider?'

Dan and Rebecca looked at each other, communicating without having to speak. Dan turned back to the Warden.

'The last thing we want to do is cause any issues for you and your staff. And you make some valid points. We haven't come here to stir up trouble, especially as you have been so accommodating in helping us to arrange this. We're happy to delay by a few days if you think it's for the best.'

Beadle clapped his hands together, the relief clear to see. 'Excellent. Then we have an agreement. I will start making the arrangements. The two of you can use the time to acclimatise to the area. I feel a lot more comfortable having time to prepare for this.'

Beadle checked his watch, stood and offered his hand, signalling the end of their meeting. 'I hate to rush you away, but I have another appointment. Blasted budget meeting.'

Dan and Rebecca took the hint. They stood and shook the Warden's hand.

'If you leave a contact number with my secretary where we can reach you, we'll be in touch to discuss the best time to plan your visit.'

'Thank you, we will,' Dan said as they headed to the door.

'One last thing,' Beadle added as they were about to leave. 'It's not too late to change your minds about any of this. If after giving it some thought you decide to go back home, having never visited, it may be for the best.'

'We can't do that, not when we've come so far.' Rebecca said.

Beadle deflated a little. Just a touch, but it was noticeable. 'I understand. I had to say it so I could tell myself I tried. We'll be in touch in a few days. Good luck to both of you.'

Dan and Rebecca left the office, the Wardens words sticking to them like their clammy, sweaty clothes.

INTERVIEW TRANSCRIPT

Present: *Interviewing officer Det Alexander Robbins*
Suspect: *James Warwick*
External Third-party observer: *Det Mike Scoon.*

AR: *I'm told you refused to speak to anyone but me. Why?*
JW: *After what happened, who else would I ever want to talk to?*
AR: *Look, I'm going to be straight with you. These games, this psychological bullshit, won't wash with me. You've been giving us the runaround for weeks, and I don't have time for that shit. You want to talk, so talk.*
JW: *(no answer given)*
AR: *You think I'm bullshitting you?*

** Detective Robbins stands as if to leave**

JW: *What exactly did ▓▓▓ tell you about me? About what we do?*

Detective Robbins re takes his seat

AR: *She told us everything. The truth. All we want is confirmation from you about what you did to ▓▓▓ and ▓▓▓. We'll find more evidence. Our teams are still up there digging as we speak. You're out of options.*

Suspect Laughs

AR: *Something funny in what I said?*
JW: *Not really. I'm just thinking, it's a big plot of land. Lots of open space. For as much as ▓▓▓ told you, even she only knows part of it.*
AR: *So cut the shit and help me out. Tell me where the rest are buried and we can help you out. Maybe get the death penalty off the table. You help us, we help you.*
JW: *That would be too easy. And after what you did to me, why should I make it easy?*

AR: You think you're something special, don't you? Sure, I know what you scored on the intelligence test. You're a smart guy. Some might say borderline genius level. But you're not so smart.

JW: Finally, an interesting conversation. Go ahead. Tell me where I went wrong.

AR: Well, you're sitting here, that's one thing. I caught you. Me. You sit there, arrogant, petulant, and think it makes you a big man. It doesn't. You think because you don't like the way the world works; you have a right to destroy it. It doesn't work that way. There are rules to follow. For all of us. Like it or not. You can't sit there and try to justify what you did. All you can do now is make it easier for the families of the victims.

JW: Victims? That depends on your point of view. You say victims. I say collateral damage. Are they any more a victim of me than I am a victim of you after what you did?

AR: I'm the one questioning you here. I won't let you drag this off into irrelevance. What I want to know is what you did to ▮▮▮▮. It's a simple question.

JW: I sometimes think there are no simple questions. Not in my situation. Why not ask ▮▮▮▮ again? I'm sure she's more than happy to talk.

AR: We're not talking about ▮▮▮▮ here. We're talking about you. Do you realise you're staring the death penalty in the face? Help yourself. Do one good thing, for Christ's sake.

JW: **laughing** You use the death penalty as some kind of carrot to entice the donkey, as if it should scare me. You forget, Detective, that I have seen death up close and I have nothing to fear from it. I looked into the eyes of God and saw myself. Trust me when I say am at peace with my situation. As for what you're looking for, all I can suggest is keep digging, Detective. You'll either find what you're looking for or you won't. Quite an exciting proposition, don't you think?

AR: Then it looks like you and I have nothing more to say to each other. Interview terminated at 14:22.

Interview ends

VISITOR

Beadle's prediction that they would become accustomed to the Texan heat turned out to be completely wrong; in fact, they found the heat more and more difficult to tolerate. The heat was unlike anything they'd experienced in England, where summers were considerably less extreme. They settled into a cramped motel room a few miles outside the prison, the air thick with the smell of stale cigarettes and cheap cleaning supplies. Because their inheritance was tied up in legal processes, they had to budget carefully.

Though a bit tired, the motel was clean and thankfully air-conditioned; a slightly warmer recycled air was better than the intense heat blasting outside. So far, their exploration had been minimal. They had tried a burger place down the street (greasy and cheap). A steak restaurant a little closer to the prison (incredible but too expensive), but had mostly stayed in their room and waited for the call from Beadle.

The hope of visiting the places their mother had frequented as a child had come to nothing. There was no information they could find about her life in America. Like her relationship with Warwick, it, too, looked to have been erased.

Dan lay on his bed, hands folded behind his head. He was in full tourist mode. Knee length cargo shorts, Faded iron Maiden T shift displaying their mascot, Eddie, a zombie Skelton in military uniform planting a flag. Even doing nothing was hard work. He wondered again how the locals could function like this. He couldn't imagine doing any kind of manual labour in these kinds of temperatures. Back home, he worked in I.T. and would sometimes have to drag in deliveries. Boxes of components. Keyboards, headsets and the like. Even that, when it was cold outside, was enough to cause a sweat. He would imagine that kind or work, shuffling boxes, fetching and carrying, would be an absolute nightmare for the average Texan. He glanced over at his sister, thumbs dancing over the screen of her phone as she talked to her friends. She was showing less difficulty adjusting to the heat. She was even wearing jeans. Jeans! He didn't know how she could do it when he was melting, doing nothing.

'Hey, Becks, are you sure we're doing the right thing?'

'About what?' she said, still distracted by her screen.

'This. Coming here. Making something of it. Before, I thought we had to come. But now…'

She set her phone down and looked over at him. 'What's on your mind?'

'I was thinking, do we even need to do this? From the stuff I've read, I don't think we're missing anything that will change our lives for the better by talking to him.'

Rebecca sat up and perched on the edge of her bed. 'I've been thinking about that myself, and I get it. It makes all the sense in the world to walk away. Then I think about the regrets we could have if we don't see this through.'

'Yeah, I suppose so,'

'Look at this big blank space in mum's life when she lived here. We've been through all her notebooks, everything, and there is zero information. He might be the only one who can fill those gaps. Maybe he won't tell us anything. All the same, I think we owe it to ourselves to try.'

'You're like her, you know. That same determination when you get an idea in your head. You'll push it through to the end.'

'I have no idea how to take that,' she fired back, half smiling.

'Oh, come off it, we both know you had mum wrapped around your little finger.'

'As if. That was you. Mummy's boy Dan.' Rebecca laughed as she said it.

'Oh yeah? Well, who was the one who got a car for her birthday? Or Archery lessons just because you saw it on TV once. Not me, Becks. Just saying.'

'First, I paid for half that car myself, and second, those archery lessons were worth the money. I'm good at it.'

'Point is, you got your own way as per, didn't you?'

A knock at their door stopped their conversation. 'Maybe it's Beadle.' Dan said, as he got up and opened the door. He didn't recognise the man on the other side.

'Can I help you?'

'Mike Beadle sent me to talk to you. I'm looking for Dan and Rebecca.'

'Yes, that's us.'

The man held out a hand. 'My name is Alex Robbins.'

Dan shook it, still cautious.

'Alex Robbins?' Rebecca said from inside the room, hurrying to the door. 'You were in charge of the Jim Warwick case. I've seen your name come up as I've been reading about it.'

Robbins nodded. 'Yeah, that was me.'

Rebecca pushed past her brother. 'Please, come in.'

'Thanks,' he said as he stepped into the hotel room.

'I didn't even realise you were still alive,' Rebecca said as she closed the door.

'Uh, thanks. As far as I know, I'm still just about kicking.'

'I'm so sorry, I didn't intend for that to sound so… weird.' She tried to hide it, but she was blushing.

'Don't mind my sister. She's weird sometimes.'

'I've been called worse than almost dead over the years. Don't worry about it.'

Dan gestured to a chair by the window. 'Please, take a seat.'

'Thanks,' Robbins sat, wincing as his knees complained.

'So why did the Warden send you?' Dan asked.

'He thought you might benefit from taking to be me about the case. He also told me you were planning to Visit Warwick, and asked if I could talk you out of it, although I'm not sure I was supposed to mention that.'

Dan glanced at his sister. 'Well, I didn't expect you to be so honest, so thank you.'

'When you get to my age, kid, you care less and less about saving people's feelings and say what you feel, good or bad. For the record, I didn't want to dig this up again. Beadle and I go a long way, so it was hard to say no. Plus, I was curious.'

'About what?' Dan asked.

'About how his kids turned out,' Rebecca said, answering for Robbins. He didn't argue.

'You know you won't be able to talk us out of this,' Rebecca added.

Robbins shrugged. 'Yeah, Mike said you were pretty determined. I know how stubborn you younger folk can be. All the same, you shouldn't be mixing with this guy. If anyone is qualified to tell you that, it's me. You'd do well to listen.'

Dan looked doubtful. Rebecca Determined. It was she who spoke on behalf of them both. 'Like we told the Warden, we know what we're getting into. We're not under any illusions here.'

Robbins smiled, but the gesture was tired. 'You might think so, but you don't know the entire story. You seem to have made up your minds regardless of what I say.'

The siblings looked at each other, surprised how perceptive the old man was.

'So, not to be rude, why did you come here if you know you can't change our minds?' Rebecca asked.

Robbins looked at his hands, considering the question. 'I don't know, and that's the truth. Other than out of obligation to Beadle, my biggest concern is that you two don't have a clue what you're getting into.'

He exhaled, shoulders slumping. 'I devoted so long to putting that man behind bars. The idea of anyone interacting with him doesn't sit right with me.'

'Everyone seems to think they know what's best for us. Shouldn't we decide that?' Dan fired back.

Robbins smiled, and this time, there was a little more vigour to it. 'Take it easy, kid. It was nothing personal. Your reaction proves my point, though. You're like a couple of mice, running to the gigantic piece of free cheese and not seeing the trap ready to slam down and break your necks.'

'Try seeing it from our side,' Rebecca said, struggling to hide the frustration in her voice. 'There are questions we need answering. What harm can come from talking?'

'Ask me anything you want to know. Believe me, nobody knows more about this case and the man in the middle than me.'

Dan and Rebecca exchanged glances. 'I don't see how having more information can hurt.' Dan said. His sister remained silent.

'Hey, it's up to you. I can't stop you. You'll do what you want to. If you would let a tired old man advise you, though, I'd recommend you consider it before you do something you might regret.'

'All right,' Rebecca said, 'If you can answer our questions enough to fill in the gaps, we might consider it. But no promises.'

'In my experience, people who have already made their decision rarely change it. You two might, though, once you know the truth.'

'And what is the truth?' Rebbeca said, her frustration growing. 'Where do we even start with this? There are so many things I want to know, but that period of our mum's life is a huge blank space. There's nothing out there. No information. Nothing.'

'The places are there. Sure enough, the names have changed and some of them don't look like they once did, but they are there if you know where to look.'

'And you'd be willing to take us? To show us?' Dan asked.

Robbins nodded. 'If it would help. Let me ask you both a question first.' Robbins replied.

'What?'

'You two eaten yet?'

'No,' Rebecca said.

'You like burgers?'

'Yeah, although we tried the place down the street and it wasn't great.'

'Francos's place? Their burgers are shitty. Don't eat there unless you are desperate.' Robbins stood, knees popping.

'Come with me. I know a place that does a burger you won't believe. My treat.'

'We have money. You don't need to pay for us.' Dan said, slipping his shoes on.

'A burger and a drink won't break the bank. We'll eat, talk a little. I warn you, though, they buried the story for a reason. You'll hear things that will make you uncomfortable. I have to ask if you're ready for that.'

'We are,' Rebecca said. Dan also nodded his approval.

'Fine, let's get moving.'

'Thank you. We appreciate it.' Dan said.

'Don't thank me yet, kid, not until you've heard what I have to say. I'll go wait in the car. You two come down when you're ready and we'll head out.'

THE BEST BURGER IN TOWN

Robbins had taken them to a spot a few miles away near a truck stop. They had passed through rolling fields and wheat, some as high as the car, others already harvested and in rolls scattered over the land. The burger place looked nothing special from outside. Glass front, small car park. Red and white awning over the entrance. There were only a couple of other cars there when they arrived and headed inside.

The atmosphere was inviting, the smell of cooking food mouth-watering. Booths lined the front windows, with more at the back. Despite the lack of cars outside, the place was pretty busy. Dan and Rebecca sat on one side of the table in the diner; Robbins sat on the other. He wasn't eating and was content to sip his coffee as the twins enjoyed their food. Robbins had recommended the house burger, and both had gone with it. Dan choosing the cheese and bacon, and Rebecca a regular hamburger. Music filtered through the diner, easy listening stuff from the 50s and 60s, making for a comfortable atmosphere.

'Oh my god, this is incredible. Are you not eating?' Rebecca said between mouthfuls.

'No, I'm supposed to be watching my cholesterol, according to my doctor. When you get old, people like that suck all the enjoyment out of life. None of this, less of that, cut down on the other. Enjoy it while you're young. How are the burgers?'

'Amazing.'

'Yeah, they're good, thanks,' Dan said.

'Didn't I tell you they were the best? I've been coming here for years, hell, since I was your age. What are you? Twenty something?'

'Twenty-one,' Dan said, taking a drink of his coke. 'Becks is older than me by six minutes. She thinks that puts her in charge.'

'Technically, I am the older sibling,' she fired back.

'I remember when your mother was carrying the two of you. I never saw you born, but it's strange how things work out, isn't it?'

Dan and Rebecca exchanged surprised glances.

'Oh shit,' Dan said. 'That's crazy when you think about it.'

'I even brought her here once.' He jabbed a thumb over his shoulder towards the tables across the room. 'Sat right over there a few weeks before she moved to England.'

They stared at him, taking it all in. Robbins went on.

'Which I suppose is as good a time as any to get into this and give you some answers. I know all there is to know about this case. I devoted the best years of my career to it. So, what is it you want to know?'

Rebecca set her burger down and stopped eating. 'I've been thinking, and to be honest, it's overwhelming. There are questions which have other questions attached. There is a lot of mention of a woman called Helen. She seemed to be a big part of his life.'

Robbins took a sip of his coffee and shifted position. 'This is what I was saying about not knowing the full story. Helen doesn't exist. The person does, but she was given a new identity to protect her from the fallout. That's why you can't find any information in any of your book or articles. Her real name was Gloria. I think before we go down that avenue, though, we should start at the beginning, and discuss your mother.'

'We're ready,' Dan said.

Robbins looked at them across the table, hoping to God he wasn't making the wrong decision is telling them everything. There was no intention of lying. He had told himself that if they were insistent and wanted to know it all, he would give it to them. Good or bad, and there would be plenty of bad.

'Detective Robbins?' Rebecca said. He realised he was staring into space.

'Sorry, I was gathering my thoughts. Alright, here we go. To understand how it all played out, you need to understand how she became involved with Warwick at all.'

'That's one thing we don't understand. In all the reports we could find, there is no mention of her. It's as if she didn't exist.' Rebecca said.

'That was deliberate.'

'You erased her from the case?' Dan asked.

'This was such a big case and so high-profile anyone coming out of it with any sense of anonymity at all is remarkable. If this case had happened today with technology how it is, there would have been no chance to protect her identity. Back then, it was easier.'

Robbins sipped his coffee, then went on. 'Your mother was younger than the two of you when I first met her. Like any teenager, she was headstrong and determined to prove hers was the right way. She should have been nowhere near that situation. Any of a million things could have been different, and she and Warwick would never have found themselves in each other's lives.'

'That's what we're struggling with. How she got mixed up in all this,' Rebecca said.

'Keep in mind, James Warwick wasn't always a monster. He was a man who was where she needed someone to be at the right time. Awful luck, granted, but back then, there was no sense that anything was wrong. It was just a meeting of two people. I'm going to tell this to you the way your mother told it to me. Are you sure you're ready?'

The siblings looked at each other, then back at Robbins.

'We're ready,' Rebecca said.

'Alright, this is how it happened.'

A STORM ON THE HORIZON
July 1973

Jim was out on a walk, as he often did, completely alone and lost in his own thoughts. He enjoyed the solitude, the time alone with his thoughts, walking without direction. He was in his jeans and work boots, T shift off and carried in one hand. There was something about being alone with nature that appealed to him. He'd been walking for about forty minutes, a light sweat on his brow, when he spotted her – a lone girl hitchhiking, her thumb pointed towards the distant horizon, and a large backpack slung across her shoulders. With her blonde hair hidden under a straw hat, she wore denim shorts and a white shirt. The girl smiled as a car approached, then gave it the middle finger as it drove past, spewing dust and exhaust fumes at her as it went. Jim crossed the road to where she stood,

'No luck?' he said as he slid up beside her.

The girl glared at him. 'None of your business.'

'I was just asking.' Up close, Jim realised she was too young to be hitchhiking alone. He estimated her age at only seventeen and suspected she might be even younger.

'How old are you?'

'I told you to leave me alone.'

'I'm saying that you need to be careful. A young girl hitchhiking alone could get into trouble.'

'Maybe *you're* the trouble,' she spat back, holding a hopeful thumb out to another car which drove by without slowing. She glared at Jim, hands planted on her hips.

'That was your fault. It would have stopped if you weren't here.

Nobody will pick up a guy with long hair and no shirt. Just leave me alone.'

'Maybe you're right. Where are you trying to get to?'

'I told you it's none of your business. Just keep walking.'

Jim nodded to the horizon where slate-coloured clouds were building, blotting out the blue of the day. 'See that? It's a storm and will be here in another couple of hours. Do you have warm clothes in your bag? Waterproof coat?' he glanced at her sandaled feet, then back to her with an eyebrow raised. 'Waterproof shoes?'

A flicker of doubt passed over the girl's face. 'No, I don't.'

'Then I'd advise you to find some shelter until it passes. If you get caught in it, you'll catch a cold, maybe get sick.'

She looked at him, still full of mistrust.

'Well, I'll leave you to it,' Jim said, flashing a smile. 'Good luck with wherever you're heading.'

He tossed his shirt over his shoulder, put his hands in his pockets and walked away from her towards the growing thunderheads.

The girl waited for him to turn back or change his mind, and when he didn't, started after him. 'Wait,' she said, jogging to catch up. He stopped to wait for her. 'What about you? You're out here in a t-shirt and jeans. Shouldn't *you* be looking for shelter from the storm if it's going to be as bad as you say?'

'I live a mile or so down the road. I'll be home before it gets here.'

He continued walking, knowing what was coming, as if he had written the script. He heard her footsteps approach as she fell in beside him. 'Then you can give me somewhere to shelter until it passes. Keep in mind, though. I've got a knife and I'll cut it off if you try to rape me.'

Jim glanced at her, drawn to the determination. Her fierce eyes, brow furrowed. 'Point taken.' He turned his attention to the road as they walked along its edge. 'Is it safe to ask you for a name?'

'Why do you need to know?'

'How can I introduce you to the people I live with when I don't know what to call you?'

'It's Mary. My name is Mary.'

'Nice to meet you, Mary. I'm Jim. Question for you. Are you running away from something or heading home?'

'That's none of your business.'

'Running away, then.' Jim said as another car passed them, spewing more dust in its wake.

'How do you know?'

Jim glanced at her and smiles. 'You wouldn't care enough to hide it if you were heading home. What are you running from?'

'You ask a lot of questions.'

'Anything wrong with trying to get to know you? Especially as we're walking buddies now.'

Mary opened her mouth to tell him to mind his own business, then changed her mind. 'My family. I'm sick of them trying to control me. If I choose not to go to school, why should I have to? It's my life.'

'School? How old are you?'

'Fifteen. I'll be sixteen next month, though.'

Before he could speak, she cut him off.

'Don't say I'm just a kid or that I don't know what I want. I *know* what I want and it's not some boring school learning about stuff I'm not interested in.'

'I was going to say, I know what you're going through.'

'Oh yeah? How do you know?'

'I ran away from home at fourteen. Similar thing. Sick of them trying to control me, although my situation was different.'

'Oh yeah, how?'

'I had an alcoholic father who used to beat me to a pulp if I so much as breathed the wrong way. That kind of thing that can make running a straightforward decision.'

'Sorry to hear that. Did you ever go back?'

Jim didn't like to talk about his past, and was more surprised he was finding it easy to open up to a stranger. 'I did for a few months, but the beatings got worse and my mother was too afraid to stand up to him, so she let it happen. I left for the last time when I was fourteen and haven't seen either of them since.'

'Oh, I'm sorry.'

'I'm not. I have no regrets.'

Mary's expression had changed. It was now one of wonder. 'How old are you now?'

'Twenty-four.'

'And you've survived all that time on your own?'

'Not on my own, but I've survived. For a while I drifted and hitchhiked like you with no idea where I wanted to go or what I'd do when I got there.'

Mary nodded, and Jim felt a flash of attraction, the same as he had seen in Gloria when they first met.

'I moved from place to place, determined to prove my family wrong. The problem was I didn't know how to do it. I knew there was something out there for me, something bigger. I just didn't know what it was.'

'You say didn't, rather than don't. What changed?' she asked, the gentle breeze moving her hair across her face. He caught a whiff of perfume. Soapy. Clean smelling. Something stirred inside him.

She's just a fucking kid. His inner monologue reminded him. He tried not to think about her and kept his focus on the road.

'I met someone who gave me the belief I could make a change. Someone who saw potential in me, who still does. We developed this idea, a dream to change the world.'

'How? You can't say something like that and not explain it.'

Jim grinned, impressed by how frank she was with him. 'Well, I can't explain it yet, as I don't know what form it will take.'

'So, you have nothing.'

'What do you mean?'

'You either have it or you don't. From what you just said, you don't. Sorry.'

'Fair enough. Smart kid,'

Mary stopped walking. 'I'm *not* a kid.'

'Take it easy.'

'I'm not dumb, you know, just because I'm a runaway. Even though I hated school, I was still was top of my classes. All of them, so don't call me a kid.'

Jim also stopped, and it felt like the world did too, waiting for them to resolve this issue. Leaves skittered across the road, and the breeze was cooling. On the horizon, those slate coloured blooms of cloud were turning black at the base.

'Alright, point made. I'm sorry, okay? Can we keep moving, please? I don't want to get drenched out here.'

Mary considered it, gave the clouds a side eye, and started walking again. For a while, neither of them spoke. Three more cars passed them before Jim broke the silence.

'Look, all I was trying to say was that it's rare somebody understands. Some people, I try to explain what I want to do, and they look at me like I'm some kind of idiot. You didn't do that. It caught me by surprise, that's all.'

'I get it. Don't worry about it.'

'Life for most people is like a lake. Flat and quiet. You ever seen a lake like that, Mary?'

'Yeah, my family went camping a few years back. Early in the morning, the lake near our campsite was like that. Like a big bowl of glass. A mirror dug into the ground. It was beautiful.'

'Yeah. So, what I want to do it take a mountain and throw it into that lake to see what ripples it causes.'

'That is what this world needs. Maybe this is some kind of fate.'

'I don't believe in fate,' Jim said.

'Maybe you should.'

'Why should I?'

'Think about it. Why did we encounter each other on the road today? What if you'd taken a different route, or if I had? What if a car had picked me up before you arrived or if that storm hadn't been building on the horizon?'

He took a moment to consider.

'Interesting.'

The wind was getting chilly now. Jim put his T-shirt back on. Somewhere in the distance, a faint rumble rolled towards them.

'What I'm saying is that a lot of stuff had to fall in to place for us to meet the way we did. There's something in that. Fate is how I explain it.'

Jim remained silent for a while, considering the idea. He looked at her in profile. Eyes determined, sun hat pulled low, cheeks flushed from walking. 'Yeah, maybe you're right.'

'I *am* right.' She said, her confidence swelling.

Jim grinned. 'You speak your mind, don't you?'

'Always.'

'All right, let me ask you this. When did you last eat?'

Mary pondered the question. 'Yesterday. Maybe the day before.'

'Well, if you promise not to come at me with that knife, you're welcome to eat with us at the Ranch, and, if you want to, you can stay. We have plenty of space.'

'Us?'

'Yeah, there's a group of us. We all started out lost, like you, and found each other along the way. They're nice people.'

Mary gave him a mistrusting glance. 'Maybe. I'll take the food, but until I've seen the place and met your friends, I'm not committing to anything. I tend not to trust people.'

'Wise,' Jim said. The sky was darkening now, the blue making that subtle shift in tone towards grey.

'Good. As long as you understand. Try anything weird and I'll use my knife, got it?'

'Got it.'

'Good.'

They walked, silent for a while. Two more cars drove by. Mary didn't try to flag them down.

'How far away is this ranch of yours?' She asked, trying to hide how out of breath she was.

'A mile or so, not far.'

'Good. I'm starving. Let's get moving.'

She increased her pace, Jim speeding to keep up. In the distance, the thunderheads continued to swell and drift closer.

II

Six months later.

'I want these people out and that's final.' Elaine shrieked as she stormed out of the kitchen. Gloria followed, stalking after her mother, incensed with rage.

'You can't do that. They have nowhere else to go. These are my friends.'

'Strangers living here, eating our food, making things uncomfortable. It's not fair.'

'They help. They work so you don't have to. I won't let you throw them out.'

Elaine turned to face her daughter. 'This is my house, and don't you forget it.'

'You're so cruel. Dad never minded.'

'He minded. Oh, it was fine at first when they were just visiting, then when he found out they were squatting in the back fields, it changed. Look at this place. It's not home anymore.'

Enraged, Gloria stepped forward, getting into her mother's

personal space. 'Don't you dare blame me for him dying. It was your fault. You and your incessant twittering.'

'How dare you even-'

'Oh, I can imagine it. You in his ear, telling him how you wanted us out, how you wanted your own daughter out so you could have your precious home back. I can't imagine how that must have affected him, how he must have got sick of your whining voice in his ear. It wouldn't surprise me if he was glad to die, so he didn't have to listen to you bleating on and -'

Elaine slapped her daughter. Gloria glared, cheek hot and tingling.

'Monster!' Elaine said, her voice cracking as she wept. 'He's changed you, that boy. You're not the daughter I raised. You've become something different.'

'Maybe I have. But it's better than growing up to be like you, a pathetic old hag who has nothing left in life but to pull other people down.'

Elaine wiped her eyes, body trembling with anger. 'I want you out. All of you. You're not welcome here and I never want to see you again. You're a stranger to me.'

'We're going nowhere. What we're building here is bigger than you.'

Elaine reared back to slap her daughter again, but this time Gloria saw it coming and blocked it with her other hand, grabbing her mother around the throat and pushing her against the wall. They were nose to nose, forehead to forehead, Gloria speaking through gritted teeth. 'Things around here will change. You might not like it, but they will change anyway.'

'This is my house. Your father and I worked for this. Worked for you to give you a good life.' This time she said it not with conviction, but through fear.

'And you did. But sometimes things change.'

Elaine grimaced. 'I won't argue with you there. Things *have* changed. You used to be such a good girl, everyone said it. Now, look at you. Smoking and drinking, spending all day with that *boy*. He's changed you all right, but for the worse.'

Gloria felt rage sweep over her. She tightened her grip. Not a lot, but enough to make her mother flinch. 'I don't deny he's changed me. The thing is, he's changed me for the better. He helped me see what I could be. What we all could be if we only took a risk.'

'You talk like he's some kind of hero. Your father, *he* was a hero. He went to war. He fought for our country. That.... person-'

'Jim.'

'-That person isn't a hero. He's another dreamer. A drifter who will achieve nothing in life.'

A swell of rage surged through Gloria and in her mind's eye she saw herself slitting her mother's throat, if only to silence the tirade coming from her mouth. 'He'll do great things. If you would support me - support us, and *listen* to him, you would understand, you would see it too. I know you would.'

'I've seen his kind before. Full of talk. He'll use you up and spit you out, then you'll be alone. Is that what you want?' She was so forceful in her delivery, she spat drool onto her chin. Gloria released her grip and stepped back, the images of blood and violence still hiding in the shadows of her mind. 'I want you to support me. Is that so hard?'

'I wanted him out from the start, long before most of the others arrived, but your father insisted we could trust you, that we'd raised you to do the right thing. I regret not stepping in when I could have told him he was wrong. It's your fault he's in an early grave, because of you and your so-called friends.'

Gloria screamed and lunged towards her mother. She didn't remember picking up the knife, nor did she know where it had come from. The sight of the blade pressed against her mother's throat, gleaming in the dim light, surprised them both. Elaine was afraid. That much was clear to see, but behind it was a steely defiance, the same trait she had passed to her daughter, the two more similar than either of them would care to admit. She smiled, causing a shadow of doubt to flicker in her child's face. 'Is this how it ends? You becoming a murderer. Killing your own mother to protect him?'

Her hands shook as the knife hovered over her mother's throat. Elaine's grin widened. 'Go on. You've come this far. Do it if you intend to do it. Get it over with so I can be with your father and away from you and this hell you're putting me through.'

'Don't push me. I'll do it. You don't think I will, but you're wrong.'

Elaine grabbed her daughter by the wrist holding the knife, pulling the blade closer to her own throat. 'Then do it. Stop talking and do it. Prove me right. Prove he's turned you from the sweet girl we raised into a monster who would kill her own mother.'

That blackness came again, the dark ooze in her brain that wanted her to fulfil her mother's wishes and open her throat. She wondered if the knife would resist or glide as it severed veins and arteries or cut through flesh and muscle. How much blood there might be, or the sound it might make as it hit the floor, how that bright red would look in the mid-morning sun.

'What's going on?'

Gloria turned to see Jim standing in by the door. If what he saw disturbed him, he said nothing. Elaine glared at him, eyes half closed in disgust.

'She's doing what you want. Getting rid of me so you can take over this place. You won.'

'That isn't what I want, Elaine. Gloria is out of line.'

Gloria flinched, feeling the sting of betrayal. 'That's your mother. She deserves respect.'

Gloria exhaled and stepped back, lowering the knife. 'I... she goaded me into it.'

Elaine rubbed her throat, staring at Jim. 'Am I supposed to thank you? Be grateful to you for saving my life?'

Jim shrugged and leaned against the door frame. 'I want nothing from you, other than a chance. You and I have never seen eye to eye, but I mean her no harm. She's important to me, and because of that, so are you. I want us to get along, or at least learn to live with each other in some kind of harmony.'

'You come into my house, take it over, brainwash my daughter, and expect us to be friends. Who do you think you are?'

'I hoped we could find a compromise.'

Elaine shook her head, the defiance still there. 'No. You might have brainwashed Gloria, but I see right through you. I gave her the chance to get you out, and she refused. Now I'm going to call the police, have them make you leave.'

'We don't have to do this, Elaine.' Jim said, locking his eyes on hers.

'There is nothing to consider. I want you off my property.' She strode towards him, her intended destination the telephone in the hallway. Jim pushed off the door frame and stepped into the room, blocking her exit. Elaine stopped, doubt and fear replacing defiance. Jim closed the door, locking all three of them in the room together.

III

Robbins sipped his coffee, already hating the memories he was pulling up from the past. Dan and Rebecca watched him, silent and waiting for him to continue.

'So, what happened next?' Rebecca asked.

'And how do you know all this in such detail?' Dan added.

Robbins felt an irrational surge of hate towards Beadle. He should have been there to help explain instead of leaving him to do this alone.

'Everything I told you was pieced together from the investigation. Interviews, statements, evidence gathering on location. Short version is, none of this is bullshit. It's the truth as close as we can know it.'

'And Gloria's mother? What happened to her?' Rebecca asked.

'We found her remains in a shallow grave at the back of the property.'

'And her own daughter would do that?' Dan said, eyebrows raised as he processed the information.

'That's our assumption. The frustrating thing is, neither of them would admit to it.'

'What about DNA evidence?' Dan said.

Robbins shook his head. 'Remember, this was a time before DNA was even a thing. It was more science fiction and in its infancy as a valid tool. We know they did it, but with no proof and no confession, we couldn't pin it on them. She wasn't declared missing until after we arrested Warwick. We found out later the war pension payments she received after the passing of her husband were still coming in. Gloria and Warwick used those to keep the house running.'

'Fuck,' Dan muttered, setting his burger down. It seemed he had lost his appetite.

'I tried to get him to confess to it once during questioning so I could give closure to the family. I remember the way he was so casual. Sat there in the chair, slumped with one arm draped over the back. That slimy grin on his face. He has this way of looking at you. It's almost as if you're not there and he's looking at something behind you. It's like he knows everything you're thinking.' Robbins shifted position. Dan and Rebecca could not take their eyes off him.

'Detective work is all about pressure. You try to trip a suspect up. Ask the same things over and over, looking for inconsistencies. Even little things you wouldn't notice go towards it. How you position the suspect in relation to yourself. How close you sit. What temperature the room is. Everything is designed to make someone who is guilty crack and confess. Anyhow, I was a few hours deep. We'd cranked up the heat, picked a small room with no windows and were relentless with the questioning. Telling him we knew it was him, and if he had any kind of humanity left, he'd admit it and give the rest of the family some respite. Tell him all he had to do was admit it and he could smoke, maybe have some food. Remember, we already had enough to get the death penalty. This was about justice for the victims and trying to get him to do what was right. It wouldn't have mattered to him to confess to it. One more death on his hands wouldn't have changed anything outcome wise, but we wanted peace for the family, so we were pushing hard.'

'Did you break him? My guess is he stayed silent.' Dan said.

'You would think so, but he was the opposite. He was full of compliments about the Pennington family, describing them as nice people who treated him like a son, and he was as shocked as anyone to learn her body was found so close to the house. He talked about how Gloria and her mother had a volatile relationship, which she admitted to later, but he was saying it in a way that implied she had been the one to kill her mother, and his hands were clean. To him, it was all a game. The bastard knew all too well we had nobody we could ask who would corroborate anything he said to us.'

He stopped as the waitress approached and asked if there was anything else they wanted. Dessert, maybe, or more coffee? Robbins said no to both and asked for the bill. He could tell from the look on Dan and Rebecca's faces as they watched him that there would be no more eating today. He couldn't blame them.

'So, you never got a confession?' Rebecca asked. She was pushing a few fries around her plate with her fork.

Robbins shook his head. 'No. We tried, God Damn did we try. The problem was, the more he could see it mattered to us, the more determined he was to fuck around and delay things. Just for his own amusement.'

Robbins drank more coffee, pausing for questions. When they didn't come, he continued.

'Murderers in my experience come in two varieties when they get caught. The first type is arrogant, proud in a way of what they've done. Once they know the game is up, they want to spill all the details, hoping for maximum exposure so people knew who was responsible.'

'Classic Narcissist,' Rebecca said, setting the fork down on the plate.

'Right.' Robbins replied. 'The second type are the quiet ones. They hate being caught and refuse to speak or cooperate, even after conviction. Fear rules that type. They have some hope that by staying silent they might get away with it, even when it's clear the game is up.'

The waitress brought the bill. She asked if it would be cash or card; Robbins said cash (he was old school and wasn't about to change the way he paid for things at this stage in his life). After Robbins settled, the waitress left. He was aware he had given them more info that he intended to, but also knew it was important they knew what kind of man they were dealing with. He pushed on, conscious that what they were learning now was the tip of a big fucking iceberg.

'Warwick didn't fall into either of those categories. He was a different breed altogether. He believed his innocence, and even talked about the things he did in third person perspective, almost as if someone else had committed those crimes and he was the one trying to help us solve them. The only other person I know of who was like that was Ted Bundy. They share a lot of traits. The charm, the unwavering belief they had done nothing wrong. Hell, it was easy to believe he could be innocent until…'

Robbins lowered his eyes and looked at the table.

'Until what?' Rebecca asked, her voice only an octave above a whisper.

'Until he got angry and let the mask slip. Those were gold for us on the rare occasions it happened, as he would have no filter. He would rant about the things he did. How he would impregnate all the girls who came to live on the ranch, and because he only wanted a son, if they gave birth to a girl, he would dispose of them. Those were his words. *Dispose*. So cold. So clinical. The way he said it would make the hairs on my arms stand up. You would look into his eyes and there was nothing there. They were like glass. Jesus, look, it's happening right now.'

Robbins held up his forearm so they could see his tanned skin mottled with goosebumps, arm hairs standing rigid.

'Holy shit,' Dan muttered.

'That's where the frustration came. We got our guy, but everyone knew we could only charge him with a fraction of the crimes we suspect he has committed. To me, that still feels like an injustice. Like he's got away with so much more than he should have. Even now, that keeps me awake sometimes. I always wonder if there was more I could have done.'

Dan glanced at his sister, then back to Robbins. 'So, if you don't mind me asking, how many do you suspect he killed?'

'It's hard to say. We went over the grounds with a fine-tooth comb. Pulled it apart, dug so many holes looking for bodies, but came up with nothing. We might not have found them, but I know they're out there somewhere. Buried deep and undiscovered. Problem was, the plot of land was big, and we didn't have the resources to dig it all up, especially with no leads on where to look. You heard of that term, needle in a haystack? That's what this was.'

Dan was pale, blinking rapidly as he processed. Robbins next looked at the girl, and something twitched in his gut. She was taking it in, calm, looking right back at him.

She's definitely his daughter.

He didn't let that thought grow. Instead, he stared at the tabletop. 'The frustrations come from not knowing more than taking an educated guess. A lot of witness statements said people came and went from there over the years. Some were in and out with no knowledge of anything wrong had happened. Others had suspicions and left the place as soon as they could, but there was never proof. Remember, it was harder to find people in those days. If you were a drifter and didn't want to be found, you could do it. We have a theory he manipulated those who stayed at the ranch into giving him what they had. Money, valuables, that kind of thing, anything he could use to grow his empire. When he had drained them of everything he could, they disappeared. The circumstances of how, we don't know.'

He glanced at the siblings, making sure the information soaked in.

'Anyway,' Robbins said, taking another drink. 'I think for today I've said enough. There's a lot to process. My suggestion is the two of you get some rest. Tomorrow, if you still want to learn more, I'll pick up where we left off. Or there's still the option to forget about this and go home, although I can see from the look on your faces that isn't an option.'

'We can't go back. Not until we know all there is to know,' Rebecca said.

'I get it, even if I don't agree. If you two finish up, I'll take you back to the hotel.'

THE DEATH AND BIRTH OF AN IDEA
1973

The ranch had expanded, its fences stretching further into the endless fields of golden wheat, the scent of hay thick in the air. Outside, where a cornfield once stood, a long, barracks-style cabin had been constructed, housing fifty people. Like a well-oiled machine, each person played their part, their combined efforts creating a small, thriving community where everyone felt a sense of belonging. The scent of charring meat and wood smoke wafted up to Jim from the barbecue in the yard below, a languid summer breeze stirring the air as he stood smoking at the bedroom window, watching his followers. Gloria had taken on a leadership role. Even now, as he watched her down in the yard, she was giving orders and handing out instructions to the others. 'You still haven't decided how to guide them yet, have you?'

Jim glanced at the bed. It first belonged to Gloria's parents, then belonged to Gloria and him, and now belonged to Gloria, him and Mary. She was waiting for an answer, one arm propped behind her head, covers pulled up over her chest. He turned back to the window, watching life go on down below.

'It's okay. We know you'll find the path. When you do, we'll be ready to follow you.'

'I know the path,' Jim muttered.

Mary sat up, paying full attention. 'You do? You know it?'

'I've known for a while. I need to take it to where it needs to be.'

'What is it? Can you tell me?'

He glanced at her, then back to the window. 'Not yet. It's not time.'

'I bet Gloria knows.' Mary said, not hiding her frustration. Jim turned and perched on the bottom of the bed.

'I thought we agreed there would be no jealousy. You and Gloria love me and I, in return, love both of you.'

'Why does it have to be a secret? Meeting when nobody else is around, having to watch as you and her are together and pretend it's fine. It's not fair to me.'

Jim ground out his cigarette in the ashtray beside the bed. 'You don't think that she's oblivious to what's going on, do you?'

'She thinks you're guiding me. Helping me find the path.' There was no conviction in her words.

'Do you believe that?' Jim was curious if she had said it to get a reaction.

'I told you; the old rules of society don't apply here. Things are different. That's what makes this so special. There is enough love for us all to share, both physical and mental. There's no place for envy here.'

As Mary gazed at him, Jim responded with a smile, his hand reaching out to caress her cheek. 'I see the doubt in you. How long have you been here with us now?'

'A year, maybe. I'm not sure.' Her eyes burned, intense as she stared at him.

'Then you're aware of our way of life. Our different way of thinking. It's vital to achieving our goals and building a better future. Don't forget the promise we all made. All love, no judgement. I know you're unsure, and that's understandable, but this is the reality.'

Jim walked to the window and knocked on it. Gloria looked at him from the yard and he motioned for her to join him in the bedroom.

'What are you doing?' Mary hissed, as she scrambled to pull her clothes on from where they were piled next to the bed.

'I'm showing you there are no secrets here.'

Flustered, Mary looked from Jim to the door, as if she were some kind of cornered animal. 'I don't want to cause trouble here. You've all made me so welcome I couldn't face being alone again.'

There was no time for Jim to reply. Gloria opened the door and entered the room. Her expression twisted, face contorting for a second as she took in the scene. Jim was slick with sweat and shirtless. Mary was dishevelled with her clothes in disarray, the smell of sex in the air. It only took a second for her to close out the pain and hide it away. Now composed, she turned to Jim. Keeping her eyes on him, anywhere but the girl sitting in her bed. 'You wanted to see me?'

'I did. I was reminding Mary that love isn't limited to one person here. She didn't believe me and thought you would be angry with us for sharing each other's love without you.'

Somehow keeping her expression neutral, Gloria blinked away tears. 'Your way is the right way.'

A smile touched Jim's lips as his eyes met Mary's. Despite the clear signs of Gloria's inner turmoil—the strained silence, her trembling hands—he ignored her. 'Do you understand now?'

Mary said nothing. She could see the pain in Gloria, even if Jim didn't want to.

'I still see a doubt in your eyes,' Jim said, his voice soft as he sat on the bed and took Mary's hand in his. 'Gloria, why don't you close the door and come join us?'

Gloria opened her mouth, wanting to speak, but no words came out. Her mind was a whirlwind of static; her heart, a volcano of rage. Then she remembered the bigger picture. Jim had been clear. There would be zero tolerance for selfishness.

Her hand shaking, she shut the door, walked to the bed, and unbuttoned her shirt. 'That's it,' Jim said as he unfastened his jeans. 'There's enough love for everyone.'

INTERVIEW TRANSCRIPT

Present: *Interviewing officer Det Alexander Robbins*
Suspect: *James Warwick*
External Third-party observers: *Det Paul Jenkins. Anna Wallner (child protective services)*

AR: *Let's talk about the living arrangements at the ranch.*
JW: ***No response***
AR: *We have testimony that states you were engaging in multiple sexual relationships for the duration of your time there.*
JW: *If that's what the testimony says.*
AR: *Do you deny it?*
JW: *Can you prove it? You say one thing; I say another. Now here we are.*
AR retrieves photographs of ▆▆▆ (Evidence no: 495B432G-2)
AR: *Do you recognise the individual in this photograph?*
JW: *Yes.*
AR: *For the benefit of the tape, could you confirm the name of the person?*
JW: *That's ▆▆▆. You know that, though.*
AR: *Did you engage in sexual activity with her?*
JW: **no answer given**
AR: *We have testimony that states–*
JW: *Did you fuck your wife last night? Can you prove it?*
** AR is heard hitting the desk**
AR: *This girl was underage. That makes you a rapist.*
JW: *if you insist James Warwick did it, then it must be true. Is that the plan? Pin it all on me and close your case, all wrapped in a bow?*
AR: *Do you deny it?*
JW: *What did she tell you? She may say we did, I may say we didn't. Where does that leave us?*
AR: *I'm asking you, just–*
JW: *How many fingers can you fit inside your wife, Alex? You have a kid, don't you? So I would guess three. Maybe four if you get her wet.*
AR: *You fucking animal....*

We hear noise as the interview room door opens.

PJ: For the record, Detective Paul Jenkins has entered the room. Go take a breather, Alex. Grab a coffee.
AR: No, I'm fine, he just…
PJ: Go now, I'll take over until you get back.

** silence until we hear the interview door slam closed.**

PJ: For the record, Detective Robbins has left the room. Now, back to the case in hand. In relation to your conduct towards–
JW: Not you.
PJ: I don't understand.
JW: I won't talk to you. Just him. Just Robbins.
PJ: He's not here, so you'll have to talk to me. Now, about the girl. Did you have sex with her knowing she was a minor?
JW: *No answer given*
PJ: Answer the question. Did you knowingly have sexual intercourse with a minor?

*Warwick continues his silence. The interview is ended shortly after.

THAT GREEN-EYED MONSTER PART 1

Jim inhaled on his cigarette, the acrid smoke burning his throat. He told himself this was a test of his devotion, a trial to prove his loyalty to the cause. Dusk had fallen, and he was sitting on the porch, dark sunglasses concealing his eyes. Mary and the boy were sitting cross-legged on the ground across the yard, their laughter drifting to Jim as they flirted. A rage, so pure in its ferocity, twisted and writhed through every part of him, yet he remained frozen, knowing his word he had tried so hard to ingrain into the others would mean nothing if he acted. He drew on his cigarette, attempting to find peace, yet the rage throbbed relentlessly.

He was unfamiliar with the boy and couldn't remember his arrival at the ranch. That in itself wasn't unusual. A steady stream of people flowed in and out, some drawn by curiosity, others by conviction; those who believed in the vision stayed, their numbers growing; the rest drifted off, never to be seen again. This one, though, whoever he was, had stayed. Jim was sure if it was because of his belief in what they were doing or because of Mary, but had his suspicions.

Deep within his consciousness, a whisper urged him to disregard the potential repercussions and act on the impulses he was trying to suppress. Jim watched as the pair talked, the boy's words lost in the distance from them to him, but her reaction wasn't. The way she laughed at whatever he had said, the way she leaned into him, her fingers touching lightly on his forearm.

Inside Jim, the inferno threatened to explode out of him. By some miracle, he kept it at bay.

As he watched them flirting, a skinny man named Adam, with acne-covered cheeks, poked his head out of the back door. He was one of those who'd chosen to stay and had been with them for a while.

'Hey, Jim, there's a guy out front asking to talk to you. Says he's a cop.'

Jim watched Mary for a few more seconds, took off his sunglasses and went into the house.

II

Jim's first impressions of the man waiting outside—a nondescript figure in a worn suit, shifting from foot to foot—didn't amount to much. His inexpensive suit, his hair greying at the temples, the deepening lines around his mouth and eyes showing time was catching up with him. He stood there, hands clasped before him, the gold of his wedding band catching the fading sunlight.

Be careful.

His inner voice only spoke up when it sensed trouble, and he had learned not to ignore it.

'Are you the owner of this property?' The man asked.

'No, this is my girlfriend's place. Well, her family home.' Jim didn't like the way his eyes moved. They were always shifting, processing. Gathering information. 'What is this about?'

The man showed a police badge. 'My name is Detective Robbins; I'm investigating the disappearance of a teenage girl who was last seen in this area. I was hoping to speak to Mrs Pennington.'

Jim showed no signs of panic as he held eye contact with the detective. He almost fell into a trap. The detective would have caught him in a lie if he'd said he was the homeowner. He may have come to the house playing dumb, but this man was no fool.

'Well? Have you seen her?' Robbins asked.

Jim realised those busy eyes had settled on him, and he didn't like it one bit.

'Possibly. As you say, we have many people come here. There's a chance she may have been through at some point. Do you have a name or picture I can look at?'

'Yes,' Robbins said. He reached into his pocket to retrieve a black-and-white photograph and handed it to Jim.

'This is the girl. She ran away last year. We've tracked her movements to this area. Answers to the name of Mary.'

Jim looked at the photograph, careful not to allow recognition to register. 'I'm sorry I haven't seen this girl before,' he said, handing the picture back to the detective.

As soon as he had taken the photograph, Robins put it back in his pocket, his eyes still fixed on Jim, never wavering. 'You sure about that? A few people we interviewed seemed to think she might live here.'

'I doubt that.'

'I see. When is Mrs Pennington due back?' Those eyes were searching again, waiting to trip him up.

'It won't be for a while.'

'Why might that be?'

'She's travelling. Towards Nevada, I think, but who knows from there? She's with a friend who has a camper van.'

Robbins wrote something in his notebook.

'I see. And they left you in charge?'

There it was, another trap.

Jim forced a laugh. 'Unlikely. This is my girlfriend's house. They left her to look after the place.'

'And can I speak to her?'

Don't say too much.

'You'd have to ask her that.'

'Can you get her to come to the door?'

'Sorry, she's not home right now. She's out with a few friends.'

A grunt escaped Robbins' lips as he continued his note-taking, pen scratching across the pages of his notebook, eyes darting, trying to see beyond Jim into the house.

'Would you mind if I came in and looked around?'

Jim shrugged, trying to keep cool. 'If it were my house and up to me, no problem at all, but it's not my place to give the okay for that. You understand, right?'

If he understood, Robbins said nothing. He scribbled something else in his notebook.

'And Mrs Pennington is fine with all these people living here when she's not at home?'

'Of course. As long as we don't wreck the place, which, as you can see, we're not, she has no issue with it.'

Robbins considered for a moment. Eyes probing, looking for a weakness. 'And the daughter, your girlfriend, that would be Gloria, would it?'

There it was again. Fishing for information he already knew. Trying to catch a lie.

'That's right,' Jim said, knowing it was pointless to deny it.

'Any idea when she'll be back?'

'Sorry, I don't. You know how girls are when they get together.'

Robbins stared for a few more agonising seconds, then put the notepad back in his pocket. 'In that case, I'll be on my way.'

He reached into his other pocket and handed Jim a card with his name and number printed on it.

'When your girlfriend gets home, please ask her to call me. I would like to speak to both her and her Mother.'

Jim took the card and read it. 'Alright, no problem, I'll pass this on.'

Robbins did one last visual sweep, then turned and jogged down the steps into the yard and got into his car. Jim watched as he drove away, kicking up a cloud of dust that swirled and settled behind him as he disappeared down the road.

Gloria came out of a side room and stood beside Jim. 'Do we have anything to worry about?'

'No. Don't worry. I'll fix everything,' Jim said as Gloria hugged him.

DIVINE INFLUENCE

Jim did not know how long he had been sitting there, eyes closed, cheeks streaked with tears. All he knew was that the day had become night, shrouding the room in shadows. This was a pivotal moment in his journey, a crossroads which would shape the course of everything that followed. The revolution would start if their faith in him proved true. If they didn't buy in, he wasn't sure what the future would hold. Failure would mean he would become the thing his drunk of a father always said he would be. Nothing. Nobody.

Jim could almost see him, the inky shadows displaying him like a grotesque TV screen. Cold eyes, waxy skin, gut overhanging his jeans. He could even hear his voice, the disgust. The shame.

You're a waster, boy. A dreamer. People like you never amount to shit. You get it from your mother. Ain't enough of me in you, that's the problem. Too much pussy in your blood and not enough pecker.

How long ago had that conversation happened? He couldn't remember. He was young, though, but old enough for the words to cut deep, the wounds even now still open, bleeding a slow death until he could prove his cunt of a father wrong. And that, he supposed, was why he had spent so long in limbo. Desperate to prove a man he hadn't seen in years wrong but afraid to commit because he wasn't sure he had what it took to see it through.

As the voice of his father continued relentless cycles in his mind, Gloria entered the room. Walking to where he sat, she stood behind him and placed her hands on his shoulders. 'They're ready,' she said, kissing him on the back of the head, then she used the sleeve of her shirt to wipe away the streaky tears from his cheeks.

'I don't know if I can do it,' he whispered in the dark.

'They believe. We all believe.'

'I'm scared, Gloria.'

'No, you're not. It's the waiting. Sometimes it's better to do something than spend too long thinking about it.'

Jim stood and turned towards her. He placed his hands on Gloria's stomach and the slight bump under her shirt. 'You carry the future inside you. *Our* future. The first of a new generation who will live in a better world than ours.'

She clasped her hands over his, tears spilling down her cheeks.

'Then go out there and shape it. Give our child the future they deserve.'

'Our Son.' He said, stroking her cheek.

'Maybe, who knows?'

'I know. I don't know how, but I do.' He pulled her hands towards his and kissed them. 'Okay, I'm ready. Tell them I'll be down in a few minutes.' He released her hands, tuning towards the window and looking out at the black silhouette of the barn across the yard, light from inside like fire spilling out of the open doors. He knew once he entered, the light would either burn him alive or fuel the change that needed to come.

II

They waited for him in expectant silence, now numbering close to a hundred, searching for meaning and hoping he would provide it. Jim strode from the house. An aura of self-assurance replaced the earlier uncertainty. He arrived not to applause, but to silence. Jim entered the barn, climbed the makeshift stage they had constructed across the back wall, and stood behind the podium as they filed in, took their seats, and waited, curious to see what would happen. He let the silence linger long enough for the anticipation to build to breaking point. The cavernous space amplified his words, projecting his voice when he spoke.

'As a family, we stand united. Our shared beliefs brought you here. We are tired of a world which is changing for the worse. The greed of those in positions of power fuels the ever-present danger of war, their relentless pursuit of profit, ruthlessly exploits the weak and vulnerable, showing no compassion as they amass their fortunes while crushing this generation underfoot.'

There were a few murmurs and nods of agreement from the crowd. 'Television tries to tell us how we should look, what we should aspire to be. That who we are is not good enough. Look different. Spend more. Stay in line or suffer the consequences. They want to condition us, to change us into mindless sheep who follow the will of the government and thank them for keeping us in the dirt.'

Cheers from the crowd as the intensity of Jim's voice increases.

'That idea, that concept, is a world which none of us agree with. We can all see it is a world which needs change. And it is our job, this generation, to make it happen and stop them taking everything and leaving nothing for the rest of us.'

More cheers erupt from the crowd as Jim gets into his stride. 'Make no mistake, our government, our society, the very people who swore to protect us, have abandoned us. Without action, history will remember us as the lost generation. A generation who did nothing to fight back against tyranny. Are you prepared, years from now, to look into the eyes of your children and grandchildren when they ask us why we did nothing to fix the world?'

The energy around the barn was building to a crescendo. At the end of each line said, the crowd erupted into cheers. The energy fed Jim, increasing the intensity of his delivery.

'I'm not willing to leave a broken world for my children to inherit. Those of us who see the truth and will do whatever it takes must make changes now.'

He let the thought hang. His skin was hot and clammy with adrenaline, making his clothes stick. The air crackled with excitement and anticipation.

The ghost of his father swam into his mind's eye.

Ain't enough of me in you, that's the problem. Too much pussy in your blood and not enough pecker.

No. He wouldn't let him in. Not now. He pushed his father back into the void and continued.

'I know what you're thinking. How can we, so few, make enough change so that it makes a difference? This is the question to which I have been seeking the answer to. These months when you have waited with patience, no, not patience. Devotion. it would have been easy to walk away, to give up, but each of you here today stayed. And now, here all together, I have the answer we've been looking for.'

He waited. The silence stretched, heavy and expectant, as his audience processed his words.

'Growing up, I was never a religious man. All of you here know that. Know me. You know it's the truth, which is why when I tell you what I'm about to tell you, each of you should know it is the absolute truth.'

Another pause. Here it was. Time to find out if he was pussy or pecker.

'That truth is this. When I was searching for the way, God came to me. Now I know what you must be thinking. Insanity. Impossible. I agree, I would have said the same, and yet the fact is, it happened. He came to show me what we must do and the path we must take. Make no mistake. God wants change as much as we do. And now, thanks to this…miracle. I know the way to do it. I know the path we have to take.'

Something had shifted. The fear of rejection, of them laughing him off the stage, had gone. In its place was borderline hysteria. Jim had to shout to make himself heard over the noise. The hairs on his arms stood to attention as they bellowed their support.

'We may be few, but we have God on our side, and we will be victorious. We will change the world for the better.'

Jim glanced towards Gloria at the side of the stage. She was clapping, tears streaming down her face, the joy and belief in his words mirrored through the crowd.

'He showed me the path, and as his vessel, I will show it to you now, along with some hard truth about what we are facing. Peaceful protest or appealing to our government will have no effect. To achieve success, we must take decisive action. We must create a legacy so powerful, a statement that demands the world's attention. We will go to any extreme, no matter how far-reaching, to make our point. If we have to blow up a building, we will. If we have to make an example of a celebrity with brutality to make them stop and listen, then absolutely, we will.'

The crowd was in a frenzy, roaring him on.

'Make no mistake, when we do this, when the powers that be realise what we are trying to do, they will come for us. We must prepare for that fight. This place, our home, must become a sanctuary to protect us. We need to fortify. We need weapons. A war is coming, make no mistake, but I don't fear it. Do you know why? Because God has already told me, we will win. If you believe in me, and if you believe in the way he has shown us, then know even death can hold no fear, because I have already guaranteed each of us a passage to Eden. It is our actions, today, that will safeguard the future. The things we must do, as terrible and violent as they may seem, will be for the greater good. We *will* succeed, we *will* be victorious, and we *will* fix this broken shell of a world together as one, our glorious family.'

Jim basked in the admiration, his eyes closed, head thrown back. The deafening cheers of the crowd enveloped him, an almost physical energy that vibrated through his very being. He had never felt so alive.

THE GREEN-EYED MONSTER PART 2

Gloria had no reason to hate Mary apart from the oldest of human emotions, jealousy. From the porch, she watched Jim say something amusing, then Mary laugh, putting a hand on his arm. She had seen enough flirting in her time to recognise it. The feeling wasn't just jealousy; it was a cocktail of envy, anger, and a nauseating sense of injustice. An ache that seemed to come from the centre of her being, white-hot tendrils of fury radiating out, nerve by nerve, vein by vein.

No matter how she tried to ignore it, or tell herself she was imagining things, she couldn't help but feel inadequate. Mary was younger. Looked better, plus she didn't have the same baggage she carried around with her like a noose waiting to pull itself taut. Things that came to her in flashes. Blood and shame, regret and fear at what she had done. She remembered her father once telling her about how some people, when they came back from the War, hadn't been the same. They couldn't shake the trauma and horror of what they experienced, and she thought she may have something similar. She watched them talk, wondering what the two of them could have to discuss with such intensity.

She had no memory of standing or walking across the yard. It wasn't until the sound of their conversation faded, and she met the silent, questioning gazes of Mary and Jim, that she understood what had happened.

'Can I speak with you?' she asked.

'Of course.' Jim said.

Gloria glared at Mary, then back to Jim. 'Alone.'

Mary sensed Gloria's hostility towards her, and left Jim and Gloria to their discussion.

'Come with me,' she said as Jim got up and fell in beside her. They walked across the yard, past the coops where the chickens, disturbed by their approach, scuffled and clucked behind the wire fence. They walked away from the house so the others wouldn't hear their conversation.

'What did you want to talk about?' Jim asked.

That was a good question. She couldn't admit to approaching him because she was jealous. That would be the worst thing she could do. She had to say something though, otherwise he might wonder why she had broken up his conversation with Mary.

'The police.' She said, unsure where she was going with it.

'We can only keep turning them away for so long.'

'There's nothing they can do, no matter what they suspect, with no evidence. They are powerless.'

'I know that, but look around. We're exposed here. So much open land around us. If they get a search warrant, we are in no position to stop them from coming into the grounds.'

'You're right. We're exposed right now,' Jim said, looking around at the fields surrounding the ranch.

'We could put up some fences, something to deter them.'

Jim shook his head. 'No. If we do this, we do it right. We need something we can defend. Concrete walls, too high to climb over.'

'If we do that, it might make the police more interested.'

Jim gave her a disarming smile. 'I don't care if they get interested. As far as I know, securing your property isn't illegal.'

'Also, about the weaponry situation. One of the new arrivals says he knows how to manufacture ammunition if we can get a workshop set up for him.'

'That's a great idea. When the fight comes to us, we need to be prepared. Find out what he needs and make it happen.' Jim said, surprised she would bring it up.

'We never have to use them, but I think it would bring comfort to everyone here to know we have a means to defend ourselves if we have to.'

He stopped walking, taking her hands and kissed her on the forehead. 'I trust your judgement.'

She thought of the fire inside. Of Mary and how she wanted those flames to burn that bitch to ash. Not now though. It wasn't the right time.

'We have a few people here who have worked in construction. We can get them to show us how to construct the walls so they are strong.' She said, pushing the thoughts of revenge away for the time being.

'It will take a lot of effort to surround the house. We should start straight as soon as we can.'

'You don't have to do the work yourself. We have people willing to do that for you.'

'You don't understand. If they see me doing the work myself, they will know how much this means and will want to help.'

None of this was what she had wanted to talk about. She had hoped Jim would notice she was upset and ask her about it, and it hurt that he hadn't. Gloria glared at Mary.

'You two are spending a lot of time together.' As calm as she said it, she could see herself jamming her thumbs into Mary's eyes until she heard the gelatinous pop as they burst.

'I assume you're talking about Mary.'

'Who else?'

'This is normal. He told me this is natural.'

'Who told you? God? how fucking convenient.' The fire was there again, white hot and raging inches under her skin.

'I thought you were with me. Why do you doubt me now after everything we've done to reach this point? Your sacrifices, especially, have been more than most would be prepared to do.'

'Don't put that on me if you're talking about my mother. Weren't you the one who said we should never mention it again?'

'You mentioned her, Gloria, not me.'

'Why can't you understand this is hard for me, Jim? After what we did -'

Gloria noticed the volume of their conversation had increased, and had drawn the attention of the others. Gloria motioned towards the house. They went inside and closed the door so they could continue their discussion in private. 'It's not that I doubt you, I just...'

'Say it. Whatever is on your mind, let it out.'

'You never mentioned God before. Not until you had to make that big speech. Before that, you were lost, but a miracle happened, and God spoke to you when you needed to give them something concrete. It all feels a little too convenient timing wise, so I'm just going to ask you. Was it a lie, so you had something to tell them?'

Jim didn't lose his temper or try to justify his actions. Instead, he looked her in the eye, his gaze intense and unwavering.

'I wondered when you would ask me about it. I'm surprised it took so long.'

Love and adoration, unexpected and powerful, now warred with the anger that still simmered in her gut, leaving her bewildered by her own feelings. She walked to the window and stared out at the garden.

'You're crying.'

Gloria wiped her eyes and looked at the floor. 'I want to understand what we're doing here. I'm so confused. It was supposed to be about us together, but we're becoming more distant and... I don't even know if we're ready for what you want us to do. I've sacrificed everything for you, and I feel like I'm not involved in whatever is going on anymore.'

'Come sit,' he said, gesturing towards the sofa as he sat in the chair opposite. Gloria complied. She was shaking, her eyes stinging from the tears. She hugged her own stomach, noticeably without baby bump.

'I'm sorry if I've upset you. It wasn't intentional. I understand you have questions and I know how much you have given so we can be here in this place. Don't think I don't appreciate the sacrifices you have made.'

'You're avoiding the question. Was God speaking to you a lie?'

'I understand why you're asking, just remember to-'

'No. none of that. None of the long-winded stuff you tell them. Tell me, right now, yes or no, was it a lie?'

Jim watched her, and she felt elated. It felt like the first time he had seen her in months.

'No, it wasn't a lie, but it's not as cut and dry as it seems.'

'Then explain it to me. No bullshit. You said you always liked how to the point I was when we first met, so I'm doing it now. Tell me how it happened.'

Jim sat back in the chair, folding his hands over his stomach. 'For as long as I can remember, I have felt as if I were two people. There was always this voice inside my head that would guide me, tell me things, even keep me calm when my dad used to come home drunk and decide to beat the shit out of me.'

You're a waster, boy. A dreamer. People like you never amount to shit. You get it from your mother. Ain't enough of me in you, that's the problem. Too much pussy in your blood and not enough pecker.

Jim exhaled, and once again, reburied his father back in the brain compartment where he lived.

'Over the years, I've grown to rely on that voice. It's like an actual other person inside me with its own thoughts and feelings, and as weird as it sounds, it has always steered me in the right direction, so the night I was about to give the speech in the barn, and you came to see me, do you remember?'

'Of course. I'll never forget that day,' she replied, realising the fire inside was dimming, now glowing red rather than white hot. He had that ability to do that to her, which she loved and hated.

'Do you remember when you came in? I had been crying?'

'I wiped your tears away. I hated seeing you that way.'

'And I appreciated that, but here's the thing. I wasn't crying because of stress or sadness. I was crying because after months of asking that voice inside for an answer and getting nothing back, it had responded when I needed it the most.'

He was sitting on the edge of his seat, eyes wide. For the first time since they met, a flicker of fear flushed through her. 'That voice I had been hearing since childhood, the one I trusted more than anything else in this world, was never a part of me. It was the voice of God. He had been guiding me my entire fucking life, I just didn't know It. It isn't a ploy or a deception for them or you or anyone else. This is a genuine revelation. It makes everything clear.'

'In what way?' Gloria asked, her voice a near whisper.

'Don't you see? God had this plan from the start. He's been with me ever since I was a kid. This entire project didn't start the day we met at that beach party. It has been in play for years, waiting for me to understand it. You know me better than anyone else, Gloria. You know I have never been a religious man; I've never been one to preach. I was chosen all the same.'

'How do you know it's God?' There was something in his eyes she had never seen before, a darkness that made her uncomfortable.

'I can't explain it. I wouldn't know how. You have to either believe in it or not. That is up to you. As Nobody is a prisoner here. If you don't want to follow the path, you are welcome to leave.'

It came again. The anger. The fury. 'So you can be with her? You don't get to fucking use me, then throw me away when you get bored.'

'Calm down. You've misunderstood.'

'You said I should leave.' she was frustrated by how much he had hurt her.

'I want you here, of course I do. My relationship with Mary has no bearing on us.'

She had never seen him so emotionless. Something had changed in him. She wondered if this version had always been there, hidden beneath the surface.

'So, you're saying you wouldn't mind if I went outside, found a guy to fuck, then scream the house down so you can hear it?'

'If that's what you want to do, I won't stop you. We have a bond, Gloria, but in no way does that mean we have to be exclusive to each other.'

She inhaled, blinking through the tears, temples pulsing as she tried to figure out where it had all gone wrong. She was still angry, but those words had knocked the fight right out of her, so that when she next spoke, it was almost a whisper.

'But we share a bed. We're supposed to be together, you and us, no matter what. That's what you said.'

'I want you to stay with us, Gloria. I love you, but I can't promise to love *only* you.'

She wanted to hug him, hit him, devote herself to him and leave him and all of this behind. In the end, she cried because it was all she could think to do. There was no reassurance from him. No words of comfort. He stood and left her alone. A few moments later, she heard him out front, chatting and laughing with Mary as if nothing had ever happened.

A LESSON IN POWER

The boy Mary had been growing close to was called Steven. Although he had tried to ignore it, Jim felt a burning sensation in his chest. What had begun as a small spark of envy had become a raging inferno threatening to consume him.

He showed Steven cold indifference in their few interactions, even though he knew it made him a hypocrite. Worst of all, he suspected Mary was aware of his feelings and still continued to flirt.

Mary and some of the others had gone to town for supplies, giving Jim a chance to get to know her admirer.

He placed a hand on his bible, the aged leather cool beneath his fingertips, the weight of history palpable in its worn pages. It had birthdays scrawled on the yellowing inside hard cover, which showed the copy of the Bible had been in the Pennington family for at least three generations. Asking for the strength to forgive and move on, Jim tucked the hefty book under his arm and went out into the garden.

Steven was mixing cement ready for the continued construction of the perimeter wall. When complete, it would surround the house and gardens, giving them the protection they wanted. For now, it was mostly trenches filled with concrete and ready for the bricks to be installed. Jim wanted a double layer, the entire thing encased in concrete for extra strength.

As the muscular, shirtless Steven mixed the cement, Jim felt a twinge of envy. He watched for a few moments. Steven noticed, but kept working.

'Come, walk with me for a while,' Jim said.

'Is there something wrong?' Steven asked.

'No, I wanted to get an update on the construction and also some time to talk to you. I realise I haven't yet with things being so busy. I thought you could join me on my morning walk.'

'Okay, let me grab my shirt.'

Jim waited as Steven pulled on his T shift, then the two of them walked away from the house towards the scrub of trees in the bordering the fields.

'I see you take this walk every day,' Steven said.

'I've always enjoyed walking. Spending time with my thoughts, that kind of thing. It's nice to leave the troubles of the world behind, if only for a while.'

Steven nodded to the Bible 'A bit of privacy to read too, I imagine.'

Jim switched the heavy book to under his other arm and nodded. 'Sometimes I read. Sometimes I walk and let my mind drift where it wants to.'

'Yeah, that makes sense, I guess.'

They had left the house behind now, the trees looming ahead.

'The wall is coming along.' Jim said. 'I noticed you've been very involved in the construction.'

Steven nodded. 'My dad works in construction. Before we drifted apart, he used to have me help in the summer holidays on whatever jobs he was working, so I picked up a lot of knowledge. Since I'm being allowed to stay here, I figured it was only fair to put those skills I learned to use.'

'And appreciated they are. You say you and your father drifted apart?'

Steven squirmed, and Jim noticed the discomfort. He lifted the tension with a smile. 'You don't have to answer that. Blame my curiosity.'

'No, it's fine, it's no secret, it's one of those things I tend not to talk about, that's all.'

They headed into the treeline. It was a cooler in the shadows, away from the glare of the sun. Jim led them deeper as Steven continued.

'Early on, my dad and me, we had a great relationship. He would take me camping, fishing, all that stuff. Then, when I was around sixteen, he started drinking. Nobody noticed it at first until the couple of beers after work became a few before work, then a couple during his breaks to take the edge off… Well, you can imagine how it went from there.'

'My dad was the same. Drink ruined him.'

Steven nodded 'So you know how the rest of this plays out. It's always everyone else's fault, never his that he can't keep it together. Eventually, my mother has enough and leaves. Tells nobody about it. I come home from working with my dad one day and she's gone and all her stuff is too. We never hear from her again. You'd think something like that would make him stop, but it has the opposite effect. He dives deeper into the bottle. Loses his job, then he takes it out on me.'

'I know all about that, too,' Jim said. 'My dad beat the hell out of me. Sometimes for nothing when he was drunk, then the day after claimed he couldn't remember. I knew he could. He was too much of a coward to admit it.'

The confession surprised Jim. He hadn't expected to open up himself, but Steven's story was such a close parallel to his own, he couldn't help it. Being able to speak with someone who understood how it felt was refreshing. For a moment, they ambled through the woods until Steven spoke again.

'Anyway, I took that shit from him for three years before I had enough. I realised my mother had the right idea and the best thing to do was to leave the bastard to his own devices. So, one morning, I packed a bag, snuck into his room where he was sleeping off the previous night's drinking, emptied his wallet and left. Let me tell you, a young kid drifting around with only a couple of hundred dollars to his name and nowhere to call home isn't a good way to live life.'

They walked on in silence. Even the birds, it seemed, were unwilling to interrupt this moment.

Jim glanced at Steven, who was the exact type of person they had been looking to recruit for the work they had to do. His envy prevented him from realising it. He waited to see if the inner voice had anything to say, but it was silent.

'What about the future?' Jim asked. 'Do you plan to stay with us or move on? I know how hard it is to settle when you've become used to drifting from place to place.'

'As long as I'm welcome here, I'll stay. It feels like something big is about to happen and I want to be a part of whatever it is.'

They had approached a clearing of sorts. There was a folding chair set up by an overturned tree stump. Jim motioned to it. 'Go ahead, take a seat.'

Steven complied, Jim paced, bible still tucked under his arm.

'What is this place?' Steven asked.

'Before you arrived, and before they built the housing block, people used to camp up here. I still like to come here and relax. It's peaceful.'

Steven looked around and could see why. As sunlight filtered through the dense tree canopy above the clearing, it created beams of golden light that illuminated the space surrounded by the trees.

'I can't thank you enough for what you have done for us. You've given us a place to call home. A lot of us have never had that. It can't be easy, doing what you do and having so many rely on you.'

'It's a heavy burden, being a leader. Sometimes, too heavy.' He turned towards Steven. 'Do you ever see yourself as a leader, Steven?'

Steven shook his head. 'No, I don't think so. I mean, I work hard, I always have, but I don't think I have that in me. Some people do, some don't, and I'm pretty sure I'm the don't kind. I'm fine with that, though. I know my strengths and they are working with my hands. Physical work. That I can do.'

'There's a lot to be said for manual work. An honesty.'

It was in that moment, his envy melted away. He could sense Steven wasn't his enemy, and was almost embarrassed at how his emotions had almost taken control.

What is it, not got the guts to do what you came out here to do?

It was the first time God had spoken to him all day. Jim closed his eyes, not wanting to do what he knew was about to be asked of him.

'Hey, are you okay?' Steven asked.

Jim blinked and somehow managed a smile. 'Yeah, I'm good. Sometimes it's nice to stop and soak it in. Nature, I mean.'

'I agree. One thing I never wanted to do was work inside. I enjoy working outdoors, knowing I've worked hard, earned my keep.'

Then what, he comes back to her...running him a bath, rubbing his shoulders, sliding her hands under the water, getting him off as he sits there and soaks.

Jim nodded to Steven, pacing some more. Trying to fight the voice.

She's yours. You know how this goes. It starts with the flirting, then it escalates. It always does.

With a purposeful stride, Jim walked toward Steven, removed the Bible from under his arm, and opened it to the page he had bookmarked. 'I want to show you something in here. I think you'll enjoy it.'

Steven struggled to read the tiny words on the aged pages, the shadows of the trees obscuring the text.

'I'm struggling to see this. Truth be told, I'm supposed to wear glasses, but they make me look a bit…well dorky, I guess.'

He wants to look good for her. For Mary.

Jim moved closer, standing behind the chair. 'it's fine, I memorised it. I'll recite it for you.'

'Okay, no problem,' Steven said. He wasn't especially religious, but didn't want to offend his host, so went along with it.

'What I wanted to show you was Psalm 41. It reads, *even my close friend with whom I trusted, who ate my bread, has lifted his heel against me,*'

'I don't un-'

In the end, there was no hesitation.

Jim threw his hands over Steven's head, the fishing wire wrapped around his fists gouging into his throat. Digging his heels into the leaf littered ground, he pulled with everything he had. Steven struggled, gasping for air, his hands flailing as he tried to reach Jim, but the fight was hopeless.

Jim hoped it would be quick, but Steven fought. He thrashed, legs kicking, the heavy bible sliding to the ground, a few of the old pages coming loose and scattering around the feet of the two men.

Jim didn't notice. Everything was static. He felt like an observer watching the scene unfold through frosted glass. Deep inside, the voice in his head laughed.

Later.

Jim was sitting in his usual spot on the back step, smoking a cigarette. Mary approached, sitting beside him. He saw she was troubled and suspected he knew why.

'Have you seen Steven anywhere?'

'Who?'

'Steven.'

'Oh, no sorry, I've not seen him.' He was amazed how easy it was to lie when he knew everything he had done was at God's command.

'He was here earlier.' Mary said, scanning the garden. 'Someone said they saw you talking to him.' She flicked her eyes at him, then focussed on the backs of her hands.

'Was he helping build the wall?' Jim asked, leaning into the lie.

'Yeah, that's him.'

Visions of Steven choking and gasping, face turning purple flashed into his mind. He pushed them away. 'You know how things are here.'

'What do you mean?'

'People come and go all the time. Maybe he decided it was time to move on.'

'I don't think he'd leave without telling me.'

A flicker of envy, even after everything that had happened. Jim ignored it. There was nothing to be jealous of anymore.

'Well, maybe he'll be back later. Could be he's gone into town or for a walk.'

'Yeah, maybe. If you see him, will you tell him I'm looking for him?'

'Absolutely.'

Mary walked away. Jim watched her go, surprised at how little he felt. He felt no guilt or sadness, only a black void inside that absorbed what he had done. He thought back to the conversation he'd had with Steven, about how some people are good at certain things. Steven was good at manual work, construction. Building. Jim thought that killing was the thing he was best at. It was a sobering thought. And as for Mary? She'd get used to Steven's absence, and things would go back to the way they used to be.

Satisfied with his day's work, Jim stood, stubbed out his cigarette under his boot and went into the house.

CONNECTING THE DOTS

Robbins was driving into what seemed like the middle of nowhere. Cornfields and farmland replaced the urban concrete, stretching as far as the eye could see on both sides of the road. There was a strange tension in the air as they left the city behind.

'So where are we going?' Dan asked.

'There are a couple of things I want to show you. It's easier if you see it first-hand so that when I tell the rest, you can put some context to it.'

'Is it a long drive?'

'No, we're making our first stop in a few minutes.'

'Since we have a little time, I have a question.' Rebecca said.

'Shoot.'

'It's not about the case, but more about you. How did you become so involved?'

'I thought we established I worked the case. Invested years into it.'

'I get that, but when you tell us about what happened, it feels like more than someone telling us about an old case. It feels like this is quite personal for you.'

Robbins switched lanes, navigating the car onto an industrial estate.

'You know, my ex-wife used to say the same thing, and I never had an answer for her either. At least, not one that would make any sense. Maybe when you know the full story and have all the information, it will make sense to tell you. Without proper context, I don't think you'd understand it from my side.'

He glanced in the mirror, saw they were about to quiz him further, and got in first before they could.

'Anyway, that will have to wait. We're at our first stop.'

Bringing the car to a halt outside the multi-level carpark, an unappealing slate grey structure that served the shopping mall behind it, Robbins squinted at the structure through the car window.

'Why are we stopping here?' Dan asked.

'This was always where we were stopping.' Robbins muttered. 'Come on, let's take a walk.'

He got out of the car. The twins followed. Their eyes scanned the bland expanse of concrete. Besides the car park, a few thrift stores and a dilapidated hall advertising Friday bingo with gaudy neon signs were nearby. At the back, overlooking these lesser structures, the immense glass and steel shopping mall. It didn't fit in there, surrounded by so much green. It was an ugly blot on the landscape.

Robbins saw the confusion on Dan and Rebecca as they took in the surroundings.

'This is where the ranch used to be. After the trial, it sat for a while. Damn thing became a goddamn magnet for tourists looking to see the horror house. Stirred the locals up too who didn't like all the attention.'

Robbins hated how vivid the memories were of how it used to be. He had hoped age and time would dull them, but they were as sharp as ever. In his mind's eye, he could still see the house – at the end, more of a fortress protecting its inhabitants.

He nodded towards an overfilled green waste bin across the car park. 'Over there is where I was shot during the raid. Lucky for me, the bullet nicked off a bone in my forearm. I can't complain, it could have been worse.'

'Did... *he* shoot you?' Dan asked.

'No, it was one of his followers. Lucky for me, I was trained, and he wasn't. He missed his chance to kill me. I made sure he didn't get a second chance.'

'You killed him?' Dan had been scuffing his shoes on the concrete as Robbins was talking, but was now watching him for his response.

'He shot at me. I returned fire. Stuff like that happens on instinct. If you stop to think, chances are you don't walk out alive. Remember, those who followed him would have done anything to protect him, even if it cost them their lives.'

'I read about the day of the Siege. One article even had a few photos taken in the aftermath of it.' Rebecca said. 'They censored the photos, blurring the bodies, but you could tell it had been bad.' She looked at Dan for his reaction, but he was stony faced and giving nothing away.

'Yeah, well, let me tell you, kid. I wish I could censor my memories. That kind of shit stays with you forever.'

'It must be hard to live with.' Dan said.

'It wasn't easy. Some guys on the team that day were never the same afterwards. I had been with the force for almost thirty years. In all that time, I only had to pull my gun ten times. I've fired it three times and hit the intended target twice. One was wounded and survived. The other who we have just been talking about, didn't.'

They were silent. By one of the thrift stores, a tired-looking mother walked hand in hand with her infant child, who was mid tantrum and demanding ice cream, which it seemed the mother had no intention of providing.

'Do you come out here often?' Rebecca asked, trying to fit the photographs she'd seen of the ranch in the articles she'd read to the scene in front of her and struggling to make it fit.

'No. When they bulldozed the place, I came out here. I hoped seeing it torn down would make those memories go away, but it never works like that. I was so happy when I heard the city had enough of the attention the place was getting and pulled it down. This is the first time I've been back since.'

'It's hard to believe it was ever here. This place looks like everywhere else.' Dan said.

'Oh, it's still here all right.' Robbins muttered.

'What do you mean?' Rebecca asked.

'You two won't feel it because you've only seen your books and websites. For me, I can still sense it. It's like a ghost.'

'What was it like on the day of the raid?' Dan asked, staring at the shopping mall as if he could see the compound.

Robbins remained silent. He watched a half-crushed Pepsi cup skitter across the carpark as the wind picked up. Dan was about to ask again when Robbins answered.

'I always wanted to become a police officer because of my father. He was a lieutenant, and I always remember people had so much respect for him. I wanted that. To be the brave guy everyone would be proud of. The day we caught our break on the case, I knew we'd get him. I'd been trying to nail him for months and this was the time. I expected we'd go over there, arrest him and that would be the end. What I didn't expect was how everything would go to shit and it would drag on until the end became inevitable.'

THE BREACH PART ONE

Few things compare to the rush of cracking a case you'd been working on for years. Third in a line of cars, Robbins followed two squad cars, their tires spitting gravel as they sped down the dusty road. His unmarked Ford kept pace as they jostled down the narrow dirt road, dust swirling around them.

If only half of what the girl had told them was true, this would be a good day all around. Robbins looked in the mirror at the blue Chevy behind and picked up his radio receiver with one hand as he steered the car with the other.

'Mack, you there?'

'Yeah, I'm here,' his partner's voice crackled over the radio. 'This better be good, Alex. I was supposed to be on vacation.'

'Trust me, this is going to be a good day.'

'Yeah, well, how often does that ever happen? You know something will fuck things up.'

'Ever the optimist, Mack.'

'I'm a realist. If things go as smoothly as you think, I'll buy you a beer. No, fuck that. You pulled me away from my time off. You buy the beer regardless.'

'Don't I always,' Robbins said, hanging up the receiver.

Robbins was feeling upbeat. He hoped to have those at the house in custody by lunchtime. Once they saw the lights and heard the sirens, he suspected they would conform and come in peacefully.

The patrol cars stopped short of the house. Robbins' last visit to the house had been a year earlier, and the change surprised him. High concrete walls lined with rings of barbed wire now surrounded the outer perimeter. He guessed as far as he could see, there was some sixty to seventy feet in every direction between walls and the ranch house, meaning what he had thought would be a straightforward arrest may be more difficult than he expected.

Robbins pulled up beside one of the patrol cars and got out. He loosened his tie and approached the officers.

'What's the holdup?'

'See for yourself.' The officer said, pointing to a hand painted sign by the side of the road.

Private property

Do not approach.

The road is unsafe for vehicles or people

You have been warned!

Robbins looked through the iron gate at the expanse of land between the walls and the house, wondering what the sign implied by unsafe. He kicked the loose stones at his feet as Mack stood beside him. A little further away from the house, a group of people were standing by a patrol car in conversation with some officers. 'Who are they?' Robbins asked.

'From inside. Apparently, they were given the option to leave this morning. Seem they got wind of what was coming.'

Mack stretched, his joints popping as he over extended. Robbins had known him for ten years, and they had been partners for eight of those. Mack was a big guy, a football player in college, but not good enough to turn pro. Nobody had expected him to join the police force, much less make a successful career out of it. He stared at the house, bald head glistening in the sun, a brush of greying stubble across his cheeks.

'Something feels off about this, Alex.'

Robbins joined him in looking at the house, squinting against the sun. It gave nothing away. Tired off-white walls and black windows like the eyes of a skull stared back at them.

'What do you think?' Mack said.

Robbins leaned his palms on the hood of the patrol car, then pulled away, the steel hot to the touch. 'I don't know.'

'You're feeling it, aren't you?'

Robbins nodded. *It* was that feeling. The ability to sense when something wasn't right. He and Mack had discussed *it* over many hours driving together or drinking beer after work, and neither of them could explain what it was. Instinct, intuition. There was no real name to describe the sensation. Whatever it was, both of them could feel it creeping around inside them.

'I don't like this, Mack, I hope I'm wrong, but I have a horrible feeling this won't end well.'

'Ahh fuck, man, don't be saying that kind of shit.'

'Maybe I'm being paranoid,' Robbins said, staring at the house again.

'Nah, there's something in the air, that's for sure.'

Robbins nodded to the warning sign by the wall. 'What do you make of that?'

'Could be a bluff, but is it worth that risk? What are you thinking? Mines?'

'It crossed my mind, but I don't think so.'

'Yeah, no signs of recent digging as far as I can see.' Mack stared at the house, cupping his face to block out the sun. 'Snipers would have a hell of a shooting gallery from the house if they have weapons. Must be fifty, sixty feet to the building and no cover. Then we'd have to breach. We'd be sitting ducks.'

'Yeah, that's my thinking, too. So much for this being easy.'

'Well, we can't stand out here with our hands on our dicks, can we?'

Despite the tension, Robbins chuckled. 'Way with words as always, Mack.'

'Do I have to remind you I should be fuckin fishing right now?'

'Alright, I get it. Let's get some kind of perimeter set up. The more I think about them having guns, the less I like us all standing around out here in the open.'

'Alright, I'll get it done.'

'I want to contact those inside.'

'You think they'll talk to you?'

'I hope so.'

'We're gonna need more than just us for this, Alex. Situation has changed since we set out here.'

'We will, but not yet. I don't want to spook them by having a ton of units down here until I've talked to them. It feels like this whole scenario is one spark away from exploding.'

'Alright, let's do this.'

As Mack went to organise the perimeter, Robbins looked at the house. Sunlight glinted from the upper windows, and he couldn't shake that feeling of being watched. He was convinced this was the calm before what would be one hell of a storm.

III

Within the hour, the perimeter had been set up a further fifty feet away from the dirt road, the squad cars parked nose to tail to offer some sort of protection. Despite wanting to keep it low profile, another half dozen patrol cars had arrived on scene to transport those who had left the Ranch back to the station for questioning. It was more activity than Robbins wanted, leaving the idea of a low-key resolution unlikely. He was seething over how big the operation was becoming when Mack walked over to him.

'Hey, I need a word.'

Robbins didn't like when Mack was so serious. It meant trouble. The two walked away from the rest of the officers. 'What is it?'

'We could have a problem.'

'Christ, what now?'

'I've been talking to some of those people who were outside the gate when we got here, the ones who came from inside.'

'What did you get from them?'

'Well, if what they say is true, it complicates things. They say they have kids in there. There's no way we can confirm it from here. No visual from where we are.'

'Alright, well, I needed to talk to the people inside, so now is as good a time as any.'

'That's not all. They also said that those remaining in the house are devoted to Warwick and will do anything to protect him. They sure as shit know we're here, though. Apparently, they've been preparing for this for months. We need to be careful how we play this.'

'Do we have a line to the house?'

Mack nodded to the tent that was situated down the road. 'In there. They're ready when you are.'

IV

Robbins entered the stuffy tent, the air thick with the smell of sweat and electronics. A technician, his face beaded with perspiration, was busy uncoiling a large spool of wire. He pointed to a desk with a quick jerk of his thumb. A telephone, notepad, and pen were on it. Robbins took a seat. 'Does this go direct to the house?' he asked.

The technician nodded, still struggling with the wire spool.

'Alright, put me through.'

Robbins waited for the call to go through. Instead of nervousness, he felt a growing sense of aggravation, as what should have been a routine arrest had already become a more challenging situation. Someone answered the phone on the fifth ring, their voice calm.

'Hello?', the voice said.

'Who is this?'

'Who is *this*?'

'My name is Detective Robbins. I was hoping to speak to whoever is in charge there.'

'Then speak away, Detective Robbins.'

'Alright, who am I speaking to?'

'This is Jim.'

'Alright, look, Jim, I think we can both agree this has all got out of hand. All we wanted to do was to come talk to you. Now there are people out here saying you have weapons and it's unsafe to approach the house. I was hoping you and I could figure out a solution.'

'What is it you want?'

'Well, I need to talk to you in person, not over the phone.'

'I don't think there's much for us to discuss.'

'If you won't be reasonable, we're going to have to come up there and remove you by force.'

'That would be a mistake.'

'That sounds like a threat, Jim.'

'Take it how you will. You're not welcome here.'

'We understand you have weapons up there. And children.'

'Who told you that?'

'Is it true?'

Robbins sat there, drenched in sweat, knuckles white as he gripped the handset.

'Jim, are you there?'

'I think this conversation is over. Don't come up here.'

Robbins had no time to respond. The connection was cut, and the voice on the other end of the line was gone, leaving only silence in his ear. Out of his depth and frustrated, he threw the handset down.

V

Two days passed. Then three. By day five, the situation had become a media circus, with constant live coverage of the ongoing stalemate. The Ranch and its surrounding had become a hive of activity as police, ambulance crews, and the fire department prepared for the worst. To add to this, media helicopters buzzed overhead, a constant droning backdrop to the operation.

Robbins had taken refuge in one of the mobile command centre tents. He could still hear the helicopters, but at least here they were muted. He sipped his coffee, hoping the headache he could feel throbbing like a rotten tooth in his temples would fade away.

The stalemate had been frustrating. There were attempts to resolve things via phone, but the conversations went nowhere. There had been no thought, so far, to entering by force, because they didn't know what they were dealing with.

He swallowed a couple of pills for his headache and washed it down with the almost cold coffee.

His radio crackled. Robbins picked it up.

'Robbins.'

'It's Mack. You better come out here. He wants to talk to you.'

'I thought he said he didn't want to deal with me anymore.'

'Yeah, well, maybe he's reconsidered. Son of a bitch is refusing to talk to anyone else.'

Robbins walked out of the tent, making his way through the command post to another tent where communications had been set up. Robbins knew the drill and also suspected nothing would come of this conversation, much like the ones which had gone before.

'What's he saying?' Robbins said, as he tried to get comfortable on the plastic chair.

'Not much, or at least not to us, at least.' Mack took a seat beside Robbins and put on a headset so he could hear the conversation.

'Jesus, Mack, why did I have to be the first one to talk to this son of a bitch?'

'Maybe he's drawn to your charm and personality.'

Robbins gave his partner the middle finger, then took a breath to compose himself.

'All right, let's get this over with,' he said as he put the handset to his ear and pressed the flashing hold button on the front of the rotary phone.

'This is Detective Robbins.'

'I was about to hang up. You kept me waiting a long time.'

'Yeah, well, things have been busy. As you can see, you've caused quite the commotion out here.'

'Detective Robbins, we've done no wrong. We're here of our own free will.'

'With the gates locked.'

'For our protection.'

Robbins sighed, making sure Warwick heard it.

'You don't agree?'

'Look, I'm done trying to sweet talk you out of there. If you want to do what's right for those you have with you, come out.'

'We're innocent.'

Mack nudged Robbins and showed him the pad he had been writing on. He had written: *How many?*

'You say we. How many is that, Jim?'

'Why does it matter?'

'It matters because I'm responsible for their safety. Come out and meet me at the gate. We can talk in person for as long as you want.'

Warwick chuckled. Mack and Robbins exchanged glances.

'I could come out there. I could hand myself over to you and you would put me in jail. Or you could have one of your snipers put a bullet in my brain the second I open the door. I think with that in mind, I'll stay where I am.'

'You'll have to come out of there, eventually. Answer the accusations against you. Everyone has to abide by the Law. You can't choose not to.'

'We don't acknowledge your laws or rules.'

Robbins took his cigarettes from his pocket and tossed them on the desk. 'Yeah, I get it. Sometimes, I don't like the rules either. But you can't make up your own because you feel like it. You're putting those people in there with you in danger.'

'I told you. We're not coming out.'

Robbins nestled the phone in the crook of his neck as he lit a cigarette, taking his time.

'Hello? Are you there?'

Robbins didn't respond. He put the cigarettes and lighter back in his pocket, then took a long drag on the cigarette, exhaling, and wafting the cloud away from Mack.

'I'm here.'

'Why the silence?'

'I was giving you time to think. Seems we keep going in circles with these conversations. I mean, how about you give us something, a goodwill gesture?'

Now it was Jim's turn to be silent. Robbins didn't chase for an answer. He smoked and let Warwick think.

'What did you have in mind?'

Mack did a silent fist pump. Robbins barely acknowledged it.

He was in the zone.

'Well, Jim, what I would like to see is you send a couple of hostages out. To show good faith.'

As soon as he said it, Robbins realised the error he'd made. Down the phone, Jim laughed.

'And when we were doing so well. How many times have I told you? Nobody here is a hostage. Everyone here is because they want to be. There are no *hostages*.'

Frustrated at his mistake, Robbins went on the offensive. 'If you care about those people, you'll put an end to this.'

'If you try to come in, we will defend ourselves.'

'Yeah, well, you say innocent, but we have a witness out here prepared to testify that you're responsible for murder. At least two, maybe more. Do the people in there with you know that?'

'Forty-one.'

'Forty-one what?' Robbins asked, as Mack wrote the number down.

'Forty-one people live here, and yes, there are women and children, too, all of them happy and not wanting to be shot by you and your men.'

'Nobody is under threat. We want to resolve this. The only one stopping that is you.'

'They will die for me. And I for them. Try to understand, Detective Robbins. Nothing matters to them more than me, and nothing matters to me more than them. Only God can judge us.'

'Last chance, Jim. You can decide how this ends. It can either be peaceful or we can go the other way. It's your choice.'

'No, Detective Robbins. It's yours. Any blood that is shed in this house will be on your hands. Just know we will defend what we have, even if it costs us our lives.'

Robbins glanced at Mack, who had written a large question mark on his pad. Robbins adjusted his position. 'Then it looks like you and I have nothing more to say to each other.'

Robbins hung up the phone, exhaled and rubbed his temples.

'So, what's the plan?' Mack asked.

Robbins took another long drag and crushed the cigarette out between this thumb and forefinger. 'Get them ready. We're going in.'

'You're sure that's the right call?'

Robbins considered the question, wishing he had a double vodka to help clear his head. 'No. but we can't afford to let the bastards dig in for much longer. This needs to end.'

Robbins headed out of the tent, glaring up at the ranch a few hundred feet away.

VI

Inside the house, Warwick watched from a darkened upstairs room overlooking the yard. As he suspected, following his conversation with Robbins, the activity outside had intensified. Ammo was being checked. The police were being grouped into teams and given instructions. Jim closed his eyes and said a silent prayer, then turned to face the others who were watching him, their expressions ghastly in the dim candlelight.

'They've made their decision. I tried to reason with them. I tried to tell them we mean no harm, but they insist on coming here to destroy what we've built. Those of you who are here knew what we might face. You stayed despite the opportunity to leave, and now we must defend what we have built. I told you it was coming, and that day has come.'

Jim took the chain from around his neck. Attached to it was a gold key. 'You all know what this is. What door it opens. A door we promised to keep locked until we had no choice. Today is that day. The women and children are to stay in this room. They know their roles. The men should follow me and arm themselves. This is it, and together we will prove our strength against intimidation. This is his will.'

There were no rousing cheers as Jim left the room. Just a few nervous glances.

VII

Dan and Rebecca waited for Robbins to go on, but he was silent. He stared at the ground, hands thrust into his pockets.

'Making that call can't have been easy.' Rebecca said.

Robbins shrugged, still not looking at them. 'I was young and stupid. An arrogant prick. I wanted the win, and yeah, I can admit it now. At all costs. I forgot how much regret I had over that conversation until now.'

'It sounds like you tried. I don't think you could have done much more.'

'Yeah, Becks is right. What else could you have done? Sounds like he backed you into a corner.'

Robbins looked beyond them to the shopping mall. 'I sometimes wonder if that's true. If the man I am now had been in that same situation, I think I could have ended it without all the shit hitting the fan. Like I said, I was different then. A stupid fucking kid with a chip on his shoulder.'

They waited for Robbins to elaborate and tell the rest of the story, but he was staring at the shopping mall, looking beyond it to something now only existed in his mind. 'I think that's about enough for today. Come on, let's get moving. This fucking place gives me the creeps.'

FAMILY MATTERS

They spent weeks building the walls, toiling in the intense heat. Concrete was mixed and poured. Deep foundations were dug. When construction was complete, a twelve-foot concrete wall topped with barbed wire encircled the ranch; a steel gate serving as the sole point of entry. Night had come; the grounds lit by a high moon in a cloudless sky. Jim was enjoying a moment alone, unable to believe what they had built from nothing. They had a functioning farm that would provide them with food. It was modest, vegetables and a few chickens, but it was already serving its purpose in allowing them to be self-sufficient. They even had a well from which to draw fresh water – a fortunate find.

Gloria's father had covered it years earlier, having no need for such a thing, but for them, under the circumstances, it was what they were looking for. Jim told the others it was a gift from God and nobody had questioned it. In addition, they now had a well-stocked armoury. Once George Pennington's downstairs office, they had bricked up the windows and reinforced the door. Over the previous months, they had stocked it with rifles and pistols. They had also manufactured their own ammunition in the outbuilding behind the barn.

Plans were in being considered. Celebrity targets to eliminate. Buildings they could destroy with explosives. Mass gatherings, food and music festivals, sporting events, all potential targets for an attack by bomb, bullet or knife. It would be dirty work, but he trusted the word of the voice in his head, which told him it was a necessary step to reach the salvation they all deserved. On the porch steps, he sipped his beer, wondering how people would remember him after his self-sacrifice, like Jesus, for the sake of their salvation.

'You're awake.'

The voice startled him. Mary came out of the house and settled next to him. They fell silent, captivated by the beauty of the night sky.

'Can't sleep?'

'No. I looked out of the window and saw you out here. Are you okay?'

'Yeah, just enjoying the quiet.'

She joined him in looking out over the bruise black sky.

'I'm pregnant.'

Jim sipped his beer and stared at the moon letting the revelation breathe.

'I'm too young to have a baby. Plus, if Gloria finds out...'

He looked at her and smiled, taking her hand. 'This has nothing to do with Gloria.'

'Tell that to her. She hates me already.'

'Gloria understands our bond.'

She looked at him, eyes betraying her fear. 'And what about God? Does he approve?' she almost whispered, the words swallowed by the night.

'Yes. And tomorrow, I will tell the others.'

'And what if...' She looked away, unable to get the words to come. 'What if it's not a boy, like what happened with Gloria?'

Jim didn't react, even as flashes of what had happened blasted into his mind's eye. The baby screaming – a girl, no good to him – Gloria screaming as well. Bathtub full of water. The voice in his head telling him what to do, to ignore the revulsion and doubt. Such a tiny thing shimmering under the surface, limbs thrashing in a fruitless fight to survive. Gloria's screams like ice on his bones, then silence. For weeks after, there was no sleep. How could there be when all he could remember were the sounds, those awful sounds?

'Jim?'

He snapped back to the present, forcing those horrors back where they came from.

Mary wanted more reassurance. She had been in the house that night, heard everything, and knew that discussing it was forbidden. It was a secret shared between the three of them, once which would haunt them forever.

'Will you talk to Gloria?'

'Of course. She will understand. She knows how things work here.'

With her head resting on Jim's shoulder, Mary watched the moon, pondering their future together.

II

Outside the Ranch, the crowd stood, their eyes focused on Jim, while Jim himself stared back at the house. Gloria's screams echoed from inside as she trashed the place and showed no sign of slowing. Jim touched the key to the armoury which hung from a chain around his neck, grateful Gloria didn't have a copy. He asked the voice in his head for guidance, but it remained silent, trusting him to resolve this himself. A test, then, from God. Jim took a deep breath, walked up the porch steps and into the house.

Glass and broken crockery covered the floor, and that seemed to be the least of the destruction. The place was a mess. Jim could hear her walking from room to room as she continued her rampage. He headed upstairs, tracking the source of the noise to the bedroom. Either she sensed him coming or had run out of things to break, as the destruction stopped, and all was quiet. He approached the open door and stood at the threshold, saying nothing as he leaned on the doorframe, hands in pockets. Gloria was sitting on the floor at the foot of the bed, cheeks streaked with spent tears, hands bloody from dozens of glass cuts. The room was, like the rest of the house, destroyed.

Jim wasn't sure if she had noticed his presence until she spoke. Even then, she didn't look at him. She was still staring into oblivion.

'How could you do this to me?' There was no fight left in her voice, no fury, just a dejected sadness.

'I understand it hurts, but this is God's way. This is what he wanted.'

'What about what *I* wanted, Jim? I wanted to give you a child. This was our dream. It's not fair.'

'If I was meant to have a child with, you would have given me a son.'

Gloria flinched, but said nothing. Jim walked into the room, broken glass crunching under his shoes. He sat on the foot of the bed beside her and stroked her hair. It was greasy and matted together, sticking to her skin where she had been sweating.

'This outburst hasn't gone unnoticed by the others.'

'Fuck the others. I don't care about them.'

'You don't mean that. It's the anger talking.'

Her eyes were full of pleading as she looked at him. 'Not her.

Anyone but her.'

'If his will is for Mary to bear my child, who are we to argue?'

She wiped her eyes with her palm, spreading blood from her cut hands across her face. 'I already gave you a child. You got rid of it because it wasn't the one you wanted.' It came out as a shriek rather than words. Jim put a hand on her shoulder. She flinched away, shaking him off.

'I have to have a son. That is the way it has to be.'

'I can't do this anymore. You've used me up and replaced me with *her*.'

'This won't feel so bad once you calm down. It's raw now. I understand that, but we've been through difficult times before. Tests of our bond. This is another.'

'You were supposed to love me.' She was hoping for reassurance. Anything to show this wasn't slipping away, but Jim said nothing.

'I hate this place and these people. I hate that bitch carrying your baby. She ruined everything. It was perfect before she arrived.'

'Remember, this is the work of God. You and I are his vessels. We do as he instructs. Our feelings don't matter,'

She glared at him, her eyes dejected and full of hatred. 'You can at least be honest and cut out the bullshit. I'm trapped here. You say I can leave if I want to, but we both know I can't.'

Jim held his silence, unwilling to engage in the conversation. Instead, he stood and walked towards the door. He looked at her, his eyes voids filled with darkness.

'Make sure you clean all this up.' Ignoring her sobs, he closed the door.

THE TRUTH HURTS

With eight months of pregnancy behind her, Mary longed for the birth to bring back a sense of normalcy and comfort. Even simple actions like sitting, sleeping, and walking were difficult and frustrating. Jim's sermons had become so in demand that as their population grew, it made sense to construct a purpose-built structure to perform them. The room was long and rectangular with no windows. They could not divert power to the new structure, and so it was lit by candles, which suited the atmosphere when those long speeches took on a life of their own. The building housed two rows of ten benches. At the front was a raised stage area with a blue carpet. When it was full, it became explosively hot. Mary had seen the humidity hanging in the air like mist as a shirtless Jim drenched in sweat delivered his message, stalking back and forth like some kind of caged animal. It was incredible to see, and for the first months of her pregnancy, she was at the front, taking it in, letting his words soak into every fibre of her being. So close to birth, she could no longer sit for long on the hard benches, so she watched from the back by the entrance, enjoying the occasional breeze which prickled against her sweat slick skin and brought a hint of relief. When Jim got into the flow of things, these sessions could take a long time to conclude, and she was often too uncomfortable to stay to the end, as she was now.

She slipped outside. Her slight frame was struggling to cope with the extra mass, so even simple things like walking the short distance to the house had left her breathless. Inside was, at least, cooler. The ceiling fan overhead thrummed as it rotated, moving the sticky air around into something resembling comfort.

She winced as the baby wriggled under her ribcage, then poured herself a glass of fresh lemonade from the fridge. The first sip was divine as she felt the change in temperature as the icy liquid slipped down her throat.

'I used to sit at the front.'

Mary almost dropped her glass as she spun around. Gloria was staring at her, a ghost of who she used to be. Pale, with tangled hair, glaring dark-rimmed eyes, and clammy skin. Her arms covered in scars, old and new. Gloria's self-harming was an open secret, which everyone ignored. She stood between the cooker and the kitchen counter, blocking the way out.

'I thought you were in there, watching.' Mary tried to appear calm and took a sip of her drink.

Gloria's expression didn't change. She was picking at the edge of her thumb with her pointer finger, the skin raw and scabbed from this recent habit.

'I used to be you. The favourite. The flavour of the month.' She took a step closer, bare feet slapping on the lino floor.

'Why did you follow me here?' Mary wanted to step back but could feel the ridge of the worktop pressing into her lower back. Instead, she stood tall, hoping her fear wouldn't show.

'Follow you? Don't flatter yourself. His sermons are something I avoid now. I've heard them all before.'

'Gloria, I have no problem with you.'

Gloria took a step, closing the gap between them.

'He'll ditch you too when something better comes around. You think you're the only one he's fucked? All these young girls here who adore him, and you think because you're having his kid, he's faithful to you? Well, he won't be. He likes them young, if you haven't noticed. He'll throw you away soon enough.'

Mary looked away, hating how Gloria had voiced what had been swimming around in her mind for a while.

Gloria grinned, but it was a haunting, pain filled gesture. 'Look at you, so young, so innocent that even now you don't see it.'

She closed the distance with the swiftness of a snake's strike, stopping inches from Mary. She lay a hand on her stomach; the skin stretched over bones, bluish ghosts of veins visible underneath. 'You mean nothing to him. His plan is bigger than us.'

She was speaking in a near whisper, eyes full of hatred and sadness, breath stinking of desperation and alcohol.

'You're not to touch me or hurt me. Jim said -'

'Jim said,' She hissed it, making Mary shrink back against the worktop.

'I know what he said. You think you can tell me anything about what he thinks, what he wants? You don't know him, not like I do. Nobody does. You're a stupid little girl with no idea of the sacrifices I've made for that man.'

Gloria touched Mary's face with her free hand, the other still resting on her stomach. 'So fragile, so clueless about the world. I can see why he likes you. He likes the innocence. The youth. Sees it as something he can shape and mould into what he wants. When that fails, you'll end up like me. You'll see.'

'I'm nothing like you,' Mary whispered, praying someone would come into the house and interrupt, but the distant sound of Jim's booming voice across the yard told her they were not about to be disturbed.

Gloria smiled. 'Do you know how easy it would be to end all this?'

The finger she was using to stroke Mary's cheek becoming a hand grabbing her face, pushing her cheeks against her teeth. The other slid past Mary and grabbed the knife from the draining board, which she touched to Mary's stomach. Mary froze, unable to take her eyes from the blade.

'It would be so easy.' Gloria whispered, lip trembling. 'You don't deserve to carry his child. Not the way I do.'

Mary wanted to argue, but was afraid one wrong word could push Gloria over the edge. She might get there either way.

'You don't care about how I feel, what I've been through. Why should you? You have what you want. What do I matter?' she traced the tip of the blade across Mary's dress. The drag of steel on cotton to Mary seemed incredibly loud. 'That should be my baby. It's not fair.' She let go of Mary's face with her free hand and placed it on her stomach. 'He'll understand if I do this. He'll know it's for the best.'

'Please, don't hurt my baby,' Mary said, the taste of fear bitter in her throat. She knew what was coming, and her mind turned towards survival. Maybe she could spin to the side, push Gloria's hand away and get something to defend herself with. She was trying to recall if there were any other knives by the sink which she might use, but her mind had been only on having something to drink. Even if there was a weapon, she wouldn't do it. She had too much to lose. Instead, she waited, wondering how it would feel as that blade was driven into her, wondering if the life inside her would understand what was happening.

With no warning, Gloria pulled her hand away, a sharp booze

laced gasp blowing in Mary's face as she took a step back, the knife hanging loose at her side.

The baby had chosen that moment to kick. For a moment, they stood there, still within each other's personal space. Gloria trembled, tears streaming down her face as she looked at Mary's stomach. She tossed the knife past Mary, where it clattered against the sink. 'You should leave this place. It's not right to bring a baby up here. It's not what you think it is.'

Mary said nothing as Gloria walked away, bare feet padding on the wooden floor. She stopped, one hand on the banister rail.

'You've taken everything from me. I want you to know that.' Then, like some kind of spectre, she headed upstairs.

DO IT OR DON'T

Checking his rearview mirror, Robbins waited for the twins to react, but they were still absorbing what he'd said. The scenery blurred past as Dan looked out the window. Rebecca was staring at her phone, thumbs dancing over the screen as she typed. Noticing Robbins looking at her in the mirror, she met his gaze.

'Sorry, just venting to my friend. I need some girl to girl advice. No offence.'

'None taken.'

'It sounds like she was smitten by this guy. I don't get it.' Dan said.

'That's because you can only see it from a guy's perspective. She loved him.'

'No, she didn't.' Robbins cut in. 'She was too young to know the difference. Warwick gave her what she needed. In our line of work, we call that grooming. Your mother wasn't in love. She was a victim.'

'I don't understand how nobody stepped in before. She was a runaway. Why didn't anyone find her and make her go back home?' Dan was growing angry and fidgeted in his seat.

'It was a different time, kid. Today you have counselling, support classes, CCTV on every street corner, the world at your fingertips to ask for advice, like your sister there. Point being, it's hard to disappear in today's world. There was none of that then. The world was a bigger place, and it was easy to go missing if you wanted to. Your mother was a victim of a dangerous, manipulative child predator who got his hooks into her and wouldn't let go.'

'She should have known better.'

'What's your problem? You've been like this since we came out here.' Rebecca asked, setting her phone aside.

'I don't have a problem other than seeming to be the only one who thinks this is a stupid idea. The thought of meeting this animal makes me sick.'

Robbins couldn't have said it better himself, but as it wasn't his place, so he concentrated on the road.

'I'm sorry finding out the truth about Mum's past is stupid to you, Dan.'

'I don't know why you can't see it. It's like you have blinkers on and can only see straight in front of you and what you want.'

'We discussed this before we came out here. You agreed. We knew what we were getting into.' She snapped at him.

'That was before I knew all the details. It's like we're digging a big hole that gets deeper and deeper the more we learn and don't have a ladder to get out.'

'April thinks we're doing the right thing.'

'What the fuck has any of this got to do with April? This is between us, not us and your friends.'

'So I'm not allowed to ask for advice from a friend?'

Dan twisted towards her, his cheeks flushed. 'Don't you think it's better to keep this between us rather than blab it out to strangers? How do you even start a conversation like that? Oh hi, April, guess what? We just found out our dad is a paedophile and a murderer. Don't worry though, we're making plans to visit him on death row for a family reunion.'

Robbins was more shaken than he cared to admit how each of

them carried so many of their father quirks and traits. It was unsettling to see.

'She's not a stranger. She's my fucking friend,' Rebecca fired back.

'I don't know her, Becks. Did you ever consider I might not want other people knowing about this? Isn't it embarrassing enough that we're related to this.... Thing. We said just us. Not us and April. You're so fucking stubborn it's unreal.'

'That's enough.' Robbins said, jamming on the brakes, the car sliding to a stop by the side of the road. The sudden change was enough to silence them both. Robbins turned in his seat to face them. His eyes had grown colder, his demeanour more authoritative. He seemed as if he had rolled back the years, returning to his prime.

'Alright, let's get something straight so we all know where we stand. I don't enjoy this. I don't *need* this. Believe it or not, dragging all this shit up from the past isn't something I wanted to do, but I owed Beadle a favour so here we are. I understood the two of you wanted to learn the truth about Warwick before deciding if you wanted to meet him, so I agreed, hoping you'd see what kind of monster he is.'

'Hey, I'm sold. It's her you need to convince.'

Rebecca was about to answer, but Robbins cut her off.

'You need to decide right now if you want to continue. For the record, nothing would please me more than to put a stop to this and not have to drag any more skeletons out of the closet. God knows, it took long enough to get them in there. I'm going to have a smoke. I expect an answer on what you intend to do when I get back, understood?'

They both nodded.

'Good. The sooner this damn thing is over with, the better.' He got out, slammed the car door, and left them alone.

II

Robbins paced by the side of the road, trying to calm down. His doctor would say to him he had to monitor his stress levels at his age, and would raise an eyebrow, maybe even both at the smoking, but the situation had shaken him more than he wanted to admit. He took out his phone to see if anyone had been in touch. He'd had one message from Sandy telling him she had arrived safely for the cruise and the cabin was lovely (Good to know another man was treating his wife so well) and that he should reconsider reconnecting with his daughter.

That felt like an issue for another day, though, so he filed that elsewhere in his mind, knowing he would most likely forget. As he smoked, he realised it wasn't so much dragging up the old memories that were bothering him; it was the twins themselves. They were nice kids and their mother had brought them up well, but they were still both pieces of Warwick, and knowing him the way he had done over the years, Robbins was struggling to ignore it.

It was the way Dan sneered sometimes, how short a fuse he had. Both traits he had seen in Warwick. And the Girl, Rebecca, the way she was so determined to pursue what she wanted at all costs, the glare in the eyes like she was looking through you, an expression he had seen so many times over the years.

The question of leaving out the parts of the story he was ashamed of, the things he had vowed to never mention again, weighed on him. He finished his cigarette, but felt no satisfaction, so took another one out of the pack. In his mind's eye, he saw those raised eyebrows of his doctor judging him, and flipped a mental middle finger.

'Fuck you, doctor Simmonds,' he muttered as he lit the cigarette and took a deep pull on it. Robbins continued to pace, no closer to finding peace.

III

In the car, the twins were silent, each of them looking out of their respective windows. Dan was staring at the blacktop, the occasional car passing by. Rebecca was looking over a dusty scrub of industrial land, and could just about see Robbins pacing back and forth a little way up the road. It was Dan who broke the silence.

'So, what do we do about this, Becks? Haven't you heard enough to know this is a bad idea?'

'It will eat at me if I don't get the answers. This is the only way I can put this behind me. It's weird, I know, but I need to do this.'

'I don't see what good it will do. Let's go home.'

Rebecca's phone vibrated twice in quick succession. Dan glanced at the phone, then at his sister.

'Seems like your pal wants an update.' There was contempt, and it was deliberate.

'I'll text her back in a minute. Dan, I need your help with this. I can't do it my myself. We only have each other. Remember what we said.'

'Don't manipulate me, Becks. That's not fair.'

'I'm not.'

'It sounds like you are. What about what I want? That doesn't seem like something you've thought about.'

'That's a fucking lie.' She glared at him across the seat.

'Is it?'

'Who sorted through all Mum's more personal stuff when you said you couldn't do it? Who made all the funeral arrangements because you said it was too hard? That was me. I did it because I didn't want you to be in more pain than you already were. That was fucking hard for me too, but I did it for you.'

Dan softened, trying to diffuse the situation. 'You're right, I get it. I didn't mean that. I'm frustrated, that's all. Hearing all this stuff is so weird. Surreal almost. It's like we're hearing about a character from a book or film, but I sit back and think this guy exists in the real world, and we might be about to have to sit face to face with him.'

Rebecca's phone vibrated again. She ignored it and stared out of the window, sniffling as she cried. Some distance away, Robbins stood with his back to them, smoke billowing out around him.

Dan grabbed his sister's hand across the seat. She turned to him.

'I won't leave you to handle this on your own. I don't like it, but I'd fret even more if I went home and left you out here by yourself.'

'So, you'll stay?' She said, wiping her eyes.

'Yeah, I'll stay. Let's get this over with and go home.'

'Thanks, Dan. I appreciate this.'

Dan turned away, trying to come to terms with the decision they had made. Rebecca picked up her phone and replied to her friend as they waited for Robbins to come back.

IV

Night had arrived.

Robbins decided that rather than bombard them with any more information, it would be better to postpone the drive out to the destination he had planned, and had instead taken them back to their hotel, telling them he would pick them up the following morning.

His intention had been to drive straight home, but those memories – both the ones he had told and the ones they had yet to learn of – screamed in his head, chastising him for trying to hide them for so long and ensuring they reminded him of every horrible detail. As he endured these long-repressed memories, he drove with no conscious direction, letting the motor skills from forty-plus years behind the wheel do the work. It had been a long time since he felt that tight feeling in his gut, of the prickle of the hairs on his arms standing to attention. He saw Mack in his mind's eye, half grin on his face.

You feeling it, Alex?

It. The thing without a name. And he *was* feeling it for the first time in a long time. Over the years, it had helped him close cases, stay alive and out of danger and know when something felt wrong, and wrong was how this situation felt.

He followed the train of brake lights, the soft red glow mesmerising as he tried to understand what this instinct he had always relied on was trying to say to him now, so many years later. Maybe it was a side effect of thinking about those awful times from the past which had ruined his life. It was deep into this train of thought when he noticed he had stopped the car. Zoning back into the real world, Robbins took in his surroundings.

The neon sign above the door was broken and flickering, the wood façade still old and in need of a lick of paint. Or, if he was being realistic, ripping down and replacing. He wound down the window, letting the cool air seep in. He could hear the muffled throb of music coming from inside, muted by the walls and poster covered windows. Even though it had been eleven years since he was last there, the place hadn't changed. It was as if it had remained frozen in time until Alexander Robbins came back to visit. He gripped the steering wheel tighter, stuck in a limbo between what he wanted in that moment and what he knew was right. One hand went to his chest.

Had anyone been passing and seen him, they may have thought he was about to have a heart attack, but Robbins wasn't in pain – not physical at least. His fingers traced the outline of his wallet through the material of his suit jacket, where it sat snug in his inner breast pocket. He thought about what it contained, what it meant to him, and how he had been here before and won. He counted back, starting at twenty, taking deep breaths with each passing number. As he reached the number five, he was under control. He started the car, spewing gravel from the wheels as he turned in a wide circle in the almost deserted car park and away from that place – another haven of terrible memories brought back into his life by James Fucking Warwick.

GHOSTS OF THE PAST

Most of the journey had been silent and tense. Dan, as always, was staring out of the window, lost in his own thoughts. Rebecca was texting. Robbins presumed whatever they had discussed the previous day in the car and the fragile peace when he returned to them had flared up again at the hotel. Robbins glanced out of the window at the black, overcast skies and thought they reflected the general mood within the vehicle.

'Well, since this atmosphere is awkward for us all, I suppose I should ask if there is anything else you want to know about what we've discussed so far.'

He waited for the usual bombardment of questions, but none came.

'We can forget this if you don't feel up to it. Neither of you seems especially interested today.'

Rebecca put her phone down. 'Sorry, Detective Robbins.'

'Jesus, Alex is fine. No need to be so formal.'

'We're fine. It was just a late-night last night. We had a lot to talk about.' Dan said.

I bet you did, and I would bet my life on who won that discussion.

Robbins focused on the road as they stopped at traffic lights. 'You need to understand something. I've seen and forgotten more than both of you combined have experienced. It's obvious you still aren't on the same page, which poses a problem today.'

'Why?' Dan asked.

'Because what I said yesterday still stands. I don't need to know details. What I need to know is if you want to still go through with this.'

'We do,' Rebecca said. 'We discussed it, and things got heated, but we agree this is what we want. I had a question, though, if that's alright.'

'We've got a way to go yet, so ask away.'

'It's about the other day, when you took us to the shopping mall where the house used to be.'

'Compound. It wasn't a house. Not at the end.'

'You were telling us the story about what happened that day you went in, but you never finished.' She let her words trail to silence, unsure how to proceed.

'I take it now is when you'd like to hear the rest of the story?'

'Yes, please, I mean, if that's alright.'

Volunteering to speak of that day again after how it ended made him scream inside, but he had promised to see it through and so he would. He took a moment to compose himself and control the anxiety which he could feel creeping up his spine. He was going back to that time, digging up those corpses he had buried from the dark recesses of his brain where they had lived for so long.

THE BREACH PART 2

It was a cocktail of sensations impossible to get used to. Adrenaline and fear, complete and total focus on the task at hand. Robbins had hoped Warwick's promise to defend themselves at all costs was a bluff, but that hope vanished when the first barrage of gunshots came.

Mack joined him, running in a half crouch as he came to rest behind the vehicle, which was protecting them from the gunfire ahead. They were wearing body armour, but that still left plenty of fleshy areas exposed if a bullet found them. Robbins peered over the edge of the car to the house, its walls riddled with bullet holes.

'Seems they are dug in pretty tight,' Mack said, ducking as a stray bullet chipped the concrete by his foot.

Robbins picked up his radio, speaking into the receiver. 'Send it in.'

The APC, or Armoured Personnel Carrier, was designed for crowd control in the event of a riot or civil unrest. The vehicle's substantial armour plating, combined with its tank-resembling structure (though lacking a turret), would offer protection against bullets fired from the house.

Mack watched the APC approach the gates, shouting to be heard over the roar of gunfire. 'What about the threat of traps once we breach?'

'It's a chance we have to take.'

'Fuck, man, the anti-terror squad should be up here dealing with this, not us. This is bigger than local.'

'You're telling me, pal. Fucking politics. They saw how big a mess this is and don't want any part of it.'

'Figures. Maybe they're the smart ones in all this.'

'Yeah, I think you might be right,' Robbins replied as the APC rumbled past them.

Accelerating, it approached the compound gates. Bullets bounced off its armour, scattering concrete as they hit the road. Robbins held his radio to his lips, shouting to be heard over the chaos. 'As soon as we breach the gate, we go in. Everyone be ready.'

The armoured personnel carrier ascended the grassy incline and hit the gates with force, causing them to sway but not collapse. The vehicle slid backward down the embankment, its tires spinning on the rough ground, trying to find purchase for another attempt. Molotov cocktails sailed over the wall from within; two struck their mark, setting the APC's armoured chassis ablaze. Still, it wasn't enough to stop it. With a surge of power, the vehicle lurched forward and broke through the gates, causing them to implode as it pushed past the wall.

'Now. Everyone move.' Robbins screamed.

The officers descended on the house, weapons drawn and ready. Whether they would be saviours or victims was yet to be determined.

II

It was like hell on earth. Hot smoke filled his lungs, and the deafening roar of gunfire seemed to encase them as they entered the inner perimeter. The design of the inner sanctum provided no cover, ensuring attackers gained no advantage now they were inside. The

APC, half-tipped into a ditch camouflaged by loose grass just inside the entrance, could go no further toward the house. It was here they cowered, waiting for a break in gunfire which never seemed to come. One thing Robbins was sure of. They had underestimated how well armed and prepared those in the house were.

The riot specialists had arrived complete with armoured shields and pushed their way towards the main doors to the house, but again, it seemed Warwick was prepared. Reinforced and blocked from the inside, the doors stopped the advance by a hail of bullets tearing through the wood. One officer dropped, hit in the leg, then another, this one going down and not moving. That was enough to see them pull back. Two more went down before they could reach the safety of the stranded APC.

The second wave, employing smoke grenades and tear gas canisters to cover their approach, proved more effective. As an endless barrage of bullets flew, they set explosive charges around the door frame.

Only for a few seconds did the tear gas delay the gunfire before it returned, filling the air with pops and crackles, fire and screams. The assault squad held firm though, and kept low, praying to avoid the fire until they could set off the charges. The explosion was deafening, wood and much of the surrounding walls reduced to shrapnel. There, at last, was a way inside.

The plan had been to assault the house in waves, yet the sheer amount of gunfire aimed at them had caused chaos. Robbins and Mack were in wave three, and were supposed to go into the house and clear the lower rooms, but they were struggling to make progress. Resistance was strong from inside, and the group had been scattered, with Robbins finding himself isolated at the side of the house and heading towards the back, trying to ignore the bullets cutting the air inches away from him. He stayed close to the wall, skirting its edge to the rear yard. There was a building off to the side, and within the open doors, Robbins could see rows of seats and a podium. Two men stood before it, setting up a table laden with Molotov cocktails. One was facing away from Robbins, using a crowbar to open crates of what Robbins presumed were weapons. The other saw Robbins coming. There was no time to think. No time to speak or ask them to surrender. Everything that happened in those next few seconds played out at half speed, every action and subsequent reaction making the eventual outcome inevitable.

The man at the table lifted his arms into view, swinging the rifle Robbins hadn't been able to see from his vantage point.

'Drop it, drop it now!' Robbins said. It was as if he were viewing this from somewhere deep within himself as he brought his weapon up to face the man, or, more accurately, the boy. He was no older than nineteen, maybe even as young as seventeen.

Don't do it kid, please don't do it

It would only be later he would remember the smallest of details, things that he saw without realising he was taking them in. The fuzz of facial hair on the boy's cheeks, not yet strong enough to be true stubble, the awkward way he was holding the weapon, a sign he was untrained. It was too heavy, too cumbersome for him. A puff of breeze cooling the sweat on Robbin's cheeks and bringing with it the smell of smoke and fire, along with the sounds of screaming and confusion. The realisation as the boy continued to turn and drew the rifle level with Robbins that this would not end well.

The kid fired.

Pain, his forearm on fire, the force staggering him. A second shot would finish him, but the years of training and muscle memory kicked in before he even knew what was happening. His return shot went where he had aimed, the centre of the chest. Two shots. There was no scream. No noise at all. The kid crumpled to the ground, rifle pinned under him, limbs twisted into awkward shapes. There was no time for Robbins to contemplate what he had done, or to think about the fire in his arm, or the blood he could feel under his jacket. His attention was already on the other man, as was his gun.

'Turn around. Slow. Are you armed?' Robbins said, wounded arm hanging by his side, blood dripping from his fingertips and soaking into the dusty ground.

'No, I'm not armed.' The man said. Robbins recognised his voice. He turned around as instructed. Alexander Robbins and James Warwick were face to face.

III

It was as if everything else had ceased to exist. The gunfire sounded more distant, the screams and confusion faint as a half tuned radio. In that moment, the world was theirs alone.

'On your knees. Hands behind your head.' Robbins said, trying not to look at the crumpled body on the floor between them.

Warwick stayed where he was. Robbins couldn't understand how he was so unflustered. No armour, not even a weapon, just him in his jeans, T-Shift and denim jacket, worn open and loose.

'How did you know to come here? To the back of the house?'

Warwick shouted to be heard above the noise. Robbins took a few cautious steps closer, teeth gritted as the adrenaline stopped being enough to hide the pain of his injury.

'You didn't strike me from our conversations as a fight to the end type. Seems I was right.'

Warwick smiled, as if the two were engaged in polite conversation over coffee.

The sounds of gunfire from inside the house were becoming more sporadic. Robbins guessed that once they were inside, the siege wouldn't last for very much longer.

'You could have avoided this. You could have come out when I asked.'

'We've done nothing wrong. As American citizens, you have violated our rights by assaulting us.'

'If you had surrendered, you could have saved your people. You're wanted on suspicion of murder.'

Warwick glanced at the body on the ground between them 'It seems the only one of us guilty of murder here is you.'

'Shut up,' Robbins said, forcing himself not to look away from Warwick. 'Don't make me do the same to you.'

'You're shot.'

'It's not serious. If you don't do what I tell you, yours might be.'

'You'd shoot an unarmed man?'

Sweat was dripping into Robbins's eyes, and his arm was on fire, but he didn't release his grip on the weapon or take Warwick out of its sights. 'I told you, no more talk.'

Warwick shifted his eyes to the crumpled corpse beside him.

'His name was Freddie. He was only fifteen. He had such a bright future. So gifted with his hands. He helped build these walls. Look what you did to him.'

Fifteen. Fifteen. Fifteen. Robbins couldn't get it out of his head. A child, he'd shot an actual child.

'They'll die for me, you know.'

'Who?' Robbins said.

'All of them.'

'Not anymore. This is over. Was it worth it? Fighting a war you can't win using women and children?'

'It's a war we didn't want. One you brought to my door. Everything that has happened here today won't live on my conscience. But I have an idea it will live on yours until the day you die.'

Robbins tried to ignore it. The man's words were like poison. He was aware there was almost no gunfire now, and could hear orders being given by his men.

'And besides, you've got this all wrong. Freddie wasn't here to fight. The gun wasn't his to pick up. He was helping me open these crates. The women and children are safe as well.'

'Seems to me you're a liar and will say anything you want people to believe.'

'See for yourself.' Warwick rolled his eyes towards the house. Robbins risked a glance. From one of the upper windows, the women and children looked at them, watching the scene before them unfold, frightened faces pressed up to the glass.

'They're barricaded in to keep them safe and have no weapons. There is a note on the door for your men to say there are unarmed people inside.'

'I wonder if they'd be so devoted if they had seen you run away, if I hadn't stopped you. What was the plan? Hidden tunnel going under the wall?'

Warwick laughed. It sounded alien under the circumstances, and despite the explosive heat and the agony in his arm, Robbins felt a chill rush from his shoulders towards his feet. 'Nothing so extravagant. There's a ladder over there in the bushes. Up and over was the plan. I would advise you to lower your weapon and let me go.'

Now, it was Robbins's turn to laugh. 'Let you go? Why would I do that?'

'Because it's the right thing to do. And because of them.'

He rolled his eyes towards those watching from upstairs. Robbins didn't follow his gaze this time.

'You have nothing left to bargain with. Do you hear how quiet it is? We have this under control and soon enough, those people locked in that room will go back to their families. Now get on your knees.'

'You hear me, but you don't listen. I won't warn you again. This is where they belong. I am their family.' he took a step towards Robbins, who took a counter step back.

'Don't move, not one more fucking step. I'm not playing around.'

Warwick showed no sign of concern or intimidation. There was no fear in him, and it was gnawing at Robbins's gut.

'If you take me away from them, they will have nothing left. I can't be responsible for what happens.'

'I won't tell you again. Knees.'

'You can't kill me. God won't allow it. If you try, you will fail, and they will love me even more.' Warwick took another step forward.

'I won't warn you again.' Robbins could feel it, the gut instinct screaming at him that this was a situation he needed to control.

'Why are you so afraid when you're the one holding the gun? What would your wife think?'

'You know nothing about me,' Robbins said, the pain in his arm now almost too much to bear.

'Come on, Alex, let's be honest with each other. I know you've been chasing me for how long now? A few years? You think I wouldn't know about you? Or the wife and daughter you try so hard to protect. Do they sit alone eating dinner wondering where you are or why you always have to work one more hour.'

Robbins could feel Warwick crawling around inside his head.

He thought of his wife and daughter in a place like this, lost forever and under his spell. Although Warwick continued talking, Robbins ignored him, imagining scenarios where his family were groomed to follow a monster like this. He knew Warwick would never stop. He would always have people who believed, even if he went to jail.

Warwick dropped to his knees, but was still smiling. 'I can see the doubt in you,' he said.

Robbins thought actual monsters had that sort of smile. The wannabes would scream or shout or plead insanity. The real ones smile the way Warwick was smiling now with their poison tongues flicking as the spoke. That was no world for his daughter. No world for anyone innocent.

Robbins squeezed the trigger.

Warwick fell silent, collapsing to the dusty yard on his back. There was no remorse and also no conscious thought he had shot an unarmed man. He was still operating from a distant place deep within himself, a stranger in his own body. He walked to where Warwick lay, gasping and spitting blood, shirt and jacket blossoming red from the hole Robbins had put in his chest. Robbins crouched beside him. He smiled, horrified at how easy it was.

'If God wanted you alive, he'd have saved you from this. Now, you'll die here with this idea of yours.'

'Two sides of the same coin, you and I.' Warwick smiled through the blood, then looked beyond to the house. Robbins followed his gaze to the upper windows, but nobody was watching anymore.

'See? Just like I said. Those people will go back to their lives. Nobody will ever remember you existed.'

Robbins stood and left Warwick to die as the house fell silent.

IV

It was over.

Robbins stood in front of the house, smoke and fire making the air thick and uncomfortable to breathe. He was exhausted, as the magnitude of what had taken place sank in. He watched as officers buzzed around, everyone with something to do apart from him. Mack approached and stood beside him, looking at the bullet riddled structure.

'It's a goddamn mess in there.' He said, pulling out his cigarettes and slipping one into his mouth. He offered the pack to Robbins, who took one, Mack lighting it for him.

'Any survivors?' Robbins asked.

'Not sure. I had to get out of there and get some air. Have you been inside yet?'

Robbins shook his head. The lie he was about to tell coming easily. 'Not yet. I got Warwick, though, around the back of the house, trying to escape over the wall. He reached for something, so I had to put him down.'

'No loss there,' Mack said, squinting up at the sun. 'It's so goddamn hot. This whole thing has been a big fucking mess.'

'Did you get the women and children out from upstairs?'

Mack glanced at him, then back at the house. 'There's nobody to take out of there as far as I know. Like I said, it's a mess.'

'There were a group of them. I saw them looking through the back window when I was with Warwick.'

'I didn't stick around for too long once we got the all clear, but look around, Alex. This is a recovery, not a rescue.'

Robbins threw his cigarette on the ground and walked towards the house, Mack following.

'You okay, Alex? You sure you want to go in there?'

Robbins wasn't listening. He had to see for himself. He remembered the faces at the window, watching him and Warwick as they faced off.

He walked over spent bullet casings and broken glass, ignoring the bloodied bodies still in the positions where they had given their lives to defend the house, and skirted around officers as they compared notes, pointed at positions, and called in help to log the mountains of evidence. He went upstairs, searching for the room which had overlooked the backyard. When he arrived, it felt as if someone had hit him in the chest with a hammer.

'You smell that?' Mack said, wrinkling his nose.

'Almonds.' Robbins muttered.

Unlike the rest of the house, there was no chaos here. No bullet holes, no destruction. It almost looked peaceful. They lay in rows on their backs, heads touching the walls, feet pointed towards the centre of the room. Mothers holding hands with sons and daughters, others who were too young cradled against their chests. Robbins saw an officer speaking to a crime scene photographer outside the door.

'What the hell happened in here?' Robbins asked, as, like fingernails on a chalkboard, Warwick's voice entered his head.

They'll die for me, you know. All of them.

Robbins counted. He couldn't help himself. Fourteen women. Nine Children. Three babies. The crime scene officer was standing beside him, both looking at the horrific sight.

'We suspect cyanide but won't know for sure until autopsy. Why the hell would they do something like this? Were they so devoted to that guy?'

Robbins's mouth watered as nausea swept over him. Mack saw it and put a hand on his shoulder.

'Come on, let's get out of here, Alex. We don't need to be looking at this.'

Robbins didn't move. He couldn't stop staring at them, the one thought in his mind repeating in an endless loop of shame.

These people are dead because of me.

An officer poked his head into the room, grimacing at the scene. 'Detective Robbins, we found Warwick in the backyard.'

'I know,' Robbins said, eyes drifting around the room again. 'He reached for something and I had to put him down.'

Mack turned away from the room. 'Bastard got off lightly. He should have to answer for this fuckin' mess.'

'You might get your chance,' the officer said. 'He's alive.'

Robbins came back from that faraway place deep in his psyche, ice filling his veins as he focussed on the officer. 'Say again?'

'He's alive, sir. He's critical, but on the way to the hospital now.'

Mack clapped Robbins on the shoulder. 'Well, at least some good might come out of this damn mess. Let's hope he pulls through, then we can nail the bastard for everything that has happened here today.'

Robbins didn't respond. He had fired at the chest from less than twenty feet away. There was no way he should have survived.

You can't kill me. God won't allow it.

That was all Robbins could take. He pushed past Mack and the officer, desperate for air which didn't taste like blood, smoke or almonds. He made it to the yard where he vomited at the side of the house, hunched over, hands on knees, dizzy with scenarios of what had and may yet happen.

V

There was no pain.

No white light.

It was a feeling of warmth and awareness that he straddled the line between two worlds. He could hear the doctors as they worked to save his life, yet it felt far away, like music heard across a great distance, with only a few notes recognisable if you strained to hear it.

Knowing his fate and where he was, he stood ready to meet his maker. He could see the frenzied actions of the medical team as they worked, performing chest compressions to save his flesh and bones from expiring. He had no interest in that. Instead, he looked beyond them to a great open field of golden corn stretching to the horizon, sitting beneath the purest blue sky he had ever seen. It was warm here; the sun making him feel safe from the trauma his physical being was enduring.

Walking through the corn, he heard the wind rustling, as if it were speaking to him. At last, he was about to meet his maker. Deeper he went, and as he did the sounds of the doctors grew more distant until, at last, they were silent.

There was a man in the field, facing away from him and looking out over the corn. His arms were folded behind his back, one hand grabbing the opposite wrist. Jim approached, coming to rest behind him, the scene so perfect in every detail he couldn't recall a more glorious sight. The corn brushed against his hands as the wind moved again, ruffling his hair in the otherwise total silence. A question came to him, the only one it felt suitable to ask.

Are you God?

He opened his mouth to say it, but before he could, the man spoke first.

No.

He turned to face Jim, and it all made sense.

It was him. Not God, but *him*. A mirror image of himself. His other self smiled, wide and white, full of ancient knowledge and understanding.

There was so much more he wanted to ask, but the perfect world he had arrived in was changing. The sky darkening, the corn rotting and collapsing around him, black flies swirling amid the decay. His twin fading, a brief pull of air and gone, as if he never existed. Then something yanked him back into that world of pain and confusion; the agony from his gunshot wound exploded in his chest. Warwick screamed, then fell silent as the medication to sedate him did its job.

His final thought before he faded into a black dreamless sleep was one of revelation.

He had been God all along.

OPENING OLD WOUNDS

As he drove, Robbins spotted a cafe and pulled over, stopping his car in front of it. In the back of the car, Dan and Rebecca remained quiet. He couldn't blame them. It was a heavy burden to land on a couple of kids who didn't know any better.

The cafe was nothing special. Pale blue walls, a list of specials written on a chalkboard behind the counter. Unlike the excitement of the last time they had eaten together, there was no enthusiasm from Dan or Rebecca. Robbins sipped his coffee. He had told them everything, although left out the part about shooting Warwick when he was unarmed and no risk. Repeating the official report, he'd told them Warwick appeared to be reaching for a weapon, leaving him no choice but to fire. He hated lying about it now as much as he had back then, but that was a burden he would have to bear alone for whatever years he had left.

He looked at the twins, the children of the man he had so much hatred for, curious about how they were handling what he had told them. Rebecca had declined food and was sipping water. She had said almost nothing since he had finished his account of the events. Dan seemed to have taken it better. He was less connected to the story than his sister. He was eating a burger, and was first to break the silence as he chewed through the quarter pounder. 'I think I understand now why you didn't want to go into it back at the mall. It sounds like it was horrible.'

'A lot of that stuff I've tried to forget over the years, but it never goes away.'

Rebecca set her glass down and stared at Robbins, her expression impossible to read. 'I have a question.'

'Go ahead.'

'Our mother. Going through all this, I can't imagine how she ever recovered from it to live a normal life. I mean, there were no signs she had ever been any part of something like this when we were growing up. It's crazy to me hearing about it. It's like there's a whole side of her we never knew.'

'The thing she had on her side was her age. Plus, we gave her support, put her in touch with the right people to help. Getting out of the country for a fresh start was a big part of it. We did everything we could to give her a normal life.'

'She was doing it to protect us, Becks. She thought it was for the best.' Dan said, nearing the end of the burger.

'Your brother is right. She was lucky. Not many people escaped Warwick once he had his claws into them.'

'I get that,' Rebecca said. 'But what happened to her after? Did she go back home to her parents? There is so much I don't know or understand.'

Robbins rubbed his eyes, wishing he could approach this situation in a less direct way. 'Alright, I know you've already taken a lot of information on board these last couple of days and it can't be easy. The story of your mother's involvement both before and after her time in the compound has one other vital factor. I'll be straight with you. This won't be easy to listen to, but it should help you understand and get into her head a little.'

He paused, ensuring they understood. 'Remember, she was young and already captivated by Warwick. Gloria's jealousy and her mental state were also getting to be out of control. It would only be a matter of time before things came to a head.'

BREAKING POINT

Mary's parents were dead. That was what she had told herself when she first ran away, and that was how she had got by for so long without thinking about them. She never expected to see them again, which was why their surprise arrival at the ranch had shaken her so much. Never did she expect to open the door to her mother, Doris, who looked so much older than she remembered, so frail and tired, clutching her handbag in front of her, headscarf tied under her chin. Her father, Michael, also seemed to have withered and shrunk somehow since she had last seen them. Like his wife, he looked tired, his blue eyes almost glazed with indifference to the world, his mouth a pursed pencil line. This unexpected family reunion conducted on the porch of the ranch began with silence as all three parties tried to come to terms with the situation.

It was only when they noticed her stomach, heavy with child, did her mother come alive, like someone had flicked a switch to activate her mouth. She launched into a tirade at the child she had already convinced herself was dead. Her father, as was his way, remained motionless, still watching, lips pursed. This commotion drew the attention of Jim, who came into the house from the back, confident as he stood beside Mary.

'You, I take it you're responsible for this,' Doris said, looking him up and down and gesturing at Mary's stomach.

It only took those few seconds for Jim to put it all together and understand who these people were.

'You must be Mary's parents. My name is Jim.'

'I don't care who you are. What have you done to my daughter? She's underage, you know. She's just a child.'

Mary gripped Jim's hand and squeezed it. 'What are you doing here? How did you find me?'

'Why do you think we're here? We thought you were dead. Raped and buried somewhere. You could have called or told us you were alright. You...' Doris became incoherent, her words lost in a barrage of sobs. Mary's father put a hand on his wife's arm. 'Now come on, Doris, try to be calm.'

'You be calm,' she said, pulling her arm away. 'We mourned you, thought you were dead. How could you be so cruel when all this time, you were here with a man who has done *this* to you?' She gestured at Mary's stomach. 'I should go to the police and report you for Rape. See how you like that.'

'Please, I think we should all calm down,' Jim was using the same smooth voice which his followers adored. Doris, however, brushed it off.

'Oh, there will be talk alright. Talk about how you took advantage of a child, yes, a child. We'll see what the police think when I tell them what you've done.'

Michael squirmed next to his wife. 'Doris, please, it's better to discuss this rationally. You're making a scene.'

'I don't care if I'm making a scene,' she screamed, fishing a handkerchief out of her purse and dabbing the corner of her eyes. 'We thought we'd lost her, but here she is, less than twenty miles from home. I want answers.'

'And you'll get them. We can figure this out,' Jim said, unused to someone not falling for his charms. 'I can assure you; Mary is here of her own free will. I just offered her a place to stay.'

'Oh, I bet you did. I bet you couldn't wait to offer her a *place to stay*. Monster. Rapist!'

'Doris, that's enough,' Michael said, embarrassed by the outburst.

'Mother, stop it. You don't understand. Jim and I are in love.'

'Love?' Doris repeated, adding a theatrical eye roll for good measure. 'You're a child. You know nothing about love, and he should know better.'

'This is why I left!' Mary screamed. 'You were smothering me, not letting me make my own decisions. It's my life to live, not yours. I didn't want to be found. I don't know how you tracked me down, but I'm happy here and I'm staying.'

'Well, it's a good job someone who lives here was responsible enough to leave us a note saying where we could find you.'

'What note?' Mary asked.

'Someone put a note through the door saying this is where you were. Probably one of these people living with you who has morals and wants to do the right thing.'

Jim said nothing, but looked over his shoulder. Gloria was sitting halfway up the steps, watching proceedings unfold, a defiant expression on her face. He made no reaction and turned back to face Mary's parents. 'Look, I think it's clear we have a lot to discuss, and it's not good for Mary to stand for so long in her condition, we can at least agree on that, can't we? Please, come in and we can work this out.'

Doris stood for a moment, eyes looking beyond Jim and Mary into the house, then nodded. 'Fine. Come on, Michael.'

Jim stood aside as Mary's parents entered the house. He glanced to the stairs, but Gloria had gone, retreated to where she had come from, the damage done. Jim closed the door and led Mary's parents to the sitting room. On the way, he looked around at the followers standing around in the kitchen, watching this unfold.

'Everybody out, please, we need some privacy.'

He waited as they filed out, leaving them alone. Gloria did not come down, however. She stayed upstairs to listen to the mess she had made unfold.

II

Doris's coffee sat untouched on the table. She was rigid on the sofa, hands folded in her lap. Michael was sipping his tea. Mary sat in the armchair, wiping her eyes, which were red ringed from spent tears. Jim sat beside her, his exterior calm masking the rage he felt towards Gloria for bringing this mess to their door.

'First, I want to apologise for the misunderstanding. Our group provides people with lodging and refuge for those who need it.'

Doris sneered and jabbed a finger towards Mary's stomach. 'That comes as part of the package, does it? You give them food, shelter and impregnate them. Very noble.'

'Mother, it's not like that,' Mary said. She looked exhausted and uncomfortable. 'Please, listen and let me explain.'

'You can explain it at home. We are bringing you back with us. You are still our daughter.'

'No, this is my home now. Jim and I will bring our baby up together, here on the Ranch. You can't tell me what to do anymore.'

If Doris heard her daughter, she didn't acknowledge it. She was on a roll now and perched even further on the edge of her seat. 'You'll do as you're told and come home. You're still not eighteen, which means you're our responsibility.'

'But mother, I-'

'And I'll tell you something else,' she said, glaring at Jim. 'You might have put it in her, but you won't be this baby's father.'

'I think we all need to calm down,' Jim said, glancing at Michael, but it seemed he was more than familiar with this wife's stubbornness and sat motionless beside her.

'You don't get a say in this, you pervert,' Doris hissed. 'You've ruined my daughter's life, and you expect me to let her stay here in this.... whatever *this* is. No. Mary is coming home, and that's final. There is no more to be said.'

'It should be Mary's choice. You have no right to speak for her,' Jim said, doing all he could to keep calm.

Unused to being challenged, Doris's eyes grew wide, her voice shrill. 'This has nothing to do with you. I'm speaking to my daughter. You've done enough.'

Jim felt a shift; his calmness gave way to a first hint of threat.

'If Mary wants to stay, she stays. It's my child too. With all due respect, you need to understand things have changed.'

Doris pointed a bony finger at him. 'What a horrible little man you are! You should show the proper respect. Look what you've what you've caused. You've ruined my daughter's life. I don't know what you do here, what this place is, but it's not somewhere my grandchild will grow up, that I can promise you.'

'I agree.'

Doris, startled, turned towards the door where Gloria stood. She was a mess. Fresh cuts on her arms were weeping blood, eyes ringed and raw from not enough sleep. She walked into the room, ignoring the glare from Jim.

'Who on earth are you? What do you have to do with this?' Doris said, thrown off by this new arrival.

'Gloria, we're busy right now. You and I can talk later,' Jim said, just about holding on to his fury. Gloria ignored him. Instead, she stood by the fireplace.

'Who am I?' she repeated, looking at Jim but addressing Doris. 'I'm the one who left you the note.'

Doris shuffled at this unexpected news. 'Oh, well, at least there's somebody with morals in this situation. Thank you.'

'I didn't do it for you.' She said, still not taking her eyes off Jim. 'I used to be her, your daughter. At the start, it was Jim and me, just the two of us. I gave him everything. Devoted my life to him. I wanted to be the one to carry his child, but circumstances meant that couldn't happen. Then she came along. Your precious daughter.'

Jim was glaring, fists clenched on his knees.

'Don't blame my daughter for this. She's the victim,'

'Maybe we're all victims.' Gloria said, a faint smile forming. 'That's my point. I left you the note because I want things back the way they used to be. Since she arrived, Jim won't even look at me. We started building this together and now I've been thrown away. It will only get worse when the baby arrives.'

'Gloria, I'm won't tell you again,' Jim was loud enough even to silence Doris. He was glaring, veins in his neck bulging. Mary, seeing this side of him for the first time, let out a gasp. Gloria saw it and smiled.

'That's him. The real him. That's who lives under the mask. The monster behind the man.'

Jim had heard enough. He stood and grabbed Gloria by the arm and tried to drag her to the door, but she pulled away from him. 'Don't you fucking touch me. Don't forget what I know.'

'What is she talking about?' Mary yelled.

'This is an outrage,' Doris chimed in.

Jim dragged Gloria towards the door, trying to get her out of the room, but she wasn't about to go without a fight. She clawed at him and squirmed away from his grasp. 'There was a boy she used to like once.'

'That's enough. We'll talk later.' Jim was struggling to keep his composure.

'Remember him, Mary? Did you ever wonder what happened to him?' Jim hit her, fist connecting with her cheek, sending her crashing off the wall and sliding to the floor. It was enough to bring the room to silence.

Doris stood. 'That's it, I've seen enough. Mary, come on, we're going home.' Doris crossed the room, bumping the table and spilling her tea. She grabbed her daughter by the arm and tried to drag her up, but Mary gripped the chair, begging for her mother to let her go.

'Doris, please. It's clear she doesn't want to go; you're making another scene.'

'I won't hear it. You're coming home, and we're calling the police. I won't stand for this.'

'Doris please why don't you - agk.'

Agk.

In the coming months, Mary would often wonder what that word her father was going to say was before everything stopped.

Agk.

Jim had the fireplace poker in his hand, the end matted with blood and hair from Michael's scalp. Michael stood there, a frozen moment in time as blood trickled from the top of his head in miniature rivers down his face.

Agk.

Jim struck again, his backswing sending blood spattering on the ceiling and his forward impact with the top of Michael's skull spattering himself, Mary and Doris with more of the same.

Agk.

Michael, who had already said so little and looked so uncomfortable listening to his overbearing wife and coping with it for years, would now never have to sigh under his breath and put up with her rambling. He would never have to think about anything again as his skull imploded, the delicate brain tissue within damaged beyond repair.

Agk.

Another blow finished the job, sending him crashing into the coffee table, blood, coffee and tea mixing into a watery soup as he crumbled to the floor on his back, his final breaths coming shallow and fast as he waited for death to take him. Doris and Mary had watched this as if paused, Doris still with her fingers embedded in her daughter's forearm, Mary holding onto the chair to resist her mother. Jim knew he couldn't stop now. There was no going back. He took a step, knowing Mary would never forgive him for what he was about to do. He struck again, taking some delight in bringing the poker down on Doris's skull. The sound was sharp and brittle, reminding him of a childhood memory of breaking up firewood in winter. Unlike Michael, Doris went down in a single hit, her arm spasming as she released her grip on her daughter. She lay on the floor, gasping. One eye blinking rapidly, the other dilated and staring straight ahead. Michael, too, was fighting the inevitable, his physical body clinging to life with a series of gurgles and twitches. Jim struck again and again until there was silence from them both. When it was done, he stood over the mangled remains of the two bodies, Mary at one side, still staring in shock, and Gloria at the other, defiant and holding her cheek, her lip bloodied and giving a crimson sheen to her teeth as she smiled.

Jim ignored her. He turned to Mary.

'You understand why I had to do that, don't you?' Jim said between breaths. 'They would have taken you away and ended all this.'

Mary could only stare and the pulpy things on the floor.

'Now she knows the truth. Now she sees the monster you are.' Gloria was smug and satisfied, defiance in her eyes, which were more alive than they had been in months.

Jim screamed, the force of it burning his throat. He lurched towards Gloria and swung the bloody poker, stopping his downswing only inches from her skull, blood splattering over her hair and face. Gloria didn't flinch or even blink. She held his gaze.

'This is the first time you've looked at me in months. That was all I wanted.'

Jim tossed the poker on the floor, for the first time taking in the destruction surrounding them. 'Get this mess cleaned up. You caused it, you can fix it.'

II

'I can't believe it,' Rebecca said. 'I mean, we knew our grandparents had died before we were born, but we had no idea they were murdered. How does something like that stay secret?'

'They never released or published their names in any of the reports. We were lucky, in a sense, because the attention was all of Warwick and the assault at the Compound. It was easy to hide the things we didn't want them to know. Protecting your mother's identity was pretty easy.'

'Would it be possible to visit their graves?' Dan asked. 'I'd like to pay my respects.'

Robbins shook his head. 'We knew what had happened because we had been told, but we never found their bodies. We spent weeks trying to get him to confess to it, to do the right thing for the good of the families, but he wouldn't admit anything. One thing about Warwick is, he likes to play games. For most people, being questioned by the police about murder would be a frightening experience, but to him, because he was the focus of everyone's attention, he thrived on it. He dragged it out, implying he would give us something, then going silent, refusing to speak at all.'

Rebecca glanced at her brother, then at Robbins. 'What if he didn't do it?'

'Of course he did it. We have eyewitness accounts. I'm not sure what you're implying.'

'I'm just saying, what if it wasn't him?'

'Jesus, Becks, are you trying to defend this guy?'

'I think it's a valid question. If he never admitted to it, and the bodies were never found, how can you be certain?'

'We'll get to the how we know in time. I don't want to jump out of the order of things or it will be hard to keep this story together. Trust me when I tell you, we know it was him, and when it gets to the telling, you'll understand it too.'

'I'm sorry. I didn't mean to offend you, Detective Robbins. This is hard to imagine someone could ever do that to someone else. I like to see the good in people and from everything you've said already, I'm struggling to do that here. The main thing I can't wrap my head around is how, after all that, and seeing it happen, why did Mum stay with him?'

'Becks, how do you think the police found out about all this stuff? That was mum, right Detective?'

'We'll get to the details.'

The sounds of other diners enjoying their breakfasts continued, but they fell silent again, the atmosphere turning sombre.

'You said this morning we had a big day today. Can you fill us in on what we're doing? It already feels like it's been quite intense.' Dan looked to be struggling to take in all that had been told so far.

'I had something planned, but after all we've talked about so far, I've been on the fence about going ahead or not. I figured we've come so far, so we may as well go all the way. First though, there's more you need to know, but not here. It's too public for my liking. I'll go over it on the way.'

NO TURNING BACK

Pre-dawn silence filled the house. Gloria hadn't slept, although of late, that wasn't unusual. Instead, she'd drifted in and out of restless nightmares, snapping awake and scanning the shadows to make sure those monsters hadn't followed her to the real world. She knew there would be repercussions for what she had done. Jim was taking his time in deciding what it would be to prolong her fear and make her feel worthless. He had chastised her in his sermon the night of the incident with Mary's parents, belittling her, telling the others, without going into details, about how she had brought shame to the group, and had acted selfishly to the detriment of the others.

He forced her to stand on the stage next to him, silent as he destroyed the few fragments of confidence she had left. Now, she was an outcast, a prisoner with the freedom to leave, yet with nowhere to go.

The thing she hated the most – beyond the blood, beyond the digging in the dead of night and cutting those people into chunks small enough to bury – was that she still loved Jim.

For all the lengths she had gone to in order to destroy the bond between them and the horror that followed, Mary was still in the house, and her relationship with Jim seemed no worse after those first days when she had stayed in the bedroom alone, refusing to see anyone.

Jim had slithered back to her during that time, slipping into her bed, pawing at her body, hot breath in her ear as she did all she could to resist his advances. It was no good. Everyone knew there was no resisting Jim if he wanted something. As he had grunted and forced himself on her, she didn't fight. She lay in silence and wept until it was over. Even after, when he saw the tears on her cheeks, he laughed and told her what had just happened didn't mean she was forgiven. For the next six nights it was the same, Jim using her in the most vile and deplorable ways imaginable, leaving her hollow and sore. On the seventh night he and Mary reconciled, leaving her, once again, alone.

She walked through the house in the hazy early morning light, every trace of the bloody events that took place a few weeks before erased as if it had never happened.

She opened the door and sat on the porch step, watching the dark bleed into morning.

The life she once knew felt like it belonged to someone else. The house she grew up in and once filled with childhood memories of summer barbeques and laughter, had become a place of death. It would be worse when Mary's baby arrived. Watching her and Jim raise that child under her nose in her own home would be more cruel than any punishment Jim could ever devise.

The first rays of sun appeared over the horizon. As the glow of the day crept over the top of the wall, she knew the time had come. People would wake up soon and she wanted to do what she had to before that happened. She walked towards the gate, stopping to pick up the package she had stashed the night before. Opening the gate, she walked down the road into town.

In the bedroom, Jim stood at the window and watched her go, forehead pressed against the glass. He did not stop her, even if he suspected what she was about to do.

Today, then, was to be the day.

II

Teasle station was a single storey office with glass windows all across the face, and three small cells in the basement level. The six officers who rotated shifts to keep the place operational had a quiet time of it mostly. Often it would be nothing more exciting than minor vandalism. Sometimes maybe a guy might have too much to drink and have to spend a night in the cells to cool off, but nothing major, and that's how they liked it. It was a good gig. The worst part of it, by far, was the night shift. Starting at 11 and finishing at 7 the next morning, it was the definition of a graveyard shift.

Most nights, nothing at all happened. That night had been another long and dull shift which was following the same pattern. Davies was due off shift in forty-five minutes, and he had been watching the clock tick down for what felt like an eternity. His only thought was what he was going to have to eat when he got back to his apartment, when the girl walked into the station and approached the desk.

'How can I help you, miss?' he asked, his mind still concentrated on food. Maybe he would have those burgers in the freezer. If not that, a cheese salad.

'Are you in charge here?' the girl asked.

'I am for the next forty-five minutes. What can I do for you?'

'I need to report a murder. Two, actually.'

Davies looked her up and down. The crazy eyes. Pale skin. Hair that looked like it had been unwashed in months. Just what he needed.

Almost through a shitty incident free night shift and a crazy bitch walks in.

'Did you hear what I said?' She was staring at him, waiting for him to react. Davies sighed and sat up in his seat, the backrest creaking in protest.

'Come on, miss, it's been a long night. I don't have time for games.'

'Actually, I want to report four murders.'

'Oh, great. Four murders? You sure? Why not report five? Or ten?'

'This isn't a joke.'

'Sounds like it to me. Unless you want a night in the cells for wasting police time, I think you better be on your way.'

The girl said nothing. Instead, she put something on the desk between them. It was long and wrapped in a flower-patterned blanket.

'What the hell is this?' Davies said as he unwrapped it.

'Careful with that. It's the murder weapon.'

Davies stopped unwrapping the package, looked at the girl and realised she was serious. He wiped his hands on his shirt. 'Maybe I should call my boss.'

The woman nodded, calm in the face of what was an intense conversation. 'Maybe you should.'

Davies picked up the phone and dialled a number, waiting for it to be answered. He was about to hang up when someone answered. 'Hey, boss, uh, it's Davies. Sorry to disturb you so early, I, uh, I think you should come down here. We have a situation.'

THE TEST

Packed into the barn, they stood shoulder to shoulder, a mixture of nervousness and anticipation in the air. Jim paced at the front of the stage, unsure what he was going to say and trusting the voice inside to do it for him.

'We've talked many times about a test. A test that would one day come to our door and one we, as a family, would have to deal with. What we didn't know was that the test would come from within.'

A few nervous murmurs filter through the crowd. There is a unique energy fuelled by anxiety over excitement.

'This morning, one of our own betrayed us. You know what she is, how she has been behaving of late. Right now, as we gather here in peace, she is telling lies, Fabricating stories. Going against my word and, by proxy, the word of God.'

Jim felt their eyes burning into him, the energy building into something, anxiety shifting towards anger and injustice.

'I won't lie to you. What is to come will be frightening. It will be a test of our resolve and there will be moments where perhaps your faith will be tested. Don't feel ashamed of those moments of doubt. They are natural, they are part of human nature, and they are part of the incredible and complex machine created by God.'

Jim stopped pacing, standing centre stage, letting his eyes drift over his followers.

'They will bring their guns and try to destroy us because they are evil. Demons disguised as men. I asked God for guidance, for what to do in this situation. God said we have to defend what we have built in his name, and that those who were worthy in this battle would ascend to be beside him for eternity. This is what we have been waiting for. Like Judas betrayed Jesus, Gloria has betrayed us.'

He raised a cautionary finger to the crowd. 'However. God understands that some of you may not feel ready to make that commitment, and it's okay. There will be no judgement. No shame in your weakness. No judgement in cowardice. In a moment, I will lead you to the gate. Those of you too weak and uncommitted will be free to leave. For those who remain, the strong, the righteous, those ready to stand side by side with God. Then we will stand together in glory and fight this war we have been preparing for.'

Jim untucked the key attached to the silver chain he wore around his neck and held it up to the crowd. 'You all know which room this key unlocks. You know what we keep inside.'

Jim hopped off the stage and walked towards the exit doors, the people parting before him. He emerged into the sunshine, a pied piper of followers as he crossed the yard towards the steel gate. He swung it open and stood by the exit.

'There is no place here for those without total commitment.'

The silence was heavy, the air itself motionless. The followers exchanged glances. There was a mixture of determination and anxiety. Some were resolute, while others were apprehensive. Somewhere close, a wasp buzzed amid the crowd, then was off on its way.

Almost thirty seconds passed before anyone moved. A woman with two small children stepped forward. The crowd parted to let her through, watching her. She stopped in front of Jim, unable to look him in the eye. She tried to speak, but appeared to be struggling to find the words. He watched as the woman led her children through the open gate. When she arrived on the other side, it was clear she did not know what to do, so she stood there, looking back and watching them. It acted like a miniature flood. More people started to move and pass through, but few. Some stayed through determination and belief. The others, through fear of being judged a coward. Fourteen left, around half the number who wanted to, but felt pressured to stay.

Jim saw Mary standing by the house, watching this scene unfold. He waved her over. She came to him, ponderous and unsteady.

'You all know who this is. The mother of my child to be. This is love. This is the dedication which Gloria and those of you unwilling to stay could not understand.'

He turned to her and brushed her cheek with his finger. He didn't have to speak. She looked from Jim to the open gate and the faces beyond, watching her. She shook her head.

'No, I want to stay.'

He said nothing. The message was obvious enough to them all.

Mary was fighting back tears. 'I don't want to.'

She clung to Jim's arm. He motioned to those outside the gate for help. They came for her, pulling her away and leading her out of the compound.

Jim watched them go. Then closed the gate and clipped the padlock into place. As he walked away, he didn't look back, even when Mary's cries transformed into anguished screams.

II

'Wow. So, he made her leave?' Rebecca said, glancing at her

brother. He met her gaze.

'Don't say it. It doesn't make him a good person.'

'I didn't say a word.'

'You didn't have to. I know how you think.'

'Jesus, take it easy.'

'I always assumed…'

'That your mother was the one who went to the police.' Robbins knew this was coming.

'Yeah.'

'I thought that too, especially after what happened with her Parents' Dan said.

'Your mother was young, impressionable. To a master manipulator like Warwick, she was an easy target. Plus, when we raided the place after the siege, we found a supply of sedatives. We suspect your mother was one of many he was drugging to keep her compliant.'

'Even when she was pregnant?' Dan said.

'Yeah, but again, we don't know for sure. We know he had the drugs, and we know they were being used, but we could never prove it.'

'Jesus,' Dan glanced at his sister, who was staring at Robbins.

'It took a lot of time to free her from his influence. She was pretty far gone. I think the pregnancy helped, especially after the two of you were born. It gave her something to focus on. Without that, maybe she wouldn't have been saveable.'

Robbins took a moment to gather his thoughts as he slowed the car, turning down a side street.

'Anyway, that wraps the story up. You wanted to know how it

happened, and now you do.'

'So if that's everything, where are you taking us now?' Rebecca asked.

'We're on our way to visit to Gloria.'

'What?'

They both said it in unison, and Robbins wished he'd have delivered the news with a little more tact. It was too late to backtrack now, as he could see they were already firing up questions.

'I assumed she'd be in prison after her involvement in everything.' Dan said, giving Rebecca a nervous flick of the eyes. His sister, though, was silent, taking it all in.

'She should have rotted behind bars for the rest of her life, but we needed info from someone who was there for when the case went to court. She was a victim as much as anyone, in a way. Nobody else, your mother included, would tell us anything about what had happened in that place. Gloria knew we needed her, so she held out for one hell of a deal. In the end, she got a six year suspended sentence, plus a change of name and identity to protect her in exchange for her telling the full story and for her testimony in court.'

'And she's free to go about her life as if nothing happened?' Rebecca asked.

'Don't expect some kind of monster based on what you've heard the last couple of days. Like everyone he came into contact with Warwick, he manipulated her, chewed her up, and would have spat her out if she hadn't left when she did. She may be free, but I don't think she has much of a life these days. The scars she has run too deep.'

Robbins tried to gauge their reactions, but both were doing a good job of hiding how they were feeling.

'Does she know we're coming?' Dan asked.

'She knows *I'm* coming. Not you two.'

'What? Is that a good idea?'

'Why would she see us if she knew?' Rebecca cut in. 'We're the kids of the woman who ruined her life. I wouldn't expect a warm welcome.'

'That's pretty accurate. If I asked her first, she'd have said no. This way, she has no choice.'

'Is she dangerous?' Dan asked, his voice a little too shrill.

'You think I'd go there if she was? Let alone bring you two with me. Just relax.'

How long until we get there? Rebecca asked.

'Not long. Unless, of course, you'd rather not. You said you wanted to know it all, but we can turn back easily enough.'

'No, we want to see her.'

To Robbins's surprise, it was Dan who said that. Even Rebecca looked shocked that their roles had, for now, at least reversed.

A MONSTER IN SUBURBIA

Robbins pulled the car to a halt in the shade of an oak tree, its base surrounded by a carpet of brown winter leaves.

'Is this it?' Rebecca asked, looking out of the window.

'Nah, it can't be,' Dan added.

Robbins could understand their confusion. They had been expecting bare concrete walls, maybe a police guard outside an ugly nondescript building. Instead, they had arrived in a picture postcard version of Suburban America. White picket fences, lawns trimmed and edged by plants in glorious reds and yellows along both sides of the tree-lined street. The houses appeared homely, and the one they had pulled up outside was no different. White façade, green painted shutters on the windows. A short gravel path leading to the black front door. A red Nissan sat in the driveway in front of the garage.

'What were you expecting? Bars and barbed wire?'

'Yeah. Kind of.' Dan muttered.

'I told you she's harmless. Come on.' Robbins said, getting out of the car. He walked towards the house, the twins following behind. He knocked and waited. A few seconds passed. They could hear a key turning and a chain being removed from the other side of the door, which was then opened.

'It's been a while, Gloria.' Robbins said.

Age had taken its toll on her. There was a perpetual tiredness in her eyes, her skin wrinkled and withered. Her hair was whiter now than brown, sticking in odd patterns away from her head resembling piano wire. She was thin, some might say undernourished.

'You're supposed to call me Anna now.' She said, her voice deep and dry from too many cigarettes.

'Yeah, well, that's for those who don't know the truth.'

Gloria looked beyond Robbins to the twins. 'I didn't realise you were bringing anyone with you. What's this? Interns? The next shining lights of the…'

Recognition, familiarity. She looked them up and down, Dan first, then Rebecca, then turned her eyes on Robbins, a flicker of rage visible despite the years that had passed.

'Is this some kind of fucking joke?'

Robbins shuffled his feet. 'Not exactly. Can we talk inside?'

'Do I have a choice?' she replied as she stepped away from the door. 'You better come in.'

Inside of the house was as classic suburbia as the outside. Plush, neat carpets, tasteful décor arranged with showroom perfection. She led them through to the sitting room, slippers padding on the wood floors.

'Shoes off. I've just had the carpets cleaned.'

They complied without comment, lining their shoes up by the door. Gloria sat in an armchair, an overstuffed ashtray on a small table beside it. Robbins sat opposite. Dan and Rebecca perched on the sofa.

'So, I suppose I should tell you why we're here.'

Gloria gave a half smile, as if there was a joke to which only she knew the punchline.

'She had twins, I see. The girl gave it away. She's a dead ringer for her mother. Noticed it the second I saw her at the door.'

'Well, that's saved me from having to explain.'

'Not really. You still haven't told me why you're here or why you've brought them with you.' she shook her head. 'Jesus, what a fucking mess.'

'Look, I don't want to get into all that again. It's in the past. You know I wouldn't be here unless I had good reason, Gloria.'

'*Anna*. You're supposed to call me *Anna*. Those are the rules. Learn your new identity. Memorise it. Who you were before no longer exists. You remember, don't you? How much you drilled it into me.'

'Like I said, I don't want any conflict. That's not why I've come.'

Gloria exhaled a cloud of smoke, stood and walked towards the kitchen. 'I need a drink. Then you can tell me what the fuck you want.'

II

Gloria sipped her coffee, eyes crawling over her unwanted guests, unwavering and hard to read. She turned her attention back towards Robbins. 'I always assumed she'd had them aborted, considering who their father is.'

The twins glared at her, which generated another of those not quite smiles. 'Nothing personal, obviously. It would have just made sense under the circumstances. It doesn't answer why you've brought them here unless it's about rubbing my nose in it.'

'Of course not,' Robbins said. 'The reason I'm here is that they found out about their father and are planning on visiting him. I'm trying to convince them it's a bad idea. I figured hearing from you might give a different perspective.'

Gloria stared out of the window, index finger tapping against the side of her mug. 'A different perspective,' she repeated. 'How much we'd all like a different perspective on Jim Warwick.'

'Please,' Dan said, glancing at his sister. 'Anything you can tell us would help.'

Gloria lit another cigarette, each motion slow and deliberate. She knew they were all waiting for her to respond, and she was making the most of it. Eventually she spoke, and it was clear from her tone that she hadn't been delaying for drama. It was because bringing this up again was hard.

'Well, where do I start? Do you want to know how that man left me broken and empty? A shell second guessing every aspect of my life? Maybe how his last kid he should have had with me wasn't what he wanted, so he drowned it in the bathtub. Or maybe you want to know how the only way I could forget what he did to me was by losing myself in drink. When that wasn't enough, drugs. Is that what you want to hear?'

She rolled up her sleeves, showing the scar tissue on her wrists. 'Or maybe how I was so destroyed by him that all I felt I could do was end it all, and I even fucked that up.'

'Jesus,' Dan whispered.

Gloria looked out of the window, focussed on nothing.

'Even when I was free of him, I couldn't go back to a normal life. How could i? Fuck, what would I go back to? Parents are dead. The only man I ever loved, taken from me by your mother and sent to jail. I sometimes wish I'd stayed in that fucking house and let them shoot me.'

She grimaced, in full flow now, but somehow managing not to let the tears come, as if showing them weakness was something she was unwilling to do. 'Maybe I should tell you about when it should have been over, when life should have gone on, it didn't go on for me. I had to become someone else. New life, new name. A fresh start, they said, but that didn't take away the memories or the scars that bastard left on me.'

She turned her attention to Dan and Rebecca, somehow keeping her emotions under control. 'If you want to know more about him, ask your damn Mother. She knew him better than anyone.'

'We can't. She's dead.' Rebecca snapped.

Gloria took a drag on her cigarette, blowing smoke out of the corner of her mouth towards the open window. 'I didn't know that. How did it happen?'

'Car accident.' Dan said. 'It wasn't until afterwards, when we were sorting through her things, that we found out who our father was.'

'It makes sense. I see why she'd hide it from you.'

Rebecca cried. It was the first time she had shown any sort of weakness so far. Even then, she tried to fight it. Jaw set, fists clenched as she stared into the middle distance and refused to give in.

'If you could tell us about her, how she was, so we can get a feel for how things were…' Dan said, as grabbed his sister's hand, but she pulled away.

'I could tell you plenty, But nothing you'd want to hear. You've heard by now how your mother and I didn't get on, to say the least. I hated her for what she did to me, and she hated me, even if she never said it. We both wanted the same thing, and neither of us wanted to share. Of course, he could have settled it and made a choice, but why would he? He had the best of both worlds and we were too fucking young and stupid to realise.'

'And what about our father? What can you tell us about him?' Dan pressed her, unsure why or if it was a question he wanted answered. But his sister wanted to know, and that was enough for him.

Gloria looked at them both, eyes coming to rest on Dan. 'You look a little like him. Same eyes. Your sister has your mother's features. A dead fucking ringer, in truth. As for Jim, what can I tell you? By now, you'll know enough to make up your own minds about him. As for how he used to be? He was the perfect man. Charming, caring, always there when you needed him. Then, there was the other side that came out later.'

She glanced at Robbins, then turned her attention back to Dan and Rebecca. 'That side of him that was cruel, and so cold it almost made you wonder if he was even human.' She took another drag of her cigarette. 'In a way, it was impressive how easily he could switch his personality. One day, he would look at you like there was nothing else in his world. The next, it was like you didn't exist at all.'

She stubbed out the cigarette in the ashtray beside her. Everyone, Robbins included, was engrossed.

'If I were you, I'd go back to wherever you came from and leave Jim Warwick to rot. You won't though.'

'How can you be so sure?' Rebecca said.

'Because you're his kids. Both him and Mary were always so headstrong. You'll go ahead with the visit, no matter what I say. You know that already though, don't you, Robbins?'

'Maybe we should go,' Robbins said, standing up and ignoring the twin pop from his knees.

'Yeah, maybe you should. And don't come here again.'

She didn't get up to see them out. Instead, she lit another

cigarette and stared out of the window. Robbins led them out of the house and back to the car, but didn't drive away. He turned to face them where they sat in the back seat.

'You okay?'

'Yeah, it's a lot to take in,' Dan said.

'How about you?' Rebecca had regained her composure, but her eyes were still red. 'I don't know what to do anymore.'

Robbins wished this was the end, but there was one more piece of news on this shittiest of days to relay to them. 'I hate to put more on you, and believe me, I wish this hadn't come today. I got a call from Beadle this morning. You're cleared to visit Warwick tomorrow, so this is it. Decision time. There's nothing else I can tell you that will make a difference. I'll drop by tomorrow and see what you want to do, then this ends for me either way.'

He gave them no time to debate. He put the car into gear and turned it around, heading back the way they had come. Thinking about Warwick had made other demons resurface, and those were proving difficult to ignore.

A MONSTER OF A DIFFERENT KIND

He parked outside the bar for almost an hour, fighting with the million reasons he wanted to go in and the one reason he knew he shouldn't. Sobriety, he had learned over the years, was a fragile thing. Sometimes it was easy, and there would be huge spells where the idea of drinking didn't even enter his head. Today was not one of those days, and his body ached with the need to pour whisky down his throat until he was too fucked up to remember anything.

It's one drink. You can handle that, can't you?

No, because he had been here before. It was never just one drink. There was always another. Then another. It was a slippery slope.

That was before. You've been in control of this for years now. You can handle it.

There was no beating addiction. He had come to terms with that reality long ago. All you could do was suppress it and try to resist falling back into its clutches for as long as possible. He reached into his shirt pocket and took out his wallet, flipped it open and slid out the silver sobriety coin, staring at it in the diffused glow of the light spilling from the bar.

You can get another one. Don't be so sentimental. Hell, you've already done ten years. What's the harm in starting again? Nobody would begrudge you this. Not after what you've been through this week. Besides, who would know? You live alone. You have nobody to justify it to.

He closed his eyes, trying every trick he knew to suppress the urge.

Think about it. All those years living as an empty, unsatisfied shell, and for what? An oversized chunk of silver. Hardly seems worth it to me.

It was then he snapped his eyes open. The voice in his head was no longer his inner monologue. It was Warwick. Robbins could imagine him in the bar, perched on a stool, a smug grin on his face as he beckoned Robbins to sit beside him, pouring him a drink, encouraging him to take a sip. He would love that. A victory from behind bars, a final fuck you to the man who put him in prison.

No.

He wouldn't allow that to happen. Especially not now. He could do one more day. Surely after all this time he could manage that, and it would be over and he could cram those fucking skeletons back into the closet where they belonged.

The voice in his head, no longer trying to disguise who he was, chuckled. Robbins imagined Warwick sipping his own drink, enjoying it, savouring it because he *could* have one and not feel the need to have another, then another. Robbins knew what he was going to say before Warwick even uttered a word.

Ahh, but tomorrow could be the day you and I speak for the first time in years. What a treat that will be. Surely that justifies one little drink?

Robbins squeezed the sobriety coin in his fist, its edges digging into his palm. It took all of his will, everything he had to not give in. To do that would mean Warwick would win, and there was no way he could accept that. He slipped the coin back into his shirt pocket and drove home, knowing he wouldn't sleep that night at the thought of what may come the next day.

DECISION TIME

The warden's office seemed darker than before, although Robbins thought that may have been his mood that was hanging over the space, an intangible sense of foreboding so thick you could almost taste it.

Beadle had been skittish since they arrived and was fidgeting behind his desk. It was a far cry from the confidence which had oozed out of him during the first meeting. Dan and Rebecca were unreadable, sitting opposite the warden as they waited for him to finish preparing the paperwork.

'I don't think it's any secret that your decision to go ahead with the visit today is the outcome I was hoping for. As I have no legal right to intervene, we must do our best to cope with the situation.'

'I'll go in with them,' Robbins said, doing all he could to hide that this was the last thing he wanted to do.

Beadle seemed satisfied with the idea, even if it didn't ease his agitation. 'Also, I need to remind you both, all of you, actually, that despite his history, Warwick isn't the same man as he once was. He's calmer these days, having long ago given up on any hope of freedom. When you meet him, you may wonder what all the fuss was about.'

Yeah, we'll see about that.

Robbins shifted, wanting this to be over so he could get back to his boring life.

Beadle paused for effect, holding up a scrawny index finger. 'All the same, I urge you all not to let your guard drop. Caution is key.'

'We're not afraid, Warden,' Dan said, trying to speak around the waver in his voice. 'We know what we're getting into.'

Beadle shook his head. 'This isn't about fear, son, not with Warwick. What I was going to say was although he may appear placid, indifferent, and even friendly, you must keep in mind why he's here. If I can tell you one thing about James Warwick, it's that his biggest weapon, his most powerful tool, is his mind. Not just his mind, but everything connected to it, things you and I would take for granted are very deliberate acts. The way he sits, the way he speaks, the way he may look at you in a certain way or word certain phrases...' Beadle trailed off, wringing his hands together. 'I'm losing my train of thought here. What I'm trying to say is, for all these years, James Warwick has been a shell of who he was. Broken, resigned to a life in his cell and no hope of ever getting out. This situation could reawaken certain traits in him. Frankly, we don't know what to expect.'

'What the warden means is, your father is a bear in a cave full of other bears who respect who he is, and we're about to go in and poke at him in places he's never been poked.'

'Well, I wouldn't have put it like that, but the sentiment is correct,' Beadle said. 'The harmony of the prison is a concern.'

'I thought he was isolated from the other prisoners?' Rebecca said.

'How do you know that?' Dan asked.

'Isn't that how it works with death row inmates? They're kept away from the general population?'

Beadle nodded. 'That's true, yes. There are four prisoners in total on the death row wing, your father being one of them. But inmates communicate information, no matter how we try to police it. Make no mistake, James Warwick has a powerful influence on the prison population, which is all the more reason to be cautious.'

Robbins was only half listening. He was eying the drinks caddy at the back of Beadle's office, the urge to take a nip of something to still his nerves growing stronger by the second. That voice, Warwick's voice that lived in his head, came out of its hiding place to tempt him again.

If ever there was a time for a drink, this is it? You and I are about to meet for the first time in what? Ten years? Fifteen? Nobody would begrudge you a little something to still the nerves.

Robbins had fought this battle before. He had survived this long without drink and he knew he could do it.

Bullshit. We both know you're a shitty day away from trading in that chunk of silver you carry around like a trophy for a shot of something warm and golden. Why not today?

He wouldn't do this. Not now. Not this way.

Go on, flip Beadle the coin and have a little drink on me. For old time's sake, if nothing else.

Robbins tore his eyes away from the drinks caddy and tried to tune back in to what was going on in the room.

'Are you okay, Detective Robbins?' Rebecca asked.

Robbins realised all eyes were on him and he shuffled his feet, uncomfortable with the attention. 'Yeah, I'm fine.'

He changed the subject, doing what his ex-wife always said he did best and redirecting attention elsewhere.

'Anyway, this isn't about me. It's about you two. Are you sure this is what you want? Once it's done, you can't undo it.'

Dan and Rebecca looked at each other and nodded, and in that moment, Robbins felt for them. They were just kids and had gone from normal lives to absolute chaos in a matter of a few weeks. It would have been tough for anyone to handle, but for a pair in their twenties, it was one hell of a burden.

'Alright,' Robbins said, forcing himself not to look over to the drinks caddy. 'Let's get this show on the road, shall we? If that's okay with you, Warden?'

Beadle seemed to have resigned himself to the fact this was happening and there was nothing he could do to stop it. 'Of course. I'll have someone escort you over to his wing. In the meantime, I'll call ahead and have him moved to the visitation room.'

Met with silence, Beadle sighed and seemed to shrink as if he was a balloon and someone had let the air out of him. 'Head downstairs to the main entrance. Someone will be there to take you over. And… good luck.'

The trio left the office and set out to whatever fate awaited them.

II

Separated from the main prison, the death row visitation area was a small building with thick walls and barred windows. Robbins had made this walk before, and even though it had been many years before, little had changed over the years. avocado walls, dim lighting from overhead fixtures encased in mesh cages. They came to a security door, and Robbins stopped, turning to the twins.

'How are you both feeling?'

'It feels like that scene in Silence of the Lambs before Starling meets Lecter,' Dan muttered. 'You ever read that book, Detective

Robbins?'

'I'm not much of a reader, but I saw the film. I know the part you mean. Don't worry though, it's not like that. No stone walls or glass cells. Just try to relax.'

'What about you? How are you coping?' he said to Rebecca.

'I'm fine,'

He had seen enough body language over the years to know it was a lie. Her skin was pale, expression tense, as if she had the weight of the world on her shoulders. He could see it all over her face, the combination of fear and anticipation, and even though these kids were strangers to him, Robbins felt a need to protect them from the monster waiting a few feet away.

'Listen, both of you. I want you to be ready for this. Let me do the talking, at least at first. I don't know how he might react to seeing you two for the first time.'

They had reached the exterior door leading to the visitation room, and Robbins gestured for the guard accompanying them to wait before taking them in.

'Remember everything you've learned. Everything I've told you about him. How his mind works, how you can't trust anything he says, even if it seems mundane. I'll be there with you to stop him if he goes too far, but you both still need to keep your guard up. He might be in a cage, but he's still dangerous. Are you ready?'

Looking at each other, Dan and Rebecca's shared expressions of fear struck Robbins as the most similar they'd ever appeared. A silent communication, possibly the unique twin bond, passed between them, leading to unspoken agreement.

'Yes. We're ready to go in.'

'All right. Then let's get this over with.'

He gestured to the guard, who unlocked the door and held it open as the three of them went inside.

OUR FATHER THE MONSTER

Like the outer building, the cell block had changed little since Robbins was last there, other than the lower half of the brick walls were now painted blue instead of green. The visiting room area was empty, as Beadle had arranged for this to be a special session outside of the regular hours. After passing through two layers of security including a metal detector, and physical checks to make sure they were carrying no weapons, they arrived in a long, narrow corridor with booths down the left hand side and chairs for those who visited. A thick sheet of plexiglass separated the space. The prisoner side was a mesh cage of sorts, enclosing them fully in the booth. When Robbins was last here, a hand phone was used to communicate, but an intercom system had since been installed. The corridor was dark aside from a singular diffused light emanating from a third of the way down the hall. Robbins led the way, stomach hot and tight with anxiety. He felt like a guitar string over tuned to the point of breaking. Risking a glance at the twins, he wondered if they were feeling the same way. They arrived at the booth and there he was. After so many battles, so many years with their lives entwined together, Alex Robbins was again face to face with James Warwick.

II

Warwick had aged poorly. Wearing regulation white prison overalls, the garment almost swallowed his skinny body. Gone was the thick, black hair that reminded Gloria of Jim Morrison, replaced by a buzz cut. A white, stubble beard speckled his gaunt cheeks, making him appear even older than he was. His eyes alone preserved their youthful intensity; though deeper-set and lined, their penetrating gaze remained unchanged. As the trio sat down, he offered a slight, almost imperceptible smile to Robbins.

Warwick's eyes drifted to Dan and Rebecca, then back to Robbins.

'You're the last person I expected to see come here.' Warwick said, almost amused at the scenario unfolding in front of him.

'Yeah, you and me both.'

'And you didn't come alone.'.

'No, I didn't.'

'Do me a favour, Alex. Please shut up so I can speak to my children.'

'We knew you were going to be informed of who they were. Don't take this as a win.'

'It wouldn't have mattered. I'd have known the second I saw them. The girl looks like her mother. The boy is like my father. Did I ruin the big reveal for you, Alex? Your big speech, the theatrics of it all?'

Robbins grunted, but didn't rise to the bait. He used to match Warwick, blow for blow verbally and mentally, but age and time had dulled his senses and his ability. He screamed at his inner monologue to come back with something – a witty retort, at least, but his brain was filled with static. It was too late anyway. Too many seconds had passed, and the gleam in Warwick's eye said Robbins he had lost this round.

'Why did you bring them here, Alex? I'm surprised Mary

would let them come.'

'Our mother is dead.' Rebecca said.

Voice unwavering, eyes unflinching.

She's her father's daughter alright, Robbins thought, and icy fingers brushed against his forearms.

Warwick's smile faded, and he lowered his eyes, staring at his cuffed hands. 'How did it happen?'

'Car accident,' Dan replied. He was a little less confident than his sister. His foot bouncing, as if he were inflating an invisible car tyre.

'That's a shame. A damn shame.'

Warwick seemed to be moved by the news, but Robbins was unconvinced. He had seen him play this game before.

'We wanted to come and see you, meet you in person. We never knew about you until she had already passed.' Dan went on.

'Fuck. A car wreck is no way to go. Still, Alex, it's better than being shot for defending your home, isn't it?'
Before Robbins could respond, he turned his attention to the twins 'So, what is it you think I can do for you?'

Dan was still fidgeting and unable to hold his father's eye, but was getting to grips with the situation. 'We wanted to know about you. Find out if you're…' He faded off, looking to his sister for help.

'He's trying to say we wanted to see if the stories about you being some kind of devil on earth were true. There's only so much you can learn from books.' No mincing of words. No hesitation. She held his eye, unwilling to be the first to blink.

Warwick broke into laughter, a sound which felt out of place under the circumstances.

'I like you, kid. You don't screw around with all the fluff. Straight to the point. You remind me of myself when I was your age.'

'They're nothing like you,' Robbins snapped, unable to ignore the anger. He couldn't explain it, but Warwick brought out all the worst traits in him.

Warwick grinned, the gesture too big and exaggerated, which Robbins thought was likely for his benefit.

'I don't see how this has anything to do with *you*, Alex. Maybe you should step outside and leave my children and I to get to know each other?'

'Not a chance. If you want to talk, talk. But I stay. I'm not letting you poison them with your shit. This either happens supervised, or not at all.'

'Even after all these years, still so angry. Still so bitter.'

Warwick sucked air through his teeth, eyes burning into Robbins, enjoying watching him squirm. Robbins had forgotten how good Warwick was at this kind of thing. The push and pull between belittling and prodding in all the sensitive areas to get a reaction.

After what felt like an age, Warwick took his all-seeing gaze from Robbins and turned it to his children. The charlatan's smile reappearing for their benefit.

'So, what did you want to know?'

There it was. The ultimate question. No more skirting around answers or debate about if they should or shouldn't be there, just the question of what they wanted to ask him.

Dan and Rebecca glanced at each other, doing that thing, the unspoken bond between siblings which has no explanation.

Dan was the first to speak. He was sitting upright in his chair, palms flat on his knees, cheeks flushed.

'We've heard stories, read the news articles, all that stuff. Since we found out about you, all we've had is people saying we shouldn't come. I didn't want to either, but here we are, and to be honest, I don't know what to say to you.'

Warwick watched Dan, eyes probing, scanning his face, taking in every imperfection, the only sound that of Warwick drumming his fingers on his side of the desk.

'That accent. Where did you grow up?'

'England. We flew over especially to visit you.'

Warwick glanced at Robbins 'Ah, so that's where you hid her. Wise to get her out of the country.'

He turned back to Dan. 'You know, all I ever wanted was a son. I often wondered about Mary's pregnancy and what she was going to have. I never imagined she would have twins. You remind me of her.' Warwick said to Dan, cuffs rattling as he pointed a finger at him. 'You try to be strong, but the uncertainty comes off you in waves. It makes everyone around you nervous.'

'That's enough. I told you, any of this bullshit and I take them out of here.'

Warwick rolled his eyes at Robbins. 'I thought we'd agreed this was none of your business.'

'Don't push it.'

'I thought we were here to have a reunion. Friends and family together.'

'I won't tell you again.'

'Isn't that what we are, Alex? Friends? The prisoner and the man who captured him. Just don't let the truth get in the way.'

Robbins stood, almost knocking his chair over. 'That's it. We're leaving.'

'Did you love her?' Rebecca's question was sudden and killed the argument in its tracks. Warwick looked at his daughter, the joy of tormenting Robbins melting away as the detective pulled his chair back into position and sat.

If he was trying to stare her down, it didn't work. In the end, it was he who broke eye contact. He spread his fingers on the desktop, staring at the space between them.

'Of course I did. She was…special. The relationship we had was special.'

This time, Warwick's smile seemed genuine, a stark contrast to his earlier predatory grin. 'It's incredible how much you look like her. The same fire, the same determination. I think your mother and I did well.'

Rebecca was stony faced and refusing to show emotion. 'You loved her?'

'Of course I did.'

Robbins was sure this was Warwick doing what he did best. Manipulation. Coercion. But it wasn't his place to say anything. He wanted a drink. The weight of the sobriety coin in his breast pocket was almost too much to bear.

'If you loved her so much, why aren't you more upset?' Dan said. Maybe, like Robbins, he could see this was a ruse. Agitated as he was, he met Warwick's gaze, his face reddening as he leaned closer to the glass.

'People grieve in different ways, kid,' Warwick replied.

'My name is Dan.'

'Dan, huh? She always said she liked Evan for a name. Must have changed her mind.'

Warwick turned to Robbins; the slick cat smile reserved just for him making a reappearance. 'Did you grieve, Alex, when you shot that boy at the house?'

Although he was screaming inside, the old muscle memory was returning, and he even forced a thin, puppeteer smile of his own back at Warwick.

'Don't even bother with that shit. That kid had a weapon. He had the option to drop it and didn't.'

'And yet, I'd bet anything it still haunts you. Not all the time. But I almost guarantee, sometimes you see his face. Maybe in the shower, or as a flash at night when you're straddling that line between being asleep or awake.'

'Fuck you. I thought you might have grown out of this kind of bullshit by now.'

Warwick wasn't listening. He had grown bored with Robbins and turned his attention back to his children.

'Did he tell you everything, I wonder?'

'He did,' Dan said. 'He left nothing out.'

'Of his version.'

'What does that mean?' Rebecca asked. It was the first time she had looked uncertain. She glanced over to Robbins, and although he could feel her eyes on him, he wouldn't look. He started straight ahead, his full focus on Warwick.

'His truth differs from mine. *Der sieger wird immer der richter und der besiegte stets der angeklagte sein,*'

Warwick looked to be about to translate, but Rebecca cut him off. '*The victor will always be the judge, and the vanquished the accused*. That was a quote from Goring at the Nuremburg trials, right?'

Everyone was looking at her. She blushed and averted her gaze to her shoes. 'I read a lot of stuff.' She muttered.

Warwick leaned back in his seat as far as his restraints would allow. 'Brilliant. And true. What happened to me has been told to you, but that's not to say it was true.'

'I won't tell you again about this, Warwick. They didn't come here for one of your damn sermons or to hear your version of retelling history.'

'Isn't it? I thought this was exactly why they were here.' He returned the volley, but now Robbins could fire back, the rivals rolling back the years as they sparred.

'Not for this. Not to hear your propaganda and twisting of the facts. I'm not about to sit here and let you manipulate them. This isn't about the past. This is about now.'

Warwick leaned close to the glass, eyes burning into Robbins. 'You can't have one without the other, Alex. How can I hope to build a relationship with my children if they don't know the truth of what went before?'

'They know the truth.'

'No, they don't.'

It was the first sign of him losing control and gave a glimpse of the monster hiding beneath Warwick's skin.

'You're wasting your time trying to manipulate them or push your agenda, because I'll be here to stop you.' Robbins could feel the blood pulsing in his temples as he pointed at Warwick behind the glass. 'Why don't you accept it? One of these days, those appeals will run out. There's no point in trying to delay the inevitable.'

'I know one day I'll be out of options. But let me tell you something, old friend. The reason I continue to appeal is you.'

'What the hell are you talking about?'

'I may die here in my shitty little cell, but death doesn't scare me.'

'Then why not get it over with? End the delays and do us all a favour.'

Warwick smiled, and when he spoke, it was so quiet it was difficult to make out via the intercom system.

'The reason I keep appealing is simple. I have made it my goal to outlive you, Alex.'

Robbins stood. 'Fuck this, come on you two, we're leaving.'

'You're old, Alex. Tired. Overweight. A whisper away from a stroke or a heart attack. That would be the ultimate win for me. To know you'd gone before you got to see me die. That's why I fight.'

Robbins stepped away from the desk, hating he was so rattled. 'I've heard enough of this. Come on, we're leaving.'

Dan and Rebecca stood, but neither of them could take their eyes from Warwick.

'You tried to kill me, Alex. I was unarmed. I'd surrendered and what did you do? You fired anyway.' Warwick looked at Dan and Rebecca, who had backed away from the booth to the wall. 'I bet he didn't tell you about that one, did he?'

Warwick pulled open his prison issue jumpsuit and lifted his T-shirt, showing the ugly scar on his chest where Robbins had shot him.

'I wear the truth of your lie on my body, Alex. If that bullet hadn't hit my bible, I'd have been dead.'

Robbins ushered Dan and Rebecca down the hall, away from Warwick, but they could still hear him shouting after them.

'Tell them the truth, Alex. You and I, we're the same monster. You belong with me on this side of the glass. Make sure you tell them. Make sure my children know the truth.'

The steel door slammed shut behind them as they left the visiting room, cutting off Warwick's ranting. They stood on the other side of the door, all of them shaken. Dan and Rebecca were pale. A tremor ran through Robbins, his breath catching in his throat, his vision blurring.

Don't you fucking dare. Not here. Not after what he said. Breathe, just breathe, damn you.

'Are you okay, Detective Robbins?' Dan said. Robbins said he was fine, even if he knew they could see it was a lie.

He used the counting technique he employed to avoid relapse. He started at twenty, and by the time he had got down to eleven, that grip on his chest loosened a little, and he could breathe again.

'I think we should get a doctor,' Rebecca said.

Robbins waved a hand at her. 'No, don't, I'm fine. I need to catch my breath, that's all.'

He thought of Warwick laughing at this unfolding a few feet away, down the hall.

He continued to count. When he got to six, he was back under control.

'Are you sure you're okay?' Dan asked.

'I'm fine, just give me a second. I need some air. It's too damn hot in here. I'll be better when I get outside.'

As much as it was true, Robbins wanted to get outside and get some air. There was one thing even over all that he desired even more. He wanted a drink.

THE WAGON

Dusk was creeping closer as Robbins drove them back to their hotel. He had recovered enough to convince himself it was anxiety, not his heart, that was to blame for what happened at the prison. He wasn't sure the twins believed it, and he was okay with that, because if he was honest, he wasn't sure he believed it either. Robbins glanced at the twins in the rear-view mirror, unsure if he should say anything and, if so, what the hell it should be. He had spent so long alone that his social skills had all but gone. Sandy always used say he was too stubborn for his own good, and he knew if she were with him now, she would tell him to stop being so selfish and start with an apology for taking over the meeting with Warwick for the sake of point scoring.

The car in front inched forward, then with a red flash of brake lights, put an end to the shortest of journeys. Robbins pulled up behind it.

'Look, I'm sorry about what happened. I know it was supposed to be your time but....'

'It's okay,' Dan said. He was staring out of the window. 'Based on everything you said about him, I get it. No apology needed.'

'I'm sorry too,' Rebecca said. She met his gaze in the mirror, but like her father, she was difficult to read with any accuracy. 'You tried to tell me what he was like. In a way, I knew it too, but I thought he would be different.'

She turned to her brother. 'I'm sorry to you too, Dan. God, we've fought about this, right from the start. Bickered and argued and I've got my way every time. I was wrong. We shouldn't have come here.'

'You are stubborn,' Dan said, giving a half smile which was eerily close to the one Warwick gave when they had first arrived at the prison. 'But none of us knew for sure how it would be. Don't worry about it, Becks.'

'In my head, I had this idea he might be reformed, or that with nothing else to lose, knowing about us might mean something to him. I see now I was wrong.'

'Does this mean we can go home?' Dan asked.

'I suppose it does.'

Robbins was relieved 'I think that's the right decision.'

'Is it true what he said? Did you try to kill him, even though he was unarmed?'

Dan's question was one he didn't want to answer, but there was no sense in holding back now.

'In a situation like that, in a hostile environment, knowing everyone inside is out to kill you, a hesitation could cost your life. The kid with the gun, I tried to warn him, but he was so brainwashed, so damn devoted to Warwick that he would never comply. I had no choice. When I saw Warwick, I thought I saw him reaching for a weapon, so I fired.'

'That's not how he said it happened. He said he had surrendered.' Rebecca said.

'He's a liar.'

'And did he have a weapon?' Dan asked.

Here it was. The key part of the scenario.

'No.'

The car went quiet. The question they wanted to ask just as

much as he didn't want to answer was coming.

'Was it intentional?' Dan asked.

'I've thought about it a lot. I've always tried to do the right thing. Part of me thinks I should have reacted differently. Another side says there's no harm done. If I made a mistake and reacted without thinking, him surviving because of the bullet deflecting off his bible may have been a second chance for both of us on that day. Don't make the mistake of thinking I don't care. Trust me, that moment is as fresh in my mind today as it was when it happened. I don't suppose that will ever change. Christ, why should it? It's a burden I deserve to carry with me.'

Neither of them asked any more questions. It seemed after everything, there wasn't much more to say.

'Look, today has been tough for all of us. Tomorrow, I'll take you both out for dinner. No more history lessons, no more depressing stories about James Warwick.'

'It's a kind of relief now it's over and we've seen for ourselves what kind of man he is.'

Robbins was surprised to hear this from Rebecca. She had built up such high expectations before meeting Warwick, and it was sad to see her deflated from it.

'Yeah, sometimes you have to see for yourself. Today reminded me of something, too. I've been carrying this case, carrying *him* with me all these years even though I didn't realise until the bastard proved it to me today. Warwick has already taken so much from me. I don't need him hanging around whatever years I have left. I guess what I'm trying to say is, this week has been a kind of closure for me.'

He stopped speaking for a moment as the traffic threatened to move more than a few inches, but the joy was short-lived and they were soon still again.

'I still have all my old case files. If you want them, they're yours. It might help fill in the blanks in a bit more detail when you get home rather than me rambling on at you. Plus, if they're in another country, I can't come knocking on your door and ask for them back.'

'We'll take them. Thank you,' Rebecca said. She hesitated, then continued on. 'Also, I know we've not said it, but I wanted to thank you for everything you've done for us. All the help you've given us, all the questions you've answered when I know it must have been hard… well, I wanted you to know we can't thank you enough.'

Robbins had spent so long by himself he had forgotten how to take someone showing him kindness. He was lucky the glow of the brake lights of the car in front masked the flush of colour which came to his cheeks.

'Like I said at the start, I was never in this for thanks. All the same, I appreciate you saying so. Your mother did a fine job of raising the both of you.'

They moved forward a little, then came to a stop again.

'Anyway,' Robbins added. 'Enough of this bleak talk. How about some music?' he flicked on the radio, the sound of his favourite vintage golden oldie station filling the car.

'What's this?' Dan asked, glancing at his sister.

'This? This is actual music,' Robbins said. 'The Rolling Stones. Surely, you've heard of them?'

'It's not my thing,' Dan said.

Rebecca smiled, embarrassing her sibling. 'Dan likes all that hard core dance stuff. He won't know who the Stones are.'

'And you do?' he fired back.

'I've heard of them.' She said, with zero confidence.

'I'll give you all the money in my wallet if you can name one song of theirs. The detective will tell you if you're right.'

Robbins half turned in his seat, curious if she would pull it off.

'Uh, I don't know… My Generation?' she gave Robbins a hopeful look.

'Not even close. That was The Who. Another amazing band, by the way, but not the Stones.'

'Yes! It looks like my cash is safe.'

'Knowing you, I'm not missing out on much.'

'I'm a good saver.' Dan chimed back.

'But a better spender.' They said in unison.

The car behind them jabbed its horn, forcing Robbins to turn his attention back to the road and the traffic, which had moved another few inches. He did his part, pulling the micro gap in the snake closed. As Dan and Rebecca bickered in the back, Robbins realised he would miss them when they left.

II

It was late when Robbins dropped them off at the hotel, and he didn't want to go home. He had enjoyed been around them, especially the journey back from the prison. It was as if they had been under a blanket created by Warwick since they had met, and now they had all pulled free of it and could talk about other things. *Nice* things.

The downside to this, he discovered now, when it was him on

his own, those not so nice thoughts were free to crawl back into his brain. The idea of going back to the house, a dark, lonely place surrounded by evidence of his failure as a husband and father, was something he couldn't face, and so he had found himself again at his once favourite bar.

There were more cars than last time, but the inner turmoil was still the same. He knew what he should do – drive away, go call his sponsor or go to a meeting, but that was easier said than done.

The first thing they used to tell him in meetings was the danger of saying one drink couldn't hurt, because for someone like him, it would.

Just one. You deserve that.

There it was. That demon in his head.

It would be so easy. There would be nobody waiting at home to chastise him or question him. No arguments if he fell through the door at three in the morning, stumbling all over the house. No guilt trips about scaring the kids. He was a single man who could do whatever the hell he wanted. Those ships where he had a responsibility towards other people, had sailed long ago, and he knew if he gave in, he would get away with it.

Then do it. Like you said, you're alone. What the hell do you have to stay sober for, anyway?

He hated when his inner voice was like this, and everything it said seemed to make perfect sense. What *did* he have to stay sober for? He'd done it for so long that it was a part of his routine. There was no joy in it, no sense of accomplishment. Along with the smoking and fatty foods, it was just another pleasure he wasn't supposed to have. All he had was the damn sobriety coin.

Exactly. No wife, she's on her cruise with the guy she replaced you with. I bet she's having a drink. She never could around you, of course. She always drank water to show support. What are the odds she's downing Martini like it's going out of fashion and not giving you a single thought?

Robbins squeezed his eyes closed, knowing this was the closest to the edge he had ever been, the closest to giving up.

And before you say it, your daughter won't care. You haven't spoken to her in how long? Hell, you haven't even seen your grandchild. To her, you're already a failure. You think that coin makes a spit of difference to her? She made her mind up long ago what you were, and she's right. Just because you're not drinking right now, you're still an alcoholic and always will be. It's just a case of how long it takes for you to realise it.

He squeezed the coin, willing the voice to retreat and leave him alone.

Just one.

Just one.

Just one.

It was drumming in his mind like a mantra, a primal chant he was finding difficult to ignore. The pain in his hand was subsiding, morphing into a dull burn as he squeezed the coin even harder.

Come on. Let's stop fucking around. We both know you're going to give in. You wouldn't have come otherwise. You know how they treat people like you. Some say it's sick. Others say it should shame you into resisting. It won't, though, will it? Not for you, you weak old fuck.

This bar saw many people like him go through the doors.

People who were close to falling off the wagon. He remembered on the bar there used to be a wicker bowl with a sign beside it offering a free drink for a sobriety coin. A sick marketing ploy, but one that worked, as that basket always had something in it, a handful of coins. Some celebrating six months, a few showing one year. All kinds of indicators that someone who came before had failed and fallen off the horse.

The owner of the bar, a pot-bellied misery of a man called Mike, insisted he designed it as a deterrent, and that those committed to staying off the booze shouldn't go to his bar. Robbins had himself traded in his first two coins for one of those free drinks, both one-year anniversary coins. Shortly after that, Sandy had left him, unable to cope with his slow self-destruction. That's what it took for him to get his shit together and commit to getting sober.

Ten years. A lot to of time to throw away for one drink which would lead to another.

His inner voice said nothing. He could feel its smug assurance as Robbins got out of the car and headed inside.

III

It was like stepping back in time. Everything was how he remembered it, the bar dark and grimy, designed for serious drinking rather than visual appeal. The smell of stale barley and hops repulsive and familiar, like an embrace from a long-lost family member. A football game was playing on the big screen TV at the rear of the room, half a dozen figures hunched around the tables in front of it. Robbins couldn't tell if they were watching the game or staring into their glasses, looking for answers they would never find. The booths down the left side of the bar were pretty full. Most people drinking alone or in small groups. The bar extended two-thirds down the right-hand side of the room; a dazzling array of upturned bottles doubled in the mirrors which covered the rear wall of the bar area. Three of the seven stools were in use by what Robbins always thought of as the serious drinkers – the kind who didn't hide why they were there. It wasn't for socialising or unwinding after a long day; it was for the business of getting shit faced. Robbins walked towards the Bar and sat on a vacant stool. Although the décor hadn't changed, Mike had. His stomach had grown even larger and his T-shirt looked to be at least a size too small for his frame. His hair had also receded, but it seemed Mike was reluctant to accept it, and so had tried as best he could to style what remained. Robbins waited, hoping his heart rate would slow a little. He couldn't decide if it was nerves or excitement and decided it was likely somewhere in between the two.

'How many years?' Mike asked.

'Ten.'

'That's a long time. Why now? What changed?'

Fuck this guy. Tell the old fuck to mind his business and get us a drink.

Robbins said nothing. Mike shrugged.

'Yeah, I figured. Most who come back here don't know why, or if they do, they prefer not to say.'

He turned away, and Robbins knew what was coming. The bowl was no longer wicker; he suspected it had perished long ago. This one was blue plastic with a snap-on lid with a closable vent hole. Robbins had one similar at home used to heat soup in the microwave.

Mike removed the lid and put the bowl on the bar. Inside were a half dozen symbols of discarded willpower from those who had already broken.

'You know the drill. Ten years will be the second highest value I have. There's a twelve somewhere in there, I think.'

Robbins looked in the bowl. 'Can't I just buy a drink?'

Mike shook his head. 'You know that's not how it works here. Not for the likes of you.'

Fuck him. Fuck this place. Let's go buy a bottle of something and drink it at home. You can even keep the coin and pretend this never happened.

Robbins considered it, and had done that the first time he had fallen off the wagon, but the shame of his lie was worse than he expected and he had promised he would never do it again.

Fine, then give him the damn coin and let's get this over with.

Robbins took the coin from his wallet and set it on the table by the bowl.

Mike folded his arms.

'It's right there,' Robbins said.

'You know the rules. Put it in the bowl yourself if you want to do this. I ain't doing it for you.'

Robbins stared at the coin sitting on the pitted bar. It somehow looked more brilliant under the overhead light.

'Ten years is a hell of a long time.' Mike said.

'Yeah, it is.'

'Let me tell you something, then I'll shut up and leave you to whatever you choose to do.' Mike moved the coins around in the bowl, picking two out. He showed the first one to Robbins.

'This guy was six years sober. Came in here and exchanged his coin. Spent the next three weeks drinking himself shitfaced. Last Christmas he realised it hadn't changed things how he thought it would. He couldn't face the shame of telling his family he'd fucked up, and the idea of starting again was too much to handle. In the end, he put a bullet in his brain.'

Robbins said nothing as Mike tossed the coin back into the bowl. He held up the next one.

'This guy was nine years. Came in here and didn't go through with it three or four times. Sat right here, just like you, coin on the bar, bowl next to him. I told him what I'm telling you now, giving some examples of those who came before him.'

'Let me guess? He blew his brains out too?'

Mike smiled, but it was thin and humourless. 'Not quite. He's sitting over there.'

Mike nodded to one booth in the corner where a man in his forties sat, a half dozen empty chaser glasses around his three quarters finished beer. He was staring into that space between something and nothing, beard flecked with stubble, eyes haunted with regret.

Robbins turned back to the bar and looked at his coin, then at Mike. He picked up the coin and tossed it into the bowl.

'Scotch. No ice.'

Mike rolled his eyes. This scene was one he had seen play out a thousand times. 'Whatever you say.' As Robbins waited for his drink, he listened for his inner voice, but it remained silent, its job done.

THE MORNING AFTER

Light.

As the sun shifted across his face, Robbins grunted, his sleep disturbed. He lay sprawled on the sofa where he had been since the night before. As consciousness swam back through the murky soup of post sleep, there was a sound, familiar but one he wasn't awake enough yet to process. He opened his eyes, realised it was too bright, and turned onto his side, away from the gaze of the sun. It was then that he understood what the strange sound was.

His phone.

He could see it on the coffee table, inching across the surface with each vibration. He fumbled for it, almost dropped it, hit the answer key and put it to his ear.

'Yeah,' he mumbled, aware of the stiffness in his neck. He listened to the voice on the other side of the phone, now wide awake and alert.

'I'm on my way.'

He hung up. A quick change and a squirt of deodorant and he was out of the door.

II

How he made it to the prison without picking up a speeding ticket was a minor miracle, and as a result, Robbins had made great time. He had spoken with the warden and was now almost at the visitation block, adrenaline making him feel more alive than he had in years. It was easier coming here on his own. Without having the twins to account for, Warwick would have less reason to play games.

Revisiting his route from the day before, he made his way to booth seven, where Warwick was waiting.

Robbins remained silent as he sat. If Warwick was surprised by the visit, he hid it well.

'Missing me already, Alex?'

Usually, a simple line like that would have been enough to trigger him, but not today. Not now. Robbins smiled and was pleased to see a flicker of uncertainty in Warwick.

'You bet. I couldn't get here fast enough today.'

Warwick folded his hands and waited. Robbins let him. Both of them held their silence until Robbins reached into his jacket and pulled out a folded brown envelope, and set it in front of him.

'I had a call from the Warden this morning. He gave me some information and I couldn't wait to come here and talk to you about in person.'

Warwick was trying to look disinterested, but couldn't hide his curiosity.

'When I was last here, you talked about how you were hanging on so you could outlive me. It's fair, I'm not getting any younger, and I don't look after myself as much as I should. I've been thinking about that a lot since. Thinking about *you* way more than I should have.'

Robbins took the documents out of the envelope and pressed them to the glass so Warwick could read them.

'It's over. No more appeals. No more delays. You've got your execution date. Two weeks from now, you're going to die.'

Warwick's eyes scanned the documentation, Robbins enjoying every second as the penny dropped.

'Two weeks. I think I can last that long at least. I'm a stubborn old bastard and I wouldn't want to miss your big day. In fact, I'm going to take extra care of myself because there's nothing on this earth that would stop me from being there when it happens.'

Robbins waited for the outburst of anger, but Warwick didn't react.

'I suppose this means you win, Alex. I'd tell you to enjoy it, but I can see you're already there. It's cruel, though.'

'You say cruel. I say long overdue.'

'You bring my children here to meet me for the first time. Now you have to tell them the father they just met is also about to die. And you're happy about this?'

'They already know. I called them on their way here to give them the news, and they don't care. They've seen enough of you to know you're a monster. They'll be back home and getting on with their lives when it happens.'

'I want to see them.'

'Were you even listening? They don't want to see you. It's over. In a few weeks, you'll be nothing to anyone. A footnote in history. Nobody will miss you, nobody will mourn you. The only person who will be there to see you die is me, and I'll be smiling when it happens.'

'You'll get to see the job through. If that's justice to you, it's warped. Maybe they should build a chair for two and we can fry together. Now *that* would be the right way to do this and you know it.'

Robbins knew what Warwick was trying to do, but nothing was going to deny him this moment. He leaned close to the glass and gave a very deliberate smile.

'Maybe I intended to kill you that day, surrender or not. God knows, you deserved it. Killing babies, raping underage girls who you brainwashed into thinking it was the right thing to do. The world will be better without you.'

'Do you remember what you said to me after you shot me, Alex? When you crouched beside me?'

'No.'

'I remember every word; My chest on fire, the copper taste of blood in my mouth. Most of all, I remember you. The look of triumph at what you had done. No remorse. No sorrow. You said if God wanted me alive, he'd have saved me.'

'That sounds about right. What's your point?'

'Don't you see? God *did* save me. Your bullet deflected by a bible. If that's not divine influence, what is?'

'It was luck. A one in a million chance. Nothing divine about it. Do you know how Dan and Rebecca reacted when I told them your date had come through? They fly home tomorrow, but I told them if they wanted to stay and squeeze in another visit to learn more about you, I would make the arrangements.'

Robbins was enjoying this, and Warwick was barely keeping up his neutral demeanour.

'They refused. Said they'd seen enough. You have nothing left, Warwick. They will head back to their lives. Your execution might be a couple of weeks away, but to them, you're already dead.'

Warwick's cheek was twitching, his eyes burning with rage, yet when he spoke, he was calm. 'I have faith in God. He saved me once. I believe he will save me again.'

'There is no God, Warwick. Not for the likes of you. God doesn't deal with monsters who murder the innocent.'

'Then I suppose I'll see you in hell.'

That one hurt, and Robbins flinched. Warwick pounced on it, leaning close to the glass, their faces inches apart.

'That boy at the house. Those women and children upstairs. All blood on your hands, Alex. You've tried to wash it away, but they're still stained. Call me a monster, but you're no different. We're the same. You just won't admit it.'

'We're not the same, because for me, life goes on. The world will tick on without you as if you never even existed.'

'We'll see. God works in mysterious ways.'

'I'll take my chances that he thinks like the rest of us, and understands that you're an evil, twisted son of a bitch who deserves to die.'

'You know this isn't over. I've got a legacy. I'll live forever.'

Robbins smiled and put the execution order back into its envelope. 'But you won't. Maybe you'll only realise it at the end when it's already too late.'

Robbins stood, the high of the adrenaline racing through his body better than the rush of any drug.

'Don't go yet, I'm not done. I still have things to say to you.' Warwick was getting frustrated, which made Robbins enjoy it even more.

'There's nothing you could say that I'd want to hear. Enjoy the time you've got left. I'll see you in a couple of weeks.'

Robbins walked away, the sounds of Warwick screaming for him to come back more satisfying than he could have imagined.

FAMILY MATTERS

Robbins couldn't remember the last time he felt so alive. He felt as if the last few years of carrying that man's weight on his back had been hacked away like the vile, cancerous growth it was, freeing him from the burden. With the James Warwick situation soon to be resolved, there was one more thing to rectify, but before that, he wanted to check in on the twins. He had forgotten how it was to have people around him, younger people especially. The last few days had made him look at his own life and set him to thinking about putting it right, which had led him to the quiet suburban street where he now sat parked across the street from his daughter's house. He took his phone out of his pocket and dialled Dan's number.

'Hey, Detective Robbins. What's up?'

'Nothing. I wanted to see how you were both getting on after the news this morning.'

'We're okay. It's another thing to add to what has been a strange few days.'

'Yeah, you're not wrong there.'

'Are you coming by this morning?'

'I can't. I've got something I have to do. But I promised you dinner, so will swing by later. Good enough?'

'Yeah, of course. Is everything alright?'

Robbins stared over at the house, wondering if he had made a mistake in going there. 'Yeah, everything's fine. Truth is, these last few days have made me think. You know I haven't seen my daughter in a long time. I think it's time to change that.'

'You're going to see her?'

'I'm parked outside her house now, but don't have any damn idea what to say.'

'Uh, hold on a second.' Robbins waited as the phone clicked and popped in his ear. He could hear Dan's muffled voice as he spoke away from the handset, then he was back. 'Becks wants to talk to you.'

'Hi, Detective Robbins.'

'Will you two ever call me Alex?'

'Sorry, we've got so used to saying it the other way.'

'I've been called worse. Are you packing?'

'We don't have much to pack, so we're going to do it tomorrow.'

'What time's your flight?'

'Five. Dan said you were visiting your daughter?'

'Yeah, I just wish I knew what to say.'

'Knock on the door. I think she'll be so pleased to see you. The words won't matter.'

'Yeah, maybe.'

'What's the worst that can happen? It sounds like you want to build bridges, so just do it. If we can face what we did yesterday, you can do this.'

'Yeah, you're right.'

He was going to leave it there, but felt there was more he needed to say.

'You know, you two are good kids, and I'm going to give you some advice. Let's call it the wise words of an old man.'

'Okay.'

'When you fly out of here tomorrow, try to put all this out of your minds. This place, Warwick, all of it. Believe me, I carried him around with me for years and it's taken until now to shake him free. I'd hate to see another two lives ruined because of him.'

'We will, don't worry. I think we had to come here and know for ourselves first hand, but now we both agreed we can move on and focus on what comes next. We have you to thank for that.'

'You don't owe me anything. This has helped me as much as it has you. Weird how things work out sometimes.'

'It is. Now stop stalling. Go speak to your daughter.'

'I will. You got a ride to the airport tomorrow?'

'We were going to get a taxi.'

'I'll drive you. I'll drop by in the afternoon.'

'That would be amazing, thank you. Dan and I are both rooting for you. Good luck.'

'Thanks. I'll need it.' he hung up the phone, got out of the car and crossed the street.

II

The area was similar in style to where Gloria lived. It had the same sort of family friendly feel, although Jill's house was a little rougher around the edges. The paint on the walls was grimy and ever so slightly worn, the grass in the garden a little too long and in need of a trim. He had gone into detective mode, the job he had done for so long taking over his motor functions, allowing him to build a picture of the person who lived there.

He opened the gate, which was missing one hinge, the wood scraping on the paved path. A scattering of toys were abandoned in the garden, becoming lost as the grass grew around them. He walked to the door, aware he couldn't put it off any longer, and pressed the bell.

You should have had a drink before you came. We both know you'll need one after this is done.

He shut down his inner voice, hating it for choosing now to break its silence. Someone was coming. He could the see the shape of them through the frosted glass window on the door. It was too late now to back out. The door opened and all thoughts of what to say went out of his mind.

He didn't recognise the man. He was holding a toddler in one arm, the boy's face covered in spaghetti sauce. The man was slim, dark eyes suspicious as he looked Robbins up and down.

'Can I help you?' the man said as the child gargled and fingered the collar of his shirt, smearing it in spaghetti sauce.

Robbins' mind was blank. He had expected his daughter, not some stranger he had never met. He willed the gears in his brain to send commands to his mouth so he didn't carry on standing mouth open but mute.

'I was looking for Jill.'

'She's not here. Can I help you with anything?'

'Who are you?' Robbins asked.

'I'm her boyfriend. Do you know her?'

Robbins looked at the child again and realised this was his grandson, the one he had never met. He realised how odd it must look; him staring at a child who, in the eyes of the homeowner, was a stranger, so he turned his attention back to the man.

'She's my daughter.'

The man bundled the child to the other arm. 'Jill said her father died before we met.'

'I can't say I'm surprised she said that.'

The man looked uncomfortable, again shifting stance as the child wriggled in his grasp. 'Look, I think this is something I shouldn't be involved with. Do you want to come in? She's gone to grab some groceries, but she's due back. I can call her and see how long.'

'No, it's fine. I think I made a mistake by coming here.'

'Please, just let me call her. Come on in. I'm Joe, by the way.'

Robbins still didn't move. This wasn't going how he had intended, and the longer it dragged on, the more he was regretting going.

'No, it's fine. I'll be on my way.'

Robbins turned to leave, and there she was, his daughter, shopping bag in each hand, staring at him as he looked right back.

III

It had been eleven years since he had last seen Jill. Even though she was approaching thirty, he still thought of her as his little girl. Even as a child, she had never been what he would have called a girl's girl. She had never been into makeup or playing with dolls. She was more into sports and crafts. This, he noticed, had carried on into adulthood. She wore little makeup, her brown hair pulled back into a rough bun at the back of her head. She wore an oversized hoodie, which Robbins would bet belonged to Joe.

He sat at one side of the kitchen table, her on the other, a sea of toys surrounding them. To call the welcome frosty would have been understating it. He reminded himself she was within her rights to be pissed at him, and this was one thing he would need to take on the chin if he had any hope of rebuilding bridges.

They were silent as Joe made them coffee. He brought it to the table and set the steaming cups in front of them. 'Okay, I'm going to leave you to it and take the little man out for an hour.'

He leaned in and kissed Jill on the cheek, then retreated out of the kitchen. They remained silent until the front door closed and it was just the two of them.

'So, what do you want?' she asked.

'I thought it was time to see if we could get past this.'

There was so much he wanted to say, but organising his thoughts into any sort of coherent order was proving impossible. He stared into the depths of his coffee cup, as if the answers may be swirling around somewhere to prompt him.

'It's been eleven years since we last saw each other. I've been married and divorced during that time, but I suppose now you've decided I'm worth the effort. It's alright.'

'I was struggling and the longer we didn't speak, it got harder and harder to reconnect.'

'Don't do that.'

'What?'

'If you're going to come here, at least be honest, otherwise what's the point? You were a monster. Drunk all the time, abusive to us.'

'I never laid a finger on either of you.'

'Words were enough. Throwing your food across the room because it didn't taste good, even though it was your fault it had to be reheated because you'd come home six hours late reeking of booze. Is it any wonder I moved out as soon as I could?'

She was tearing open old wounds, but he had no intention of stopping her. If it was to be his penance, then so be it.

'All I can say is I'm sorry. That's not who I am anymore. Not who I've been for years now.'

She pulled her hoodie sleeve down over her hand and dabbed the tears from her eyes. 'It wasn't even just the booze. It was your work. Do you even know how many plans you broke? How many of my birthdays you missed?'

'I was trying to give you a good life.'

'You think we cared about how much money we had? You think either of us wouldn't have traded the new carpets or stereo system to have you at home? Do you know how it felt to grow up thinking you cared more about a dead stranger or some fucking rapist or murderer than you did about us?'

'That's not how it was. I thought I was doing the right thing.'

'We tried to tell you, both of us, time after time, but you wouldn't hear it. Your priorities were work and drinking. Nothing else came into the equation.'

She let out a sigh as she slumped in her seat.

'I know what I was and you're right in everything you've said. Things are different now. I'll be sixty-four next month and I don't want the years I have left to be empty.'

'What do you want? Sympathy? Forgiveness? Because I don't have either of those to give you.'

'I've had some demons, and I've carried them with me for more years than I should have, but that's not who I am anymore. Please, tell me what I need to do and I'll do it.'

'You know I used to write letters to you when I was a kid

asking you to stop drinking and to be kind to us? I used to wish they would come true, only to hear you stumble into the house at God knows what time. Jesus, you could have killed us. Pan of bacon in flames, smoke alarm going wild and you didn't even stir because you'd passed out on the floor. Every time something like that happened, I would tear up those letters I'd written you and throw them away because I knew they would never come true.'

The depth of their hurt dawned on him. It was no wonder she was telling people he was dead. That was the minimum he deserved. He'd been clinging to the hope of reconciliation, even a tiny chance, but now realised it was hopeless.

Jill took a sip of her drink, calmer now she had got things out in the open. 'I know you've quit the drink. Mum said you've been sober for years now, and that's good for you. But she also said you still obsess over old cases.'

'Until recently, that was true, but I can let all that stuff go. That's why I'm here.'

'I won't expose my son to the same life I had growing up.'

'Jesus, you make it sound like I'm some kind of animal. I was a poor father, but that I'm here now and want to fix what I've broken.'

'It's too late.' She said, walking to the sink and pouring her unfinished drink away. She stood there, back to him, looking out of the window. He could hear her crying. Robbins picked up one of the soft toys from the table, a blue elephant with oversized ears. He turned the toy over in his hand. Jill turned to face him, for now composed. 'Put that down, please.'

Robbins nodded and put the toy back where he found it. 'How old is he now?'

'Four.'

'He's a good-looking kid. Looks a little like you when you were that age.'

'We're not doing this.' She gathered the toys from the table and deposited them into a white painted wooden box with the rest of their kin.

'I don't understand.'

'I won't let you worm your way back into my life, and certainly not Joey's. I won't do it.'

'Jill, please…'

'No. It's not fair of you to come here like this without warning. Damn you, why did you have to come here?' she was close to losing it, her eyes pools of hatred.

'I didn't come to upset you.'

'But you have. *Again*. Even after all these years.'

'Jill…'

'Get out. I don't want you here. You're not welcome.'

He stood as she waited by the door, wringing her hands.

'Jill, please,'

'Just go.' Robbins knew that was it. There would be no reconciliation. He had his own scars left by Warwick over the years, so he knew the hurt they caused. They were nothing compared to the ones he had left in his daughter's psyche, though, and for that, he could never forgive himself. He went down the hall and opened the door, letting the light of the day spill into the house. Looking back, he saw Jill by the kitchen door, crying. She wouldn't look at him, and he could think of nothing to say even if she did, so he left. Walking back to the car, he had never wanted a drink more in his life.

I know a place. Just get in the car.

He wasn't surprised to hear the voice pipe up now. It always did when things had gone to shit.

CHECKMATE

Robbins woke early. He had replayed his disastrous meeting with Jill countless times, imagining alternative scenarios and what he could have done differently. It was self-torture, but so what? He deserved to feel as shitty as he did. In the end, tired of shifting position and further tangling up his sheets, he got up when the surrounding houses were still dark tombs as their inhabitants slept on. He must have fallen asleep in the chair after, because he woke with a start to his angry buzzing phone and daylight streaming through the window. He squinted at the screen, trying to focus his blurry eyes on the unknown number; there was no caller ID. He answered, grunting a barely formed greeting into the handset. He sat up, perched on the edge of his seat as the voice on the other end of the line relayed information. By the time the call had ended, Robbins was already in the car, throwing it into reverse and out into the early morning street, tyres protesting at this unusual punishment.

II

As he arrived at the motel, the sun was high in the sky, a beautiful pastel blue, a stark contrast to the churning black fear in his stomach. The Police had already taped the area off, and two uniformed officers kept onlookers at a safe distance. He got out of the car, wondering how to talk his way in when he saw the man who had called him – A detective called Jonas Bloom – one guy from his generation who was still active, for a few more years at least. Robbins whistled, getting Bloom's attention, who waved for one of the uniformed officers to let him beyond the tape. Robbins approached his former colleague, the two of them shaking hands.

'Thanks for coming, Alex,' Jonas said, his voice hoarse and cracked. He expected the next question and answered before it could be asked. 'Tonsillitis. Fucking thing is stopping me from sleeping.'

He was spared further small talk as an officer led Dan out of the motel room, his eyes darting as he spoke, the words all ramming together to the point of becoming incoherent.

'I only went to grab us coffee. I was only gone half an hour…'

Robbins had seen this before. Disbelief. Shock. Fear. Each was bad enough on its own. Combined like this, it was dangerous.

'Take a deep breath and slow down. Tell me what happened,' Robbins said.

'We were up early to pack, and Becks asked if I would do a coffee run. I was only gone half an hour at most. When I came back, the door was open, and she was gone. She's gone missing, Detective Robbins.'

Robbins felt his stomach plunge towards his feet, and that horrible clamping sensation around his chest again. He had learned not to believe in coincidence, and as much as he promised to be free of that man, only one name came to mind who was responsible. He did not know how, but he just knew.

Robbins turned his attention to the officer beside Dan.

'He's in shock. Get him something sweet to drink. Any medical crews on scene?'

'Inbound,' the officer replied.

'Good. Make sure he gets some attention.'

This wasn't Robbin's scene. He hadn't done the Cop thing for a long time and yet, it had come back as if he had never been away. Robbins tuned to Jonas, who was looking on. He popped a throat lozenge into his mouth, sucking it loudly as he regarded the former detective.

'Seems you still have the knack, Alex.'

'What the hell happened here?'

'Like the kid said. He went out this morning to get coffee for him and his sister. When he came back, the door was open, and the room trashed.'

'Jesus. Did anyone see anything?'

Jonas shook his head. 'No. Also, no CCTV that we know of, but we're still looking into it.'

Jonas frowned, perhaps his own intuition dragging itself to the same place Robbins had already reached. 'Right now, a robbery is looking plausible. Maybe the girl ran away when they broke in and will make her way back. Anything could have happened.'

'Do you know who their father is?'

'Should I?'

'James Warwick.'

'The serial killer? Isn't he on death row?'

'Yeah.'

'So, what does that have to do with this?'

'Come on, Jonas, are you telling me you don't think he's linked to this?'

Jonas moved the lozenge to the other side of his mouth, slurping loudly. 'Sorry, I can't see how it could be anything to do with him. The man has been locked up for years. Why would he attack his own kids? I mean, who even knew they were staying at this motel?'

'Just me. And Beadle, the prison warden, although, now I think about it, I don't think he knows the specifics. Just that they were staying in the area.'

'Exactly,' Jonas said, puffing his chest out and looking smug.

Prick.

'I know this means a lot to you, but you've been out of the game for a while. The senses lose their sharpness. In truth, the only reason I called you down here is because the kid only had your number as a contact. Nothing personal, Alex. No offence meant.'

'None taken,' he grunted, only half tuned in to Jonas's ramblings. He was well on with processing his own investigation. The last thing he needed was Jonas getting in his way.

'You're right,' Robbins conceded, feigning defeat. 'Seeing the son of a bitch again got to me, you know? Got me thinking the worst.'

Jonas nodded. 'I get it, Alex. Retirement gives you lots of time to think and stew on things. Everyone remembers how close you got to the case, but think about it. There was no way he could have known they were here, or that they were alone, or do anything about it even if he did. It stinks like an opportunist robbery. Nothing more.'

'Yeah, I guess so,' Robbins said, raging at the stupidity of his former colleague. He looked over to Dan, who was sitting in one of the patrol cars sipping a hot drink from a polystyrene cup.

'Any chance I can get a look at the scene?'

Jonas smiled, but there was no humour. Worse. It was filled with pity. 'You know I can't do that. It's more than my job's worth.'

'What about photos?'

Jonas shook his head. 'We're still waiting for forensics. Leave this to us, Alex. We'll solve this, don't worry. It's not your problem anymore,'

The jab was deliberate, but Robbins did a masterful job of rolling with it and not letting it land as intended.

'Yeah, I get it. Loud and clear.'

Jonas nodded again, surprised at how little resistance there had been. 'Look, it's not exactly protocol, but if you want to take the kid, you can. Get him some rest. There's nothing much we can do now anyway until forensics is done and, in truth, I don't think we'd get much out of him, anyway. You good to both swing by the station later so we can get statements?'

Robbins nodded, bewildered by how little interest Jonas seemed to have in resolving this. 'Yeah, no problem.'

Jonas flashed an arrogant smile 'Thanks, Alex. You know, I always thought you were a great cop, despite what some people said. But I need to ask you to step back outside the tape now.'

II

Forensics had arrived, a half dozen white paper suit clad ghosts. They spoke to a uniformed officer, who directed them to the steps leading to Dan and Rebecca's room. Robbins watched them ascend, disappearing out of sight around the corner. He ushered Dan into the passenger seat of the car. He was still shaken, but the colour was returning to his cheeks.

Robbins got in and stared at the steering wheel, then at the road beyond, already shimmering with a heat haze. He knew what the right thing to do would be. He should go home, let Dan get some rest, and wait for Jonas to update him. That would be right, as this was no longer any of his business. He was yesterday's news, with none of the privileges he once had. And yet, despite all the reasoning, the old instinct screamed for attention deep in his gut. Robbins put the car into gear and pulled into traffic, not turning left towards his home, but going right, heading towards Huntsville Prison.

III

Robbins was about to explode as he paced the reception area. He was being refused entry, and so far, every attempt to make headway had resulted in pushback from the young officer behind the reception desk.

'Look, I get it. You're doing your job, but this is urgent police business.'

'I'm sorry, but you've already stated you're not with the police.'

'Get Beadle on the phone. We're friends. He knows the situation. I Need to speak to James Warwick.'

'Sir, Warden Beadle isn't here. He's taking a personal day.'

'Then call him at home, damn it.'

'I'm sorry, sir. But I can't help you. If you would like to make an appointment to speak to the Warden, I'd be happy to take some details.'

Robbins no longer had a badge he could flash or any way to put pressure on this kid who was trying to do his job. He was just a civilian, and like it or not, he couldn't force this issue. Before saying anything else which might have got him arrested, Robbins walked out of the prison. Dan was waiting in the car, head down. He had barely said a word since they left the hotel, and Robins realised he'd done it again and put work before people, even when it wasn't even his job anymore.

He got into the car and turned to Dan, feeling guilty at disregarding how traumatised he was.

'Try not to worry. I'm sure your sister is fine.'

Dan met his gaze, eyes hollow and haunted, not buying the half-hearted lie Robins had tried to sell him. 'This isn't like her. She wouldn't do this. Something's happened.'

Robins agreed, but knew putting any more stress on Dan was a bad idea, and was trying to decide the best way to present this to him without sounding too full of shit when Dan's phone rang. He grabbed it out of his jeans pocket, squirming to one side in the seat to free it from the tight denim.

'It's her, it's Becks,' he said as he answered the call. 'Becks, where are you? What happened? Are you safe?'

Dan listened, his expression changing as the person on the other end of the line spoke. Robins knew this was coming. The big plot twist, the cliffhanger to keep this story rolling.

Dan held the phone out to Robins. 'They want to talk to you.'

Robins took the handset, lifting it to his ear. 'Where is she?'

'If you want to find out, you'll shut up and listen.'

Despite it being impossible, he had convinced himself it would be Warwick on the other end of the line, so much so that it took a second or two to register that it wasn't him, although it was still someone he knew.

Gloria.

'I should have known. Jesus Christ, Gloria, you were free of all this.'

Gloria let out a single note of laughter. 'It's Anna now, remember? Fuck, that name never suited me.'

'Where's Rebecca?' Robbins was in no mood to play along.

'We have her. Before you say anything, she's safe. How long it stays that way is up to you.'

'Spit it out.'

'We don't want the girl. We have no interest in her other than as a bargaining chip.'

'Stop right there. I know what you're about to ask, and before you get some stupid bullshit idea about an exchange with that evil son of a bitch, I don't have any power to make that call. It will never happen. Jesus, Gloria, listen to yourself. This isn't some shitty cop tv show.'

'I owe him.'

'Owe him? you don't owe him shit. He owes *you* for taking your life from you when you were a kid. He's a monster and you know it.'

'For years, I tried to convince myself I had done the right thing by going to the police, but…I was wrong. I was selfish and now I owe him this. I need to make things right.'

'Jesus, listen to yourself. You think he cares about you? Remember what he did to your baby, for Christ's sake. How long have you been in contact with him for?'

'Stop that.'

'What?'

'Trying to manipulate me. Trying to talk me out of it.'

'It isn't me who is manipulating you. I'm trying to stop you from making a stupid fucking mistake. If you hurt Rebecca, I'll-'

'The girl is fine. If you want her to stay that way, you need to come get her.'

He drummed his fingertips on the steering wheel, trying to plan the best way forward.

'Where?'

'It might be cop show fantasy to you, but this is how it has to happen. Bring Jim with you. You hand him over, the girl goes back to you and everyone is happy. Nobody has to get hurt this time. All you have to do differently is swallow your pride and get it done.'

'Did you not get the part about me being retired? This isn't my show anymore.'

'Tough shit. You do whatever you have to do to make this happen.'

'Or what?'

'Or I'll kill her.'

'You think you have that in you? To take an innocent life?'

'Why not? I've done it before.'

'Gloria, come on, this is madness.'

'All I want to do is make amends to Jim. I can't see him executed.'

'How did you know about the Execution? That was new information.'

'You think his lawyers weren't told? Who do you think pays for them?'

'You're still not listening. I don't have the power to do anything. I'm fucking retired.'

'Then go to whoever you have to. The police. Government. I don't care. The one rule is that you are the one to bring Jim. Nobody else. Bring the brother too.'

'No. Even if I could, I wouldn't put Dan at risk.'

'No, it's okay. If it will get my sister back, I'll do it.'

'There you go. At least one of you has guts. It's not a negotiation. If he isn't with you, and believe me, we'll know, this bitch gets ripped open.'

'Gloria…'

'Twelve hours. Otherwise, I'm going to cut pieces of this cunt off one by one and leave a trail for you to follow like breadcrumbs. Understood?'

'You haven't even told me where I'm supposed to go.'

'Jim knows. You'll have to have him guide you. Tell him I'm at the failsafe. He'll know where to go.'

The line disconnected, leaving him stunned and enraged, frozen between a hundred things he knew he needed to do as soon as the jam in his brain freed itself. He lashed out, hitting the steering wheel with an outstretched palm.

'Will my sister be okay?' Dan asked.

Robbins composed himself and nodded. 'Don't worry, kid. We'll get her back.'

It was easier to lie than to be honest. Deep down, he thought it would be a miracle if everyone came out of the other side of this unscathed.

TICK TOCK

Within the first twenty minutes, Robbins had made enough calls to get things in motion.

Ten minutes after that, Beadle had been called back from his day off playing golf and was on his way back to the jail, having made a call of his own to the police chief and filling him in on the situation.

Forty-five minutes after receiving the call from Gloria, Robbins was at the prison, making his way to Beadle's office. That Warwick would ever see the outside of the jail again filled him with a rage more intense than anything he had ever experienced.

He realised he was powerless. People much higher up a food chain he no longer belonged to would decide what happened. Sure enough, he could offer some input and would be involved because of the demands Gloria had set – but the decision making would be in the hands of someone else.

On the drive back, he had experienced another bout of crushing tightness in his chest, and was sure he was going to pass out. Either through luck or determination, the feeling passed, and he tried to ignore the nausea it left behind.

They allowed him into Beadle's office, where he found the Warden still dressed in his golfing clothes—a garish pink shirt and beige shorts. It seemed he had wasted no time in getting back to deal with this situation.

'Alex, come in, take a seat,' Beadle said, gesturing to a chair against the wall that someone had placed there. Someone else already occupied the other two seats. One, Robbins knew – Owen Stacey, one of those guys who had kissed enough asses to drag himself to a position of prominence, and with it had grown arrogant. Stacey wanted to be sure everyone knew his role, as he was wearing a blue jacket with *Negotiator* written back and front in a bold white font.

It was posturing to show he had the biggest dick in the room without getting it out and swinging it around to show everyone he meant business. Stacey was late forties and trying to pass himself off as ten years younger without success. His hair was brown, the front gelled into spikes, which looked ridiculous on someone of his age. He had ratty eyes and a crooked mouth, teeth a shade of smoker's yellow.

Robbins didn't recognise the other man, although it was ironic that without even trying, he gave off more of an air of authority than Stacey. He was sitting silent, hands folded in his lap, only his eyes moving as he took everything in. In another irony, Robbins suspected this man was older than Stacey, yet somehow looked younger. Beadle sank into his chair, looking at the three men in the room. 'On my way back, I learned most of what's going on. Now we need to find a solution to this problem.'

'It's a trap. I think that much is obvious.' Robbins glanced at Stacey and the man he didn't know. Both remained silent. 'What do you plan to do?'

'We were hoping you could tell us.' The unknown man said. He was robotic, without emotion or expression.

'And you are?'

The man stood and offered a hand, which Robbins shook. 'Vernon Martin. F.B.I. My understanding is you're the closest thing we have to an expert on this situation.'

Robbins squirmed, uncomfortable with all eyes on him. 'Yeah, you could say that.'

'Good. I'm glad to hear it. We were hoping you might have an idea about where they are holding the girl. Did anything about a failsafe come up during any of your sessions with the prisoner?'

Robbins shook his head. 'No, I've been thinking about it ever since the call. I have no idea what it could be.'

Martin turned to Stacey. 'I guess it's over to you to find out.'

'Him?' Robbins said, wondering why the idea made him so angry.

'I'm the negotiator,' Stacey said, arrogance oozing from him. 'I'll question Warwick and get the location of the hostage. We still have eleven hours. That's plenty of time to break him.'

'He won't talk to you.'

'I'm an expert in negotiation, and have been for the last fourteen years. With his execution hanging over his head. I expect he'll be quite keen to talk about making a deal.'

'He won't.'

'Who the fuck is this guy?' Stacey said to nobody in particular.

'Take it easy, pal. I'm trying to stop you from wasting time we don't have.'

Beadle threw his palms up. 'Gentlemen, please. We're on the same team here.'

Stacey was turning the colour of beetroot, unused to having anyone question him. 'Tell that to your so-called expert. He knows all the answers.'

Robbins had dealt with this type before. Wannabe alpha males who are quick to back down the second someone stood up to their bullshit.

'What are you going to do? Offer him a transfer? Get him a pardon from his death sentence? You're wasting your time.'

Stacy glared at him, left eye twitching. 'I don't think a civilian has any right to tell me how to do my job. Frankly, I don't agree with your presence here at all.'

'Yeah, well, tough shit for you.'

Martin seemed amused by this exchange. Robbins got the impression he wasn't Stacey's biggest fan either.

'You think you can do a better job than me?'

'As a negotiator? No. Talking to Warwick? Yes.'

'Things have changed since you retired. We have methods. Techniques to get the results we want.'

'They won't work. This will all be a game to him.'

'Alright, so what do you suggest? Do we hand him over?' Stacey said it with such venom he spat on himself, slick drool sitting on his chin.

'That's enough.' Martin said. 'This isn't helping. We need to work together to figure this out.'

'Let me talk to him.' Robbins said, ignoring the stare he could feel burning into him from Stacey. 'If anyone can get anything out of him, it's me.'

Stacey snorted and shook his head.

'Listen to yourself. Time is short and you think a retired officer out of the game for years would stand a better chance than me? It's an insult. If anything, seeing you would make Warwick *more* inclined to play games and waste time. You have a history, you put him where he is. The idea he would divulge information to you is, frankly, ludicrous.'

Beadle chimed in, glancing from Robbins to Stacey. 'In fairness, Alex, I remember when you went to see him last time. It didn't end well. You lost control.'

'He caught me off guard, but it was just because I was rusty.'

Stacey stood. 'I've heard enough. I'm not prepared to waste any more time going around in circles. Warden, would you have someone escort me to speak to the prisoner?'

Beadle looked at Martin, who nodded his approval. Stacey was loving it. Enjoying being the centre of attention, metaphorical dick in full swing as he walked, chest out towards the door.

'Let's get this show on the road. Have teams ready to go as soon as I get the information.'

Robbins laughed, making no effort to hide it.

'Something funny?' Stacey asked.

Robbins checked his watch. 'Just remember, that kid's life is at stake.'

'I do this for a fucking living. I've confronted and talked down suicide bombers and terrorists, the absolute worst. A washed-up old man with nothing to live for is something I can handle. It's a new age, Robbins. You'll see that soon enough.'

Robbins had a head full of creative insults he could have thrown back, but said nothing. If anything, a sense of calm had overcome him. He knew Stacey would fail, and soon enough, it would fall to him to talk to Warwick. He hoped they wouldn't waste too much time. His eyes slid to Beadles overstocked drinks cabinet until he forced himself to look away.

II

It took less than two hours for Stacey to return, and when he walked back into Beadle's office, frustration and confusion had replaced the swagger and arrogance he had left with. For a second, Robbins felt guilty until he remembered how arrogant he had been. During Stacey's absence, Robbins had gone over every aspect of the conversation with Gloria at least three times, with Martin cross checking facts as if he had forgotten Robbins used to be a detective and knew the value of giving through information. Stacey returned to his seat and flopped down. He looked exhausted.

'I take it he wouldn't talk?' Martin said.

'Oh, he talked. Talked his ass off. Problem was, it was all bullshit. What a waste of time.'

Stacey gave a weary glance towards Robbins. 'He's all yours. If you can get anything out of him, all power to you.'

'Do you need anything before you go? Any support?' Martin asked.

Robbins glanced at the drinks cabinet, then forced himself to make eye contact with Martin. 'No nothing. There's no time to waste. Hopefully, he'll give me something.' Robbins left the office, ignoring the rush of white spots in his vision and the agony in his chest. There was a job to do.

III

Robbins sat opposite his nemesis, who stared back at him as unreadable as ever.

'I wondered when they'd send you. The other guy wasn't so entertaining.'

Robbins had no specific strategy for this. There was no plan or scheme to trick him into talking.

'Alright, here it is. No games. I'm going to ask you to help me find Gloria. She's got your daughter at a place called the Failsafe. You know how unstable she is, how far she'd go if she had to. You might think she won't hurt her, but I wouldn't be so sure. Do you think when the pressure is on, she'll hesitate to kill?'

The silence hung for what felt like an age before Warwick spoke, his eyes never leaving Robbins.

'I know where she is. I could point it out right now for you on a map and you'd be able to save the day.' The smile as he said it told Robbins this would not go the way he hoped.

'This is your family. For once, why don't you do the right thing?'

The smile grew wider, lips parting into a sly grin. 'Depending on your perspective, maybe this is the right thing.'

Robbins was seeing those white spots again, but tried to hide it. There was no way he was prepared to drop dead in front of the man he hated most. He willed his heart to get its shit together and focus on the job at hand. Somehow, it worked. His vision cleared, and the pressure released. He unleashed a sly smile of his own, knowing that here, he didn't have to hide his hatred or pretend to be anyone other than himself.

'You can't think they will free you, can you? If you think this is going to become some kind of escape attempt, I want you to know this right here, right now, it won't work. I won't let it happen.'

'What are you going to do, Alex? Put another bullet in me? Finish what you started all those years ago?' Warwick chuckled and shook his head. 'You think about me every day, don't you? Alone in that little house of yours, wife estranged, daughter wanting nothing to do with you…'

Robbins couldn't hide his surprise, and Warwick pounced on the crack in his armour, ripping it open to peer inside and see how much more damage he could cause.

'Oh, I know all about you, Alex. How you've lived. You think I wouldn't have ways to find out everything I wanted to know? I know what you are. A shell of a man with nothing to live for other than trying to outlive me, so you can say your life had a purpose.'

Warwick jammed a thumb towards his own chest, handcuffs rattling in protest. '*I* had a purpose. I had a vison, a plan to make the world a better place. You and I are on the wrong side of the bars.'

Robbins couldn't speak. His tongue sat useless against the roof of his mouth as blood pulsed around his body with such ferocity he imagined he could feel it moving. He waited for that horrible constriction to come back, but for now, at least, that stayed away.

'Even now, you don't realise how weak you are. Spending your days thinking about the family you lost and the bottle you want to pick up. And even though I'm locked away in here, I'm still out there with you. The itch you can't quite get rid of day after day, year after year. Scratch scratch. Scratch scratch. Even as your fingers dig through flesh and muscle, gristle and nerves, you still can't stop. Scratch scratch.'

Warwick relaxed in his chair and smiled, a carefree expression of a man without concern. On the other side of the glass, Robbins was sweating, heart drumming, unable to think or breathe or respond to this monster who he was once equal to but now realised was ahead of him. The psychological battle was no longer fair or one he could win. Worse, Warwick knew it too. His crocodile grin grew even wider.

'Run along now, civilian. Go tell the people in charge there will be no deal. If you want to know where the failsafe is, you'll need me to take you there.'

'They'll beat it out of you if they have to.'

Warwick shrugged. 'They would eventually, but I think I could hold out long enough for it to be too late to save the girl.'

Robbins slammed his palms on the desk in front of him. 'The girl? Christ, she's your daughter. Don't you have any compassion?'

Warwick leaned close again, eyes burning with hatred. 'If she'd been born when I was around, she'd have ended up in the bottom of the bathtub like the last one.'

'What is wrong with you?' Robbins could feel his entire body shaking. 'I should have put a bullet in your head that day,'

He could feel it coming, the constriction, the white spots and dimming of vision, but he was, by some force of will, able to keep it at bay.

Warwick tapped his wrist. 'Time's ticking, Alex, and where we need to go is quite a drive. You better run along and tell the people in charge you couldn't get anything out of me.'

Robbins stood, chair legs scraping on the concrete floor. He walked as steadily as he could until he was out of Warwick's field of view, then had to lean on the wall for support, staggering towards the door as the vice on his chest re engaged. Blinking through the white spots, screaming inside that there was no time for this, he made his way out of the visiting block, telling himself he would be fine. He just needed to splash some water on his face and get some air. When all this was over, he would rest. God, how he would kill for some rest. But not now. Now there was too much to do, and he was determined to see it through, no matter the consequences.

FREEBIRD

Beadle watched as Robbins tried to squeeze into the bullet-proof vest. He wasn't as slim as in his prime, and the vest would go nowhere near.

'You okay, Alex? You don't look so good,' Beadle said.

'I'm fine,' Robbins snapped back as he tried to fasten the side straps. As far as lies went, that was a big one. He felt about as bad as he had ever felt in his life, but he couldn't tell anyone. He couldn't afford to be taken out of the game or Warwick would win.

'Got anything bigger?' he asked, embarrassed at how much weight he had gained.

Beadle shook his head. 'Not here, sorry.'

Robbins gave up, tossing the vest onto Beadle's desk. 'Fuck it.'

'I'm sure we can botch it together and make it fit.'

'No time. Besides, if they wanted me dead, I'd be dead. That fucker knew all about me. Where I live, where my family lives. I don't know how. Have you started digging into his visitation log? His letters? This all feels too well planned for a snap decision thing.'

'It's in progress. We're having his cell searched.' Beadle looked his friend up and down. 'You look like death, and I don't mean that as an insult. For Christ's sake, your skin is grey, Alex.'

'How's the kid?' There it is. The classic swerve he was so good at. Avoid the question. Redirect.

'He's being briefed. I wish there was a way not to involve him in this. For his part, he seems calm.'

'He's still in shock. He's been through hell already. I don't think this has sunk in yet.'

'He's a variable I wish we didn't have to worry about on top of everything else.'

'Bastards are trying to make sure we comply. Extra civilian risk means less chance of us doing something stupid.'

Beadle grimaced but still couldn't sit still. 'This whole thing is a risk. I don't like it.'

'That makes two of us.' He felt the room tilt, a sudden shift to the side. He put a hand on Robbins's desk to steady himself. His gut churned with nausea, and for a few seconds, tiny white explosions filled his vision.

'Jesus Christ, are you okay?' Beadle said, half standing.

'I'm fine. I just lost my balance for a second.'

They both knew that was bullshit, and may have got into the specifics of it more if Martin hadn't chosen that moment to walk into the office. He was all business, chest out, enjoying the show. He had a black case with him, which he set on Beadle's desk, then turned to Robbins, unaware of what had happened before he walked in.

'Alright, here's the deal. I know you're retired, but under the circumstances I've been authorised to give you weapon holding privileges for the duration of this operation.'

Martin snapped the clasps of the case and opened it. The bulk of the inside was charcoal coloured foam. Cut into a recess was a handgun. Two clips of ammunition were in the two cutouts beside it. Martin pulled out the gun and handed it to Robbins.

'You remember how to use one of these?'

If it had been Stacey who had asked, Robbins would have been sure it was an intentional dig at him, but he detected no malice in Martin. He was gathering information in the most direct way possible.

'I've been handling firearms longer than you've been able to buy beer,' Robbins replied, praying to God he wouldn't ruin the bravado by vomiting all over the office or collapsing and dying.

'Good,' Martin said, not responding to the jibe. He pulled out one of the ammo clips and handed it to Robbins. '15 round mag. I hope you don't need it.'

Robbins hadn't seen this model before. It was more modern than anything he used in his time, but the principles looked the same. He checked the safety was engaged, then loaded the weapon, slamming the magazine home with the flat of his hand.

Martin seemed satisfied with his competence and nodded his approval. 'Good. Here, there's a spare mag and they have a body holster for you downstairs. Are you ready for this?'

'Do I have a choice?'

Martin cleared his throat and clapped his hands together. 'Come on. The parking garage is this way. I'll walk with you and brief you again on the way.'

'I know what I have to do.'

'Good, but indulge me and let me go through it with you one more time for my sake.'

'Fine.'

'Alright, let's go. Warden, you coming?'

'Absolutely. It's my duty since this involves one of my inmates.'

Martin led them out of the office. As a man who had always trusted his gut, Robbins hoped this time it was wrong, as it was telling him this entire situation was wrong.

II

The corridor of the admin building seemed darker and smaller than before as the trio headed towards the elevator. Martin and Robbins walked side by side, Beadle behind. Robbins listened to information he already knew, only half paying attention.

'Warwick is already in the car. He's chained in tight in the back by the wrists and ankles. It also has reinforced glass and a dividing screen between him and you. Believe me, he's not getting to you. He'll be like the fucking Pope in his little bubble car.'

Robbins nodded, more focused on walking without losing his balance. The nausea and dizziness were coming in waves, each stronger than the one before. It was taking everything he had to hide it.

'You and the kid will ride up front. We've got a team following you, but the expectation is she'll make you call them off. Don't worry if she does, we've planned for it.'

'I know, I know, you have a GPS on the car. Phone too. They briefed me.'

They arrived at the elevator. Martin pushed the button to call it.

'You used to be a cop, and from the research I did a damn good one. You also know this case, so I won't insult you by telling you what kind of man you're dealing with. The priority is keeping you and the boy safe.'

The elevator arrived, and they stepped inside. Beadle pressed the button for the ground floor. Robbins was grateful for the elevator wall to lean against for the blissful few seconds it would take to get to the parking garage.

'Wherever he takes you, we'll find you. You need to stall the exchange for as long as you can. We'll be coming in covert, but you need to buy us some time.'

The elevator door chimed, and Robbins felt his stomach tighten. At the end of the short concrete walled corridor was the door to the parking garage, and beyond, Warwick. They walked towards it, Robbins in a state of utter disbelief that this was happening.

'If things go wrong, if you get into any kind of situation that is deemed to be high risk, you retreat. Don't hesitate, just get out of there.'

Robbins stopped walking. 'And what about Rebecca?'

Martin held his gaze. 'We want to save her. That goes without saying. But one victim is preferable to two. Three if you count you as a civilian. If things look bad, get you and the boy out. We'll do what we can to save the girl to the best of our ability.'

'If you go in hot, she won't stand a chance and you know it. First thing they'll do is kill her.'

'Then, for all our sakes, we better hope this works.'

'And what about Warwick? If he tries anything, if he becomes a danger…'

Martin looked him dead in the eye, gaze unwavering. 'Then you do what you have to. No hesitation. Your primary aim is to keep the civilians safe. Now, are you ready?'

Robbins looked at the steel door, reminded himself what was beyond and how much could, and likely would go wrong.

'Hang on. Give me a second, would you?'

'Of course.' Martin said.

Robbins walked back towards the elevator, putting some distance between himself and the others, and then took out his phone.

He scrolled to Sandy's number, knowing he should speak to her in case something bad happened. He hovered his thumb over the green dial button, but stopped short of pressing it. What would he say? How would he explain he had again sacrificed everything for James Warwick? He closed his eyes and could almost see her, that look in her eye of weary resignation that no matter what she said, he would be too stubborn to listen.

'Hey, you good? We need to do this,' Martin said.

Robbins closed the phone and shoved it into his pocket. 'Yeah, I'm ready.'

They waited for him to join them, then Martin pushed open the door and led the way into the parking garage.

III

The car was a charcoal sedan. Armed officers surrounded it, weapons poised and pointed at the sole inhabitant of the vehicle in his orange jumpsuit, wrists and ankles shackled where he sat in the centre of the back seat, watching the attention he was getting with some bemusement.

Besides the Sedan, there were six squad cars, which would make up the rear of the convoy.

'We have you covered, as you can see. Six cars, each with four armed officers. These guys are the best men you could have for support. Trust me, if it all goes down bad, these guys will be ready. You won't be given a key to Warwick's restraints. Nothing personal, just a security measure, so you can't be forced to free him. Even if the exchange goes ahead, he won't get very far shackled the way he is.'

'Good idea,' Robbins said, staring at the shadowy figure in the car. 'Where's Dan?'

'He's with Stacey going over the brief again. Short version for him is he sits up front with you and is not to interact with the prisoner. That goes for you too, Robbins. Don't let this motherfucker get under your skin. You get the directions, you drive to where he tells you, you stall, then we come and find you and take over. That's it. No heroics. Don't let him get in your head.'

'Do I look like a hero to you?'

'No, and that's good because it's not what we need in this situation. We're relying on your years of experience and knowledge here, Alex. Remember, this is all about the girl and getting her back.'

'I know.'

Martin nodded past Robbins. 'Here he comes now.'

Stacey led Dan towards where Robbins and Martin were waiting. Something struck Robbins as they approached. The blank expression and unreadable eyes of Dan were remarkably similar to the man who had given birth to him.

Stacey too looked out of it, but having experienced the mood Warwick had been in that day, Robbins wasn't about to hold it against him, even if he was an asshole.

'You okay, kid?' Robbins said.

Dan nodded. 'I have no idea how we got to this point.'

'All you have to do is sit up front with me and say nothing. Leave the rest to me and the team. We'll get your sister back.'

Stacey pulled Robbins aside. 'I'll be monitoring everything. Here, wear this.'

He handed Robbins a Bluetooth earpiece. 'It's a secure channel. Connects to the speakers installed in the car so we can hear everything that is said. Depending on how much he gives you directions wise we might get ahead and narrow down where he's taking you, so drive slow, stick to the speed limits, even if the temptation is to race ahead and get to the girl. The slower you drive, the more time we have to figure out where you're going. The earpiece is so I can talk to you without Warwick knowing about it.'

'Thanks,' Robbins said, slipping the earpiece on. With the bravado knocked out of him, Stacey had come down a few notches on the prick scale.

'Alright, let's get this show on the road. You ready?' Martin said.

'Ready as I'll ever be. Let's get this done.'

Robbins and Dan walked towards the car, unable to shake the feeling that everything about the situation was wrong, and that if the day ended without bloodshed, it would be a miracle.

'Hey, kid, hang back a second,' he said to Dan as he walked to the passenger side. 'I want a word with Warwick alone before you get in.'

Dan nodded as Robbins got into the vehicle and shut the door, closing out everything other than him and Warwick. Robbins didn't turn to face him. Hands on the wheel, he stared straight ahead. He checked his rearview mirror, meeting Warwick's gaze.

'I wanted to tell you straight up, man to man, that I see through this. The first sniff I get of anything that looks suspicious or wrong, I'll put a bullet in you, and believe me, there won't be any bible to save you this time. The best way for you to stay alive is to do as you're told. You do that, and you might live to see tomorrow.'

'Just in time for my execution,' Warwick replied, mouth

widening into a grin. 'Besides, what is it you think I could do when there are so many guns aimed at me?'

Robbins ignored the goading attempt. He was feeling nauseous again and trying to fight it. 'Also, you don't try talking to the kid. He's been told he's not to interact with you, and I'm telling you the same.'

'I know. Directions only.'

'Where are we heading?'

'For now, head towards my old home.'

Robbins half turned in the seat, looking at Warwick in person rather than through the mirror. 'The compound?'

'You call it what you will. It was my home.'

'Fine.' Robbins reached across the seat and opened the passenger side door so Dan could get in, then waved a hand of acknowledgement to Martin, who gave an unheard command into his radio. The officers who had been surrounding them exploded into action, moving to designated vehicles, firing up engines ready for the journey to start. Robbins was waiting for a signal from Martin to say that they could set out, but was surprised to hear him come through the Bluetooth headset. Robbins had already forgotten he was wearing it.

'Alright, you're clear to move out. We're with you, Alex. We'll keep you and the boy safe.'

Robbins started the car, slipped it into gear, and eased towards the shutter door. He watched as it opened, steel rattling and allowing the warmth of the day to spill in. Head pounding, nausea surging and the now ever-present tightness in his chest showing no sign of leaving, Robbins drove out into the heat of the day.

THE ROAD

Robbins had prepared for the journey to be a battle of wills between him and Warwick, but so far, it had taken place in silence. Despite having a window cranked and the air con set to full, Robbins couldn't stop sweating. He felt as if he were holding on to consciousness by his fingertips, and prayed he didn't have one of those vertigo-like dizzy spells, or he would roll the car. It was getting harder to breathe, each inhale seeming to tighten that grip around his heart a little more. If he was dying, so be it. He was fine with that as long as he got to see this through first and save the kid. Her life for his felt like a pretty fair trade. His eyes shifted to the mirror as he checked on Warwick. He sat in the middle seat, cuffed hands clasped together and hanging loose between his legs. He was watching the scenery go by.

'We'll be at the location soon. Where next?' Robbins asked.

'I'll tell you when we get there.'

'You know it's not there anymore, don't you? If you were expecting some kind of reunion with the house or-'

'I know. But that's where we're going, for now.'

Robbins heard Martin's voice come through the earpiece, startling him.

'Alright, I heard that and I don't like it. Do me a favour and slow down a touch. We're going to go on ahead and check out the mall to be safe.'

Robbins was already a couple of miles under the speed limit, and lifted his foot, shaving another couple of notches off the speedometer. Ahead, in the distance he could see the glass dome of the shopping mall drift into view, sunlight shimmering like diamonds and reminding him of the white spots he saw in front of his eyes when he was having one of his spells.

'It's not a trap,' Warwick said from the back. The sudden breaking of the silence startled both Dan and Warwick.

'They wouldn't do anything to put me at risk. Too many of your kind with twitchy fingers and narrow minds for that.'

Not feeling well enough to engage, Robbins ignored him and focused on reaching their destination.

The shopping mall was getting closer. In his mind's eye, Robbins could still see the compound. The high concrete walls and the glint of sunlight on the mall's dome transformed into muzzle flashes from when they came under fire. He was interrupted by the phone ringing on the dashboard. He answered, putting it on loudspeaker.

'So far, so good,' Gloria said. 'We've been watching. That's quite the convoy you've got there.'

'You thought it would be just me and him?'

'No, of course not. You should be almost at the shopping mall now.'

'Yeah.'

'Pull in to the carpark. Around the back.'

Robbins hadn't got there yet, but knew the layout well. The car park surrounded the mall, which itself was encased by walls to keep intruders at bay. That, at least, should offer a little protection from the wider world and any prying eyes who might wonder what the hell was going on. With room for six hundred vehicles by his best guess, the Car Park had plenty of places where someone could hide or spring an ambush. His gut gnawed as he slid his eyes to the rearview mirror.

'Are you still there?'

Robbins snapped back to the present. 'Yeah. I'm here. This doesn't sit right.'

'I don't care.'

'Why are we pulling in here? What's the play?'

'Because this is what I want to happen. If you want to see the girl alive again, you'll do as I say.'

Robbins was trying to think, playing a thousand different scenarios in his head about what might or might not happen. Before he could go too far down that rabbit hole, Gloria was speaking again. 'Don't overthink this, Robbins. All I'm having you do it swap cars.'

'Why?'

'Why do you think? I'd bet my life your car has a tracker or something on it. This way I make sure.'

It was too late to say more, as they had arrived at the Mall. Robbins pulled into the car park, eyes scanning the ocean of vehicles and the thousands of hiding places they represented. 'We're here,' Robbins said, Gloria now secondary as he tried to sniff out any potential danger.

'Head to the back.'

Robbins led the train towards the rear of the building, every sense, every year of experience focused on checking every vehicle, searching for any sense of movement in and between each row, but the carpark was silent.

'Alright, what now?' Robbins asked.

'Back corner. There's a red ford. Old. You can't miss it.'

Robbins drove to the back of the mall as instructed until he saw it. Old was an understatement. Rust and mud splattered the frame.

'You see it?' Gloria asked.

'Yeah, I see it.'

'Then go on, get in. All of you. Keys are in the ignition.'

'I need to make sure no weapons are stashed in there first.'

'It's your time you're wasting. Clock is still ticking, Robbins. Just one thing.'

'What's that?'

'We're watching. If anyone other than the three of you approaches the car, you won't like what happens. I don't want anyone planting a fresh tracker or anything on there.'

'Alright, but I need to hang up so I can focus on this.'

'Fine. take the phone with you.'

The line went dead, and Robbins slipped the phone into his jacket pocket.

He turned to Dan, who still looked to be in a daze. Robbins felt for him; everything was happening so quickly it must be hell.

'Alright, kid. You heard her. Now we're going to do as she said, because we want to keep your sister safe, okay?'

Dan nodded. 'Yeah, okay.'

'You'll be safe, no matter what. I got you covered.'

'Careful,' Warwick said from the back. 'When he says things like that, innocent kids end up dead.'

'You shut your fucking mouth.' Robbins fired back.

Warwick smiled and leaned back in his seat, happy to have got the reaction he wanted.

Robbins considered for a second, then pulled out the earpiece, speaking into it

'Martin, you hear me?'

'What the hell are you doing, Robbins?'

'I'm not taking the risk anymore. You heard her, they're watching. Have your guys make a perimeter so we can transfer.'

'If you move to that other car, we have no way of tracking you other than visual.'

And the phone, Robbins thought, but Martin had been careful not to mention that. All part of the game. Smart move.

'Then you better keep a close eye on us from now. Make the perimeter and make sure none of your men go anywhere near that damn car.'

Robbins pulled the wires and pack for the earpiece from his jacket and tossed them on the console. The convoy behind split, officers training weapons in every conceivable ambush space, with several others trained on their vehicle and their dangerous passenger in the back. Robbins waited until they were in position, his heart beating so loudly that he was convinced everyone could hear it. No worsening of the chest pains yet, though, that was one sliver of good news. He grabbed the tangled wires of the earpiece and spoke into it again.

'Alright, keep your guys focused on Warwick. I'm going to get the kid out first, but have him hang back. Then I'm going over to check the car before we transfer. I doubt they will do anything to risk Warwick, but who the fuck knows what these pricks are thinking? Eyes sharp, I'm coming out now.'

He tossed the earpiece on the console between the seats and turned to Dan.

'Alright, kid. You get out, but don't approach the car. Wait by your door. The guys are watching.'

Dan nodded.

'Alright, let's do this.'

'Good luck, *son*,' Warwick said from the back, flashing a glimpse of that awful crocodile grin,

'I told you to keep your fucking mouth shut unless it's giving directions.' Robbins said.

Dan ignored Warwick and got out of the car, standing close to the front wheel. Ignoring the vice around his heart, the nervous tremble in his knees as he stood upright, Robbins followed. His eyes scanned the surroundings. The cars, the mall itself. All those windows. All those places to stage an ambush.

He approached the parked car from the rear. His mind flashing back to that day they assaulted the Ranch. Cowered behind the armoured car, tense and waiting for all hell to break loose. Same location, same feeling, but a fresh set of surroundings. He wished to God that hadn't sprung into his mind, and it took all his effort to force himself not to think about it. At a glance, nothing seemed out of the ordinary about the car. Rather than go to the driver's side, he approached the car parked next to it, a silver truck. He cupped his hands against the glare of the sun and looked in through the passenger side window.

As he suspected, there was no ambush waiting. Nobody was there to spring out as they swapped vehicles. Satisfied, he went to the Ford and looked it over. Rust had eaten through the wheel arches, leaving them uneven and rotten. The windows were filthy, the interior an ocean of swirling dust motes made visible by the glare of the sun. He moved to the driver's side door, and opened it, holding his breath in half expectation of some kind of trap left for him, but there was no explosion. No nail bomb set to fire at whoever was unlucky enough to open the door (He'd seen that in a case once back in the day). Just the gentle click as the door swung open. Robbins poked his head inside, surveying everything. The car smelled like dust with an undertone of mould. He suspected it had been a long time in storage before that day. As promised, the keys were in the ignition. Robbins didn't get in, though. He reached in and removed them, then made his way to the back of the vehicle and opened the trunk, stepping aside as he swung it open.

As with the rest, there was no ambush, no trap. Just a tatty brownish carpet and the spare wheel. He checked the space anyway, looking for hidden panels or weapons. Satisfied, he closed the door and stood upright, checking the surroundings, aware of the heat, aware he was being watched. He looked back at the car they had arrived in and, although he could only see the silhouette of his head; he knew Warwick was watching.

Robbins went to the rear door next and opened it. He got down on his knees with some effort, fighting off a wave of vertigo, which forced him to lean against the open door to catch his breath. Once it had passed and he could function again, he checked the inside of the doors, the seats, the footwells, covering every inch of the rear. Even handcuffed, he didn't want to take any chances where Warwick was concerned.

Satisfied, he stood and waved Dan over to where he was standing.

'You okay, kid?'

Dan nodded but said nothing.

'Alright, come on, sit up front. Remember, keep doing what you're doing. Don't engage with him.'

Dan did as he was told and got into the car. Robbins wished he had the time to check the kid was alright, but the job had to come first. A flicker of Sandy appeared in his mind's eye. That look which reminded him that was the exact attitude that had cost him his marriage. He took a breath to compose himself and settle the dizziness, then returned to get Warwick. Although it was only a matter of a few feet, it felt like the longest walk he had ever taken. As he approached, he addressed the officers with their weapons trained on the rear of the car, making sure Warwick heard.

'Watch him. If he does anything unexpected, take the shot.' He moved to the rear door and opened it.

'Out.' Robbins said. He grabbed Warwick by the arm and helped him to shuffle out of the car, the shackles rattling in protest.

Robbins led Warwick to the waiting vehicle, the armed officers walking with them at a distance, weapons ready. They stopped by the rear door of the car. Robbins checked the wrist shackles to make sure they were secure and connected to the ones on his feet. Satisfied, he ushered Warwick into the rear of the vehicle and closed the door.

He almost went again, his world tipping out from under him. He put a hand on the roof of the car to steady himself, and it came, the pressure in his chest so tight this time he couldn't breathe. Those white flashes appeared, dancing in patterns across his vison.

No. don't you fucking dare. Not now. Breathe. The hard part is over. Get your shit together and get in the car. Everyone is looking at you.

And they were. Robbins could feel it. Dan. The armed officers. Warwick, hell, even Gloria. He only had to look at the faces of the armed officers to know he must look in a pretty bad way. What a way to go out. So close to seeing it through, then dropping dead before the finish line. It wasn't fair. He had to push a little longer.

Breathe, you old fuck. Don't die and let him see it happen.

That seemed to do the trick. His vision cleared, and by God, he could breathe again. He sucked in air and thought he could keep the vomit down. He stood upright, locking his gaze on the armed officers.

'I'm fine, just a dizzy spell.' Before anyone could argue or, more importantly, pull him out of the mission, he hurried around to the driver's side on legs that were unsteady and got in. He was sweating, alternating between hot and cold, but there was no time to think about that yet. He wiped his brow on the arm of his jacket and pulled on his seatbelt.

'What now?' Dan asked. Robbins could see the concern, but the boy knew enough not to say anything in front of Warwick.

'I don't know. We wait, I guess.' Robbins fished out the phone from his pocket and set it on the dashboard, then slipped the keys into the ignition, all the time keeping a close eye on Warwick, who for his part was sitting still, hands folded in his lap.

'No need to wait. I know where we need to go,' Warwick said.

'So where to?'

'Head to the exit.'

Robbins expected such an old piece of shit car to struggle to fire up, but to his surprise, it started without issue, grumbling to life.

'Interesting,' Warwick said.

Robbins was in no mood for games. He was barely hanging on, his body falling apart, but he couldn't help himself. 'What is? What are you talking about?'

'You're slipping, Alex. You didn't even test the ignition until we were all in the car. What if there had been a car bomb? Boom.

Game over for all three of us.'

He was right. In his prime, he wouldn't have missed it, but now, so broken, he had missed a pretty obvious risk. It enraged him more than it should have.

'Lucky for me, your people don't want to blow you to smithereens.'

He slipped the vehicle into gear and made his way towards the exit, paying extra attention to Warwick now there was no divide between the front and rear of the car.

The phone rang, and Robbins answered, still keeping his focus on his surroundings.

'Exit the Mall and Turn right. Head out of town, towards the highway.'

'Then what I-'

'No questions. Just do it. If you slow down, stop, or do anything else, I kill the girl.'

'Yeah, I get it. Understood.'

'Good. Throw the phone out of the window when I hang up. No doubt they are tracking it. Jim will guide you to the next location. Remember, we're watching.'

The line went dead, and Robbins did as he was told, and tossed the phone. He didn't like the way this was going and was asking himself how far he might have to go to resolve this. His priority was to see Rebecca rescued and unharmed, but he also wasn't sure if he could bring himself to do that if it meant letting Warwick escape.

Pulling up to the mall exit, he waited for a break in the traffic. Several cars passed, all oblivious to the dangerous passenger he was carrying and not slowing to be courteous enough to let him pull out.

As an eighteen-wheeler approached, it slowed and flashed its lights, giving him a chance to leave.

Thanking the other driver with a raised hand, Robbins turned right after exiting. The rest of the convoy went to follow, when the eighteen-wheeler sped up and swerved across the exit, blocking the rest from joining the train. A few seconds later, multiple car bombs exploded in several vehicles near the convoy's exit. From the truck, the driver unleashed a hail of bullets through the window, causing the convoy to become pinned down.

Robbins heard the chaos and saw the eighteen-wheeler where it was now parked across the exit. He drove away from the scene, knowing this was how it was supposed to play out. He shifted his eyes to Warwick, unsurprised to see he was smiling.

STANDOFF

The car park was in chaos. Stacey was crouched behind one of the chase cars, arms overhead, as he tried to protect himself from the rain of glass as the world seemed to explode around him. He saw at least four burning cars scattered in the parking lot from where he stood, and he knew what had happened. They had driven into an ambush.

There was a break in the gunfire, but Stacey suspected it wouldn't be for long. He eyed the tanker attached to the truck, and couldn't comprehend the destruction if it exploded. He yelled into his headset, opening the channel so that all the officers could hear.

'Fall back. Don't return fire. Repeat, don't return fire. Do not compromise the tanker.'

Just as he finished speaking, a fresh rain of bullets sprayed into the air. Stacey covered his head, gritting his teeth as glass swirled around like winter snow. He knew it would be a miracle if they survived for long, so exposed and in the open. He spoke again, hoping the others could hear him over the sheer volume of the gunfire.

'Next time he stops to reload, fall back. Stay close to the walkways if you can. Any of these cars could be rigged to explode. I repeat, stay away from the parked cars.'

Although it could have been only a minute, maybe two, waiting for the gunfire to stop seemed to take an eternity. Stacey realised he had blood on his hands, but did not know where it had come from. He touched his face and was surprised to see more crimson on his fingertips. There was no time to worry about that now, though. He was alive, and that was all that mattered. The gunfire stopped, the only sound now the chorus of car alarms, the screams of the wounded and the roar of fire. Stacey couldn't breathe. Heat and smoke, the taste of gasoline coating the back of his throat.

'Now. Fall back now!' he screamed into the headset, himself taking off in a crouched run towards safety. Those few seconds of silence were the most terrifying he had ever encountered, a thought which lasted only as long as it took for the firing to start again. Concrete chipped, windows shattered, tyres exploded all around him in a horrifying soundscape. There was no time to stop for those who hadn't made it. Two in his path, one face down and motionless, blood pooling out onto the concrete, the other off to one side, half under a parked car, moaning in agony, his blue shirt stained red where he had been gut shot.

Stacey weaved between the parked vehicles, aware that at any point, one could explode, tearing him to shreds and turning his body to mulch before he was even aware it was happening. He was close to the mall now; its concrete outer frame would give them protection, or at least a chance to regroup.

He reached the mall, skirting around the corner and out of range of the gunman. Hunched over, hands on hips, breathing ragged as the unseen wound from his head dripped a pattern of crimson on the concrete between his feet.

'Call it in,' He gasped between breaths. 'Get everyone out here right now. And tell someone we lost Warwick. We need a team out to find them now.'

Once again, the gunfire fell silent, but this time, it didn't start again. Each side was waiting for the other to make a move.

RISK VS REWARD

Apart from the ugly cut in his hairline caused by a stray shard of glass, Stacey had escaped with no serious injury. He had expected that once they had called it in, officers would swarm to the scene and bring much needed reinforcements with them, but it seemed whoever planned this spot for the ambush had ensured the police had every disadvantage. The danger of hundreds of potential explosives attached to the vehicles surrounding the mall prevented them from sending anyone in. Instead, they had set up a perimeter around the mall, a no-go zone within which there was just him and the four officers who got to safety, the mall staff and security, and one hundred and forty-three members of the public.

The other concern for Stacey was the shooter in the truck. His initial blasts had been semi-automatic fire of some kind. Far too rapid for manual firing, and although silent for now, Stacey wouldn't be surprised if there was more to come. Safe from incoming fire, the driver had taken cover in the armoured cab, customised with firing slits.

It wasn't all bad news for Stacey, though, as the search for Warwick and Robbins was well under way. There were choppers in the air looking for the vehicle as well as all the patrol cars they could pull together to conduct a grid-based search. Stacey was told there was every confidence they would find the car before it got too far. An officer approached him with a mobile phone, holding it out to Stacey. 'It's them. They want to talk to you.'

Stacey took the phone.

'Who is this?'

'Are you the one in charge?'

Stacey expected it to be the shooter, who he knew was male, however the person on the phone was female.

'I am.'

'Then listen. If you stay where you are and don't leave, there's no reason anyone else will get hurt. Our brother in the truck is watching, but has instruction not to open fire unless you do first.'

'Tell that to the two men he's already killed.'

The few seconds of silence told Stacey this was new information to the person he was speaking to. 'Well, I'm sorry about that. Unfortunate collateral damage.'

'Collateral damage? I knew those people. They had families.'

'I assume you want this to all be over. We do too, and it will be. All you have to do is call off your search teams.'

'I can't do that. No way. Sorry.'

'You're not in any position to negotiate.'

Stacey looked down at his vest emblazoned with the word *negotiator*. It was now grubby and flecked with blood.

'Way, I see it. This is a stalemate. Your boy in the truck there isn't going anywhere. He's surrounded. You might have broken us away from the convoy, but don't think it's going to make a difference. We have choppers, squad cars, officers on foot all looking for that car and the people inside it. We'll find it. Then this little standoff won't make a difference.'

'Mustard gas.'

'What?' Stacey said, knowing he'd heard right the first time.

'Mustard Gas. I assume you've heard of it.'

'What about it?'

'The tanker is filled with it. We rigged the tanker's interior with explosives, and our brother has the detonator. In addition, sixty of the cars surrounding your position have canisters of it hidden inside them, all rigged to explode at the press of a button. Imagine the devastation on a breezy day like this. You can't hold gas back behind a barricade.'

Stacey couldn't speak. His mind was struggling to compute both the situation and the consequences and didn't like the results of either.

'So, what is it you expect me to do? I've got innocent people down here.'

'Let this go. Call off your search. After the exchange, we will instruct our brother to surrender. No more death. No more chaos. All you have to do, is do nothing.'

The line went dead, and Stacey sprang into action. 'Get all remaining officers in here now, including the mall security.'

'What's going on, sir?' the officer said.

'Trouble, that's what. A whole shitstorm of trouble. Someone needs to get me a line to the outer perimeter.'

Stacey made the call, relaying the phone conversation. The watching officers, hearing it for the first time, shot nervous glances at each other as Stacey relayed how deeply in the shit they were.

TIME WAITS FOR NOBODY

Stacey got off calls to the F.B.I., chief of police and half a dozen other decision makers, getting everyone up to speed on what he had been told. Some information had also flowed the opposite way. The outer perimeter teams had done some recon of the truck and found out some more information.

It had been stolen three weeks earlier, and the information about the cab being fortified was accurate. Despite positioning several snipers around the perimeter, there was no shot into the reinforced truck, and there was no line of sight to the driver.

The biggest uncertainty had been about the Mustard Gas. The F.B.I. thought it unlikely that anyone could acquire or produce as much as the caller had claimed, but conceded it was possible if there was enough time to plan and determination to do it. Because of their uncertainty and the high risk of calling the bluff, they decided to follow instructions and do nothing for now. They did, however, provide a solution to the request to call off the search, which was ingenious in its simplicity. Stacey had been told all squad cars would be withdrawn, as would the choppers. Waves of other officers, undercover in plain clothes and driving their own unmarked vehicles, would replace them, an invisible continuation of the search so that little to no time would be lost. The only thing they couldn't replace would be the helicopters, but it was an acceptable sacrifice. The age of the vehicle made it likely to stand out against the more modern models, and there was some hope they would soon find it. They were also searching through traffic cameras to aid with the search, but so far, there had been no results. All they could do was sit and wait. All eyes of both officers and mall security on the eighteen-wheeler blocking the exit.

II

The waiting was unbearable.

With each passing second, Stacey knew Warwick was getting further away. It was clear this plan had been far more elaborate and well thought out than anyone had expected. Despite all their plans to cover off any eventuality, they were now reduced to sitting on their hands and doing nothing.

A sudden commotion outside broke Stacey's concentration. Officers were shouting and gesturing, responding to something unseen. As he went outside, an officer met him.

'Sir, there's movement from the shooter.'

Stacey followed the officer outside to get a look at the truck, the concrete wall keeping them out of range from any potential gunfire. From the passenger side window, a white t-shirt was being waved.

'Keep me covered. I'm heading over there.'

'Shouldn't we call this in?'

Stacey nodded. 'Do it. Meantime, I'm still heading over there. Every second we lose is killing our chances of catching Warwick. I'm going to stay in cover until I'm closer. Nobody does anything unless they see a good reason to, got it?'

'Yes sir,' the officer said.

'I'm keeping my radio open so you can hear everything. When you call it in, tell them not to do anything stupid.'

'Yes, sir.'

Stacey was already moving. Hesitation, he knew, would cause him to question the sanity of his actions. He moved in a half crouch, skirting around the parked cars, each potentially a lethal trap waiting to maim him if it blew. He had moved to within twenty feet of the truck and was crouched by a station wagon, eyes locked on the cabin of the truck, the white flag now motionless in the window.

He typically conducted his work over the phone or radio, attempting to de-escalate situations. Here now, amid the blood and smoke with that giddy sense of danger all around him, it was all so different.

'You in the truck. Can you hear me?' Stacey shouted, bracing himself for the onslaught of bullets.

'I'm coming out. Don't shoot me, okay?'

He wasn't sure what he had been expecting to hear, but it wasn't a voice so young. 'Nobody is going to shoot you if you come out unarmed and slow.'

'I get it. I'm coming out now.'

'Remember, do it slow. You make any sudden moves, and I can't guarantee your safety.'

Stacey could taste it. Fear, adrenaline, anticipation. It was the thing he both loved and hated most about his job. He saw a hunched figure move the flag and open the door.

'No sudden moves. Nobody else needs to get hurt today.'

The driver did as he was told, climbing down, arms in the air. Stacey felt sick when he saw him. The face and voice matched, and Stacey would be shocked if the kid was any older than twenty-two.

He was wearing a zip up grey hoodie, and Stacey could see the fear in the kid's features. Eyes wide, acne pocked cheeks, skin pale. He could also see there was something in his hand.

'Don't shoot me,' he said, his voice breaking. 'I didn't want any of this. It's not my fault.'

'Are you armed?'

'I don't have a gun.'

Those inner alarms were screaming at Stacey, his belly full of ice. 'The jacket, unzip it, show me underneath, then we can talk.'

'You don't understand,'

'Do it, kid, or I can't guarantee your safety. Open the jacket and drop whatever you're holding on the ground.'

The driver was looking around, trying to locate Stacey, who was still crouched behind a car, out of sight. 'Where are you? I just want to explain.'

Stacey wasn't the impulsive type, which is why it came as a surprise, even to him, when he stepped out of his hiding place and stood in front of the youngster, ten feet of open ground between them.

'You don't want this to get any worse, kid. I can see that clear enough. You need to do as I say. What are you holding?'

'Are you the one in charge? The one I'm supposed to talk to?' His voice was shrill, too high, filled with too much fear.

'That's me. Now open the jacket.'

'I'm not one of them. Believe me. Please.'

'Jacket. Now.'

'You're gonna shoot me. I know it.'

'If I was armed, I'd already have my gun on you. See for yourself.' Stacey raised his arms and opened his jacket to show he had no holster underneath.

The driver seemed satisfied, and with his free hand, pulled the zip of his hoodie down to reveal the intricate suicide vest he was wearing underneath.

'It's armed,' the kid said. 'If I lift my thumb from this detonator, it will explode. The tanker too.'

Stacey didn't cower or run for cover. From this range, there was no point.

'Alright, let's take it easy. What is it you want?'

'I don't want anything. I have nothing to do with this. They've got my girlfriend. They said If I didn't do what they said, they'd kill her. She's having my kid ….'

He trailed off, then looked Stacey in the eye. 'Please, help me out of this, man. I don't wanna die.'

And in that one sentence, everything had changed. The scenarios Stacey had prepared for hadn't included this, that the driver too might be another victim of this awful mess.

'Alright, relax, and whatever you do, don't drop that detonator.'

'I know that. You think I don't know not to drop the fucking thing?' the kid was close to losing it.

'Take it easy. Just breathe and stay calm. I need to ask you a few things, okay? Just so we can set about putting this right. Can you do that?'

The kid nodded.

'Good. Now what's your name?'

'Gary.'

'Okay, Gary, my name is Owen. Now why don't you tell me what happened and we'll do what we can to help. Is this your truck?'

Gary shook his head. 'No. They made me drive it. I don't even have a licence for one of these. I work for UPS.'

'Why did you open fire at my men?'

Gary was agitated. Stacey could see the anguish in him. 'I tried not to hurt anyone. I tried to aim towards the sky or at the cars, but it's so cramped in there and I couldn't see. They said they were watching me, and if they didn't shoot, they'd kill my girlfriend. I didn't want to hurt anyone. Was anyone hurt?'

Stacey's mind flashed to the men he had passed when he was running for his life, but that was information best kept to himself for now. That kind of information might push someone over the edge. A lie, then.

'No. Everyone is fine. What's the game here? What are you supposed to do?'

'This vest they made me wear; it was switched off at first. They said when it activated, I was supposed to surrender and keep hold of this detonator until they shut it off again. They said they could switch it on and off by phone and would know if I didn't do as they said. That's all I know, man. Now please, help me.'

'Just stay where you are and keep pressure on that trigger. I need to reach for my radio so I can call for some explosives experts to help resolve this. I'm not reaching or a weapon, so stay calm, okay?'

'Please, they have my girl...'

Stacey took his radio and spoke into it. 'You get all that?'

'Yes sir,' the voice crackled back.

'Report to the outer perimeter. Tell them we need the bomb squad down here.'

Stacey closed the channel and clipped the radio onto his belt.

'There you go. We'll get you out of that thing, but they might be awhile. Why don't you tell me everything from the start.'

'I don't know what else to tell you. I got a call when I was on my way to work, a picture message from my girlfriend's phone. When I opened it, she was tied to a chair with this crazy fucker with a knife at her throat. Then they told me I had to....'

Stacey was taking it all in, but was also listening to that screaming instinct inside. His eyes drifted to the truck. Could someone with no experience of driving such a large vehicle have been able to do so with apparent ease? Possibly. Some people are quick learners, and if the kid worked for UPS, their trucks wouldn't be too dissimilar. Stacey nodded as the kid talked, his words a droning buzz somewhere in the back of his mind. Stacey flicked his eyes into the cab of the truck through the open door, processing what he saw. An open can of coke in the drinks holder stood out.

Sure enough, it could be old and been there from when the truck was taken, but maybe not.

He turned his focus to Gary. Hands rough and calloused, the way someone spending hours and hours driving a rig such as this would be. A pale band of exposed skin on the third finger of his left hand, where it was still raised in surrender. A removed wedding ring? Maybe. Although he had said girlfriend. Not a wife, which meant there should be no wedding ring. Gary was still giving details, but Stacey wasn't listening anymore. He was looking into Gary's eyes, realising he had made a mistake. He thought it was fear he had seen in them, but now realised as he looked, there was nothing there. A line from one of his favourite movies, Jaws, sprang into his mind when Quint had been explaining his horrific experiences on the USS Indianapolis. Stacey had seen the movie dozens of times and remembered the line well.

Sometimes the shark looks at ya. And the thing about a Shark he's got lifeless eyes. Black Eyes. Like a doll's eyes.

That was how Gary was looking at Stacey as he told his story. This wasn't a man who was terrified of what might happen to a wife or girlfriend. Another voice popped into his head. This time, not that of Robert Shaw's Quint, but his own reminding him of his own stupidity.

He knows you're unarmed.

Stacey tried to stay focused and not give anything away while assessing his options. Where was the best cover and could he get anywhere safe if things turned nasty? As he was contemplating this, Gary stopped speaking, causing Stacey to refocus. Now, his expression had become as blank as his shark's eyes.

'You're not buying any of this, are you?' Gary said, his tone calm and flat.

'I was. Not anymore.'

Gary grinned, the gesture as lifeless as his eyes. 'Yeah, I figured you might work it out, but not so fast. What gave it away?'

Stacey shrugged. 'Just good at my job, I guess. So, what happens now?'

'Nothing. This all ends. This is in the name of our father, James Warwick.'

'Wait, don't!' Stacey shouted as Gary lifted his thumb from the detonator. He turned away, closed his eyes, and waited for the heat and agony as his body would be ripped to shreds, but it never came. He looked back to Gary and now, at last, saw emotion. It was panic. He was pressing the detonator, but nothing was happening. Stacy reacted without thought. Where most would flee for cover, he charged towards Gary, tackling him to the ground and wrestling the detonator from his grip, doing his best to restrain him as he screamed and writhed to get free. The other officers were coming. He could hear their footsteps getting louder, but he couldn't look away. All he could think of was what would happen if whatever had broken on the bomb, be it loose wire or an incorrectly configured detonator, suddenly fixed itself. He pushed it aside, pulling the Velcro straps from the harness and somehow wrestling the device over Gary's head, using his size and strength to overpower the youngster. He knew, of course, that he violated countless rules and procedures, and would likely face disciplinary action for it, but he figured since he had already lost a high value prisoner on his watch, he may as well go all in. With the vest removed, Stacey dragged Gary away from it, pinning him face down, one knee over his upper back, arm pinned behind him so he couldn't move.

'Bring some damn cuffs.' He screamed, aware that his voice was now the one too high and shrill from fear. Two officers took over as Stacey fell backward onto the concrete, winded and watching Gary get handcuffed and dragged away from the truck and bomb vest. Stacey, too, was dragged away, but was hardly aware of it. There was still work to be done, though. There was still a fugitive out there who they needed to find and get back behind bars. He hoped they weren't too late.

III

Within minutes, the scene was swarming with officers. They put Gary in the back of a squad car, and the bomb squad was inbound. Based on the photographs of the device that they had received, they were confident it was a fake. The truck, too, was deemed safe, the tanker on its back empty.

Stacey had gone from being in control to another cog in the wheel as officers went about their business. The F.B.I. were also on scene and were doing a better job of coordinating the operation.

He approached one agent, Dark-skinned, cold eyes and a thin moustache. He looked suave, far too pleasant for his voice as he distributed orders. The agent was on the phone as Stacey approached in the middle of what looked to be an intense conversation. Stacey waited for a few seconds, then, with time critical if they wanted to catch Warwick, He started to walk away, when the agent clicked his fingers in Stacey's direction and held up a hand for him to wait. The agent ended his call, then turned to Stacey.

'You're the guy who took down the shooter.'

Stacey wasn't sure if it was a question or statement, so nodded instead. The agent held out a hand.

'Great work. Unorthodox, but under the circumstances, Brave.'

'Thanks,' Stacey said, as he shook the man's hand.

'I'm Special Agent Gallagher. F.B.I., as if you couldn't tell from the vest and jacket.'

'Owen Stacey.'

'I'll need to go through a full debrief with you as soon as I get all this bullshit organised, so don't go anywhere. How you holding up?'

'Fine, I was just wanting an update on Warwick. Have they tracked the car yet?'

'You're behind the curve here.'

'Why?'

'We already found the car. Abandoned around five miles away. Looks like they switched again.'

'Switched to what? When?'

'We don't know yet.'

'Someone must have seen something. Anything for us to go on?'

'Take it easy. We've got people on it. Good people. Right now, it's a waiting game.'

Stacey walked away and sat on the curb, head in hands, wondering how everything could have gone so wrong.

HANDOVER

After the success of separating them from the group, Robbins had expected Warwick to be full of bravado, but apart from giving one- or two-word instructions to guide them on their way, he had been silent. The second car swap had gone much like the first, only without the benefit of a small army of police officers keeping watch. Robbins had expected this would be where they would have come in and snatched Warwick when there was no protection, but no ambush had come and as quickly as they had entered it the red ford had been abandoned in favour of a slate-coloured station wagon. It was the definition of anonymous. Old enough to blend in, but not so old someone might remember seeing it. He had to hand it to them. So far, their plan had worked almost perfectly.

For a while, he wasn't sure Warwick even knew where to guide them, and twice, they had doubled back on themselves. He supposed the outside world looked a lot different now than how it had when he had last seen it, so Robbins gave him the benefit of the doubt. As steel and concrete gave way to open fields and countryside, Warwick's instructions became more definitive, as the surroundings untouched by progress felt more familiar. They were heading into open country, the heat of the day shimmering on the blacktop as they rolled towards whatever end this game had for them. Dan had withdrawn further into himself, silent as he stared out of the window. The only one of them who still looked cool was Warwick.

'How much further?' Robbins asked.

'Not far now. There's a dirt road coming up on your left. Take it.'

Robbins slowed the vehicle and took the turn. To call it a road was an overstatement. Robbins followed the bumpy ruts. Ahead, shimmering beyond the heat of the day like a mirage, was a structure. It was too far away for Robbins to make out what it was, but as there was nothing else in sight, he assumed this was where they were heading.

'Is that it?' Robbins asked.

Warwick leaned closer to look, causing Robbins to half turn. 'Back. No leaning forward.'

Warwick grinned and did as he was told. 'Sorry, my eyes aren't as good as they once were. Yeah, that's the place.'

'What is it? Some kind of warehouse?'

'Not exactly. Lumber mill. Or at least, it was until I bought it.'

Robbins glanced over his shoulder at Warwick, who flashed a slimy grin.

'You didn't dig that up on your investigation, did you?'

Robbins turned his attention back to the road. Choosing not to reply.

'The plan had been to move down here because the old house was getting full. Gloria accessed her father's savings, so we had the money to buy the land. We never got around to building the new house before you attacked us.'

Robbins didn't rise to the bait. He gripped the steering wheel tighter as their destination loomed ever closer.

'The land was purchased in her mother's name, and passed on to Gloria when she was declared dead.'

Declared dead was one way for Warwick to put it, considering the circumstances, but again, Robbins fought the urge to get into another verbal battle.

'Makes sense how you knew where we'd be heading today.'

'Where else? Only Gloria and I knew about it. When I was asked where this trade off would happen, it could only be here. Our forgotten piece of land in the middle of nowhere. A fitting place for the story to end.'

II

The derelict mill loomed, its sun-bleached whitewash peeling in tired strips from the sagging walls. A faint, dusty smell hung in the air. Cracks spider-webbed across the façade, the silence broken only by the crunch of gravel under their wheels. Black-painted windows, like vacant eyes, stared out from the crumbling stone, hiding whatever secrets lay within.

Robbins brought the car to a halt in the building's shadow, shut off the engine, and turned in his seat to look at Warwick.

'You do what I say when I say it, understood?'

Warwick said nothing.

'What about me? Should I stay here?' Dan asked.

Robbins looked around. He couldn't see anyone, but was sure they were there all the same. It felt as if a thousand pairs of eyes were staring at them from unseen places.

'No. I want you with me. I'm not leaving you here as another hostage for them to take. Just stay close. And keep your eyes open. If you see anything unusual, speak up. Got it?'

Dan nodded. 'Okay, yeah, I can do that.' Robbins had his doubts. Dan had withdrawn further into himself as the day had gone on and had said almost nothing, but there was no choice now other than to hope he would be alert enough if something went wrong.

Robbins got out of the car and looked around, doing a slow circle, scanning the obvious hiding places, waiting for the ambush, but there was nothing. Far above, the silver glint of an aircraft on the way to a place better than this was the only blemish in the sky.

Dan got out next. He too looked around; hands thrust into his pockets.

Robbins opened the rear door of the car and dragged Warwick out. He didn't fight. The Mill blotted out the sky when they came to rest in front of it. One of the two dirty wood doors was ajar, whatever lay beyond hidden in darkness.

'Stay behind me,' he said to Dan, then led Warwick to the door. It was old, the paint on the frame chipped and cracked. The glass in its centre had long ago been sprayed black, its corners filled with old nets of cobweb. Robbins pushed the door, which opened with a tired creak.

The door opened onto what would have once been an office. Ugly wood panelling, warped with damp, adorned the walls and the carpet was dusty and stained where rain water had found its way in from somewhere above. Opposite was another door, which was open. Beyond was the shadow draped factory floor. Robbins didn't go in. He paused at the threshold, listening, trying to stretch his hearing to reach into the darkness. A wave of dizziness, not as severe as the last one, threatened to stagger him, but he rode it out. Even the chest pain, which was now ever present and something he was forcing himself to ignore, seemed to let up a touch.

Warwick chuckled, breaking the silence. 'Still paranoid after all these years?'

'Shut up. You don't speak unless I say you can. Go on, inside.'

Robbins led Warwick through the office, Dan at the rear. They walked across the grubby carpets and came to a halt at the door leading to the cavernous space of the warehouse floor. The dirty skylight gave some visibility, but not enough to banish the shadows from the darkest spaces. Old hulks of broken, rusted machinery stood silent, everything coated in dust. The floors were filthy, covered in rubbish which had collected over the years. Robbins stared into the gloom, unwilling to step forward.

'Is that your instinct, Alex? Not allowing you to step into the unknown?'

Robbins didn't respond. Though he strained his senses, the space's secrets remained hidden from him. 'Move,' he grunted, shoving Warwick over the threshold.

If the feeling of being watched was bad outside, in here, it was worse. Robbins took the gun from its holster and pressed it to Warwick's temple, then whistled. The sound reverberated around the room, reaching in to those dark places where eyes could not see. Seconds passed, each feeling as if it had lasted a lifetime, and then they came. Like spirits out of the shadows. Robbins had expected lots of them, coming in waves to surround them, but if there were others, they were still in hiding. Gloria was with Rebecca, who was gagged, hands behind her back. Gloria came to a stop around forty feet in front of them. She had a box cutter, which she held towards Rebecca's throat.

'Stop there,' she said.

Apart from looking dishevelled and grubby, Rebecca looked to be otherwise unharmed.

'Alright,' Robbins said, his voice echoing around the cavernous space. 'First off, everyone, stay calm. If you have people here, tell them to take it easy.'

'They know, they're hanging back as long as you do as I tell you.' she replied, eyes flicking and darting.

That inner instinct, the one Mack referred to as *it*, pulled at his innards again. This time, instead of addressing Gloria, he shouted, voice bouncing into those unseen areas of the space.

'Whoever else is here, come out and show yourselves, otherwise no deal.'

'Don't listen to him. Stay where you are,' Gloria said, her expression twisting for a second, into a grimace. For most people, it would be meaningless. To someone like Robbins, it said far more than that, and proved his hunch.

She's here alone.

It made sense and played into the theory he'd been pondering since he found out where they were doing the switch. If this was the failsafe, the fewer people who knew about it, the better. Gloria was doing her best to bluff that she held all the cards, and that was fine, as Robbins also knew how to bluff. He could bluff his fucking ass off if he needed to.

'Let her go. This is over, Gloria.'

'You don't make up the rules here, I do.'

Robbins almost felt sorry for her. She still believed that to be the case. 'No, you don't. Right now, the police are on the way and will surround this place. There's no way out. Your best chance is to give up.'

'Bullshit, we made you switch cars twice and throw your phone away.' Desperation was replacing confidence by the second. Robbins leaned into it. Piling on the lies. 'Losing the phone meant nothing. I have a micro tracker on the heel of my shoe. We could have changed cars a hundred times and it wouldn't have mattered. It's over.'

'If you want the girl to live, we do the exchange. No more talk.'

Robbins knew it was over. She was close to breaking and needed one last nudge to bring this mess to an end. He put the barrel of his gun to Warwick's temple. 'There won't be any exchange, Gloria. I know you're here alone. I wouldn't expect this operation to have more than a handful of people involved. You. The guy in the eighteen-wheeler. Someone to pass information to and from Warwick at the prison, maybe a couple of others to do a bit of dirty work. Times have changed. Give it up and let her go.'

'You want me to see her bleed out here in this room? Do you think I won't do it?'

'Do that, and I pull this trigger.' He pressed the barrel harder into Warwick's temple for emphasis. He had never felt so alive.

'You wouldn't do it.' Gloria said, still shuffling and twitching.

'You think I won't pull the trigger once I have a valid excuse? Why do you think he's been so quiet? Because he knows I'll do it.'

'No. you hand him over to me right now,' Gloria said, cheek twitching as she peered out from behind Rebecca's shoulder.

'I can't let him walk out of here. You had to know that when you set this up. That was the mistake you made, Gloria, insisting I be the one to do this. Someone else might have given in, but not me. Not after everything that has passed between us. The second you made that demand, you were never going to win.'

'Another word, and I'll get the others to gun you down. They're all around us.'

Robbins looked around. 'We both know that's not true, Gloria. I've seen the people who still follow your cause. A handful of curious or lonely people looking for something to do on a weekend. Not the people you could ever influence enough to do this. This shitbox in cuffs maybe could have pulled it off, but not you. I'm calling your bluff.'

Robbins felt she was close to breaking now and pushed harder, using all his experience to know how far to go.

'You can still walk away from this. Put the knife down and go. I won't follow. You don't need to do this, especially for this animal.'

Gloria looked uncertain. 'I can't do that to him.'

'You don't owe him a damn thing. He never loved you or cared for you. Like everyone he brainwashed and manipulated, you were a tool. A puppet to help him make some false God of himself. You were nothing to him.'

'I don't... I can't...'

'He's not worth it, Gloria. He'll go back to jail, and after a couple of weeks, he'll be gone and all this will be over.'

Her voice was trembling, her eyes uncertain, but the words hit Robbins like a sucker punch to the gut. 'Then why does he look so unafraid?'

Robbins glanced at Warwick. So smug, so confident. So... sure. He had been so focussed on Gloria; he hadn't noticed. The puzzle pieces in Robbin's mind fit themselves together quickly.

Why would he be so confident unless he knew he had an advantage? And if he did, what would that advantage be? The next question that came to him was almost enough to render him useless, as it was a thought so horrific, he couldn't imagine a scenario where it could be true.

What if the ace up his sleeve of one of his children?

Robbins turned to Dan. The man who reported Rebecca missing. He who, at the sight of his sister, bound and threatened, hadn't panicked or rushed to her aid. He hadn't looked at all surprised. Why would Gloria insist he came along? Robbins assumed as an extra risk factor, but now something else came to him.

We'll be watching.

She had said it over the phone countless times, and what better way to be always watching than have a pair of eyes along for the ride? Dan, who all during the journey to the Mill had seemed distant, as if he had the weight of the world on his shoulders. He should have seen it coming. The one thing Warwick had always wanted was a son. It hit Robbins hard, throat constricting as tightly as his chest at his own blind hatred causing him to miss what should have been obvious.

This was never about Rebecca.

The next few seconds played out at half speed.

He looked from Gloria, still twitching and on edge, then to Warwick, a smile forming as he saw Robbins putting the pieces together. Then to Dan beside him. Eyes focused as he met Robbin's gaze, in that instant he was the mirror image of his father. Robbins wondered why he had never noticed before how alike they were. The roar of gunfire interrupted the thought, so loud in such a large space. Robbins inhaled, waiting for the lead to rip apart his innards, but no pain came. Dan was falling, eyes growing wide as the bullet impact threw him off his feet. Robbins realised too late that the look he had mistaken for defiance was confusion and fear at what he could see.

Another gunshot rang out, and this time Robbins felt the searing heat in his chest as the impact spun him away from Warwick, sending him tumbling to the cold concrete. He couldn't breathe, couldn't do anything. Instinct screamed at him to get up and fix this, but his body was on fire, and all he could do was lay on his back as the iron taste of blood spread into his throat.

He lifted his head towards Gloria, wondering where she got the gun from, and saw how wrong he has been. How completely and devastatingly wrong.

It wasn't like Father, like Son.

Daughter.

Like Father like daughter.

Rebecca stood, feet spread, gun held with both hands as it smoked from the barrel. Her hands had never been bound at all. She was just holding them, and the weapon until this moment arrived. She looked on now, expressionless, dead eyed, the gag pulled down so it hung loose around her neck. Robbins tried to speak, but his throat was filling with blood. He turned his head to the side to let it out, allowing it to pour down his whiskered cheeks. Every breath was like inhaling lava. He glanced to Dan, who lay next to him on his back, shirt a red horror as he bled out.

Robbins tried again to get up, but the agony was too great. He couldn't move. Death, it seemed, wasn't quite ready for him yet. He would have to suffer one last humiliation. Warwick stood over him, chest out, an arrogant sneer on his lips. He crouched by Robbins, smile melting into a grin as Gloria and Rebecca joined him.

'This is like that day you arrested me, remember? Only this time, our roles are reversed. Even for someone who doesn't believe, you have to admit there's some beautiful symmetry to this.'

The pain was too intense for Robbins to speak. He gargled blood and each breath felt as if someone were sitting on his chest. Those white spots came worse than ever, the edges of his vision dimming. He flailed an arm towards Warwick to grab him, in a final desperate attempt to restrain him, but there was no strength left. Nothing but agony, fire, and the taste of blood. He looked past Warwick to Rebecca, unable to piece it together. The how and why things had come to be this way. Warwick followed his gaze, loving every second of this. He grinned again, at his happiest, surrounded by death and chaos.

'I'm going to tell you a little secret, Alex. I've been in touch with my daughter for the last four years, in case you were wondering. She found those journals belonging to her mother an age ago and acted on them to contact me. It's not as difficult as you might imagine. A letter in a false name was enough to start the lines of communication.' Warwick leaned closer to wipe some of the blood from Robbins's cheek. 'During that time, we've got to know each other well. Well, enough to devise a way for us to be reunited. Mary's death was too good a chance to miss. A happy accident.'

He shifted his eyes to Dan, who lay motionless beside Robbins. 'He had too many of his mother's genes. Weak and indecisive. Not of interest to me. Rebecca, however. She's just like me. The next generation. It's a pity you won't be around to see how it goes, my old friend.'

Robbins squirmed, each breath he could take a gift as he clung to life.

'I know how you think, Alex. You want to tell my daughter not to listen, that it's not too late, or that she still has a choice to do the right thing. I want you to see how wrong you are.'

Warwick stood and kissed his daughter on the head, then gave her a nod.

Robbins knew this was it. The person he came to save was about to end his life. Rebecca took a step forward, but instead of pointing the gun at Robbins, she turned and shot Gloria in the face. She never saw it coming. Blood and brain tissue, skull fragments and hair. All of it exploded in a gore shower as Gloria crumpled to the ground. Robbins screamed in rage, causing another wave of agony to surge through him.

Warwick stared down at his nemesis again, indifferent to the destroyed remains of Gloria.

'You were right about her, Alex. She was nothing to me in the end. At first she was a big help in being the bridge between myself and Rebecca so we could communicate, but she became a hindrance. She was too weak. And if we plan to rebuild what you once took from me, there is no place for the weak. Rebecca, however. She's my blood. Just look at how committed she is. You can't teach that, Alex, you just can't.'

Robbins glared through his fading vision.

Warwick turned to his daughter and smiled. 'Go start the car. Make sure the bolt cutters are there.'

She kissed him on the cheek; took a last glance at the chaos she had created and was gone into the shadows. Warwick picked up Robbin's gun, chains rattling, and crouched beside him.

'It kills you how this has happened, doesn't it, Alex? How can a good girl become like her father?' Well, is it a surprise when she learned her own grandparents wanted to have her aborted? You know who stopped that from happening? Me. She's alive because I took action and put an end to those awful people. I gave her life.'

Robbins was fading, his protests becoming less animated.

'That bullet seems to have torn you up inside. Better to lie still.' Warwick took a second to compose his thoughts. 'Once a child learns her own mother never wanted her, is it any surprise she turns to her father? Over these years, we have become close. You lost, Alex. In the end, when it mattered, you failed.'

Warwick stood and checked the gun was loaded, then pointed it at Robbins. 'I could finish this right now. I should. But I think back to that day when you shot me. I could see you wanted to finish the job. Even though you lied and made up a different version of events, I can appreciate you didn't shoot me dead like a dog. I'm going to extend you the same courtesy of leaving you here, bleeding and dying, wondering if you've done enough in your life to gain passage to heaven.'

Warwick lowered the gun and spoke with what appeared to be genuine sincerity. 'I've enjoyed our little cat and mouse games over the years. But now, the time for games is over and I have work to do. I hope death finds you quickly.'

Warwick flashed a smile, then shuffled away into the dark.

SYMMETRY

There was no pain.

No white light.

It was a feeling of warmth and awareness that he straddled the line between two worlds. He could hear the doctors as they worked to save his life, yet it felt as if that frenzied activity was far away, like music heard across a great distance, with only a few notes recognisable if you strained to hear it.

He could see the frenzied actions of the medical team as they worked, performing chest compressions to save him. Robbins looked beyond them to a great field of golden corn stretching as far as the eye could see, blocked off by a cloudless sky, the vision of those trying to save him fading like mist. He walked into the corn, and as he went deeper, the sounds of the doctors grew more distant until, at last, they were silent.

There was a man in the field.

Arms folded behind his back, one hand grabbing the opposite wrist. Dressed in white, black hair pulled into a ponytail as he stared out over the horizon.

Is this God?

Robbins approached the man, stopping a few feet away. The corn brushed against his hands as the wind moved again, ruffling his hair in the otherwise total silence. A question came to him, the only one it felt suitable to ask. He didn't say the words; he didn't have to.

Are you God?

The man responded and turned to face Robbins, a familiarity

which ripped the tranquillity away from Robbins in an instant.

'Yes.' Warwick said, holding his arms wide to the surrounding fields.

Robbins screamed, but instead of words, blood spewed from his mouth in endless torrents. All around him, the perfect world he had arrived in was changing. The sky darkening, the corn rotting and collapsing to the ground as he was yanked back into that world of pain and confusion, the agony in his chest exploding from the gunshot wound. Robbins screamed, then fell silent as the medication to sedate him did its job.

His final thought before he faded into a black dreamless sleep was fair.

How the hell did I survive?

II

A week had passed.

Wires and tubes snaked out of Robbins as he lay in his hospital bed, police guard on the door. For the first days, he had flitted in and out of consciousness, plagued by horrific nightmares. Somehow, he had pulled through, although how, he did not know. He lay staring out of the window at the grey cityscape, the one question he had been asking all along refusing to go away.

Where was Jim Warwick?

The door to his room opened, and a man walked in. He looked familiar to Robbins, and he thought he may have been into his room during one of his in and out of consciousness phases. One thing he knew for sure was he was a cop, although the name escaped him.

'How are you feeling?' The man said as he sat beside Robbins.

'Who the hell are you?'

'My name is Adam Banks. I was hoping I could have a quick word. I'm heading up the Warwick manhunt.'

Robbins stared out of the window. 'I'd hoped you'd have tracked that prick down by the time I'd woken up.'

Banks shook his head. 'Trail's gone cold. As for the daughter, we're still trying to find out her level of her involvement. I was hoping you could fill me in.'

Robbins shook his head. 'Level of involvement? She shot me and killed two others. I'd say that's pretty fucking involved. If you're asking how it got to that point, I have no fucking idea,'

'One other,' Banks said. 'Daniel survived. He's critical, but we're hopeful he'll recover.'

Robbins exhaled, overcome with emotion. 'Thank God, at least something good came out of this fucking mess.'

'As for the girl, we've been working with our teams in the UK to seize her laptop and search the family home for anything that might help us. I suspect we'll find quite the trail of evidence of the planning of this whole scenario. We traced a number on her phone to the same one Gloria was using. It seemed she had been giving regular updates during your time together.'

Robbins recalled Rebecca in the car, texting, fingers moving furiously as she updated her so-called friend. Girl advice, she had called it. 'Jesus, what a mess,' Robbins muttered.

'Are you feeling any better? Docs said it was touch and go. Not only were you shot; you had a series of micro heart attacks, too. You're one tough old man, if you don't mind me saying.'

'I don't even know how I survived. I mean, the poor kid is fighting for his life and here I am, sitting up in bed and chatting shit with you. It seems unfair.'

'Ah, now that is something I can answer.' He walked to a drawer across the room and took something out, handing Robbins a distorted shard of metal. Robbins took it and turned it over.

'What the hell? Is this?'

'Your sobriety coin. Turns out the bullet hit that in your wallet and sheared off. It still fucked you up, but it missed your vital internal organs. That thing saved your life. Without it, you'd be dead, no doubt about it.'

Robbins looked at the twisted fragment of coin. 'Symmetry,' He muttered.

'What's that?'

'Symmetry. Something Warwick said about how our lives have mirrored each other in certain ways.' He held the coin up to the light. 'Back when I arrested him, I shot him. Turns out he only survived because the bullet hit the bible he had in his pocket and deflected away some of the impact. Same situation here with this.'

'Damn,' Banks said, watching as Robbins turned the shredded coin over in his hands. 'Thing is, I almost traded this in a few days ago. There's this bar that trades sobriety coins for a free drink. Got a big old container on the bar there full of coins like this. I traded mine in, then realised if I drank it, Warwick would win, so I gave the drink back to the bartender and got my coin back. If I hadn't....'

'Symmetry.' Banks said.

Robbins nodded. 'Right. Symmetry. Now how about you spit out what you're doing here rather than keep squirming there on your seat?'

Banks gave a sheepish smile. 'It's that obvious?'

'It is to a grumpy, long in the tooth fuck like me, yeah.'

'Alright, I'll be straight up. I've been put on this case and am doing all I can to find this guy, but the fact is, nobody knows him more than you. Nobody knows the man like you do. I want you to help me hunt this guy down and bring him in. A special consultant of sorts.'

Robbins sighed and looked out of the window. For a moment, he didn't speak. 'I don't know what I can offer you, kid. That son of a bitch has dominated my whole life and, no matter what, he always wins. I got so much about this wrong that in my prime I'd have got right. I'm not sure I have what you need anymore.'

'You won't need to go into the field or do any of the dirty work. I'll be working with another officer, a guy named Owen Stacey. Says you and he met.'

'Oh yeah, the negotiator. Seems a bit out of his wheelhouse.'

'It is, but he stopped the guy in the eighteen wheeler that blockaded the mall. Took a huge risk to save lives at the scene and impressed some of the higher ups in the F.B.I. with his actions. He requested assignment to this case, and they granted his request.'

'So it's just the two of you leading this?'

'For now, yeah, but I won't lie. Without your help, finding him is going to be even harder. Sure enough, there's a chance we may bring him in by a chance encounter. Traffic stop or something, but from what I've seen already, this guy is careful. With your help, we have a chance.'

Robbins turned away from the window to face Banks. 'I'll help you. How can I not? I feel responsible for this. As soon as they unhook me from all these damn wires, anyway.'

The relief in Banks was obvious. He looked ready to hand out the high fives, then remembered where he was and kept his composure.

'Alright, that's what I'm talking about. Do you think he's likely to be lying low for a while? That's our working theory.'

Robbins shook his head. 'With arrogance like that and knowing him like I do? No. My guess is he's enjoying his newfound freedom somewhere. Mexico, maybe. At this point he won't be giving much thought to the consequences of getting caught.'

'Any idea what he'll do next?'

'He said something about rebuilding what I took from him.'

'What do you think he means by that?'

Robbins wanted to know that too, and as much as he would love to drag himself out of bed, he was aware he was too weak to do anything yet.

'I'll give it some thought, but right now, I'm wiped out, kid. Pain meds are strong, you know?'

'Of course, yes, get some rest. Build up your strength. I'll be in touch.' Robbins nodded as Banks left, more than ready to rest. Despite those intentions, however, there would be no sleep. He stared out over the city until the day faded to night. Contemplating all that had happened, and all that was yet to come. He hoped he would be up to the task.

THE END OF A LIFE (REPRISE)

The red Cadillac rolled along the black vein of blacktop cut through the Mexico desert. It was brash and loud, the engine growling as it chased the horizon.

Warwick was driving, his hair growing back from the prison buzz cut, his face clean shaven. That alone had rolled back the years. As the cool breeze washed over him, he drove with one hand on the wheel. He was dressed in jeans and a white t-shirt, arms tanned from the sun, eyes hidden behind aviator sunglasses. He glanced to the passenger seat, where Rebecca watched the passing landscape. Summer floral dress and the sweetness of her smile hiding the monster within. Warwick reached across to her and held out a hand. She smiled and took it, returning the gesture. On the console between them, a gun lay in easy reach.

A tanker truck, chrome glinting under the sun's gaze, was coming in the opposite direction. Rebecca stood on her seat, holding on to the frame of the windshield. She whooped and cheered, dress and hair billowing in the wind behind her. She gestured to the truck to honk the horn as they passed. The driver complied, honking in response, and then they were past each other, heading off to their respective destinations. Rebecca sat back in her seat, grinning at her father. He smiled back, as they went on, deeper into the future and wherever the road would take them.

This was the story of the end of a life and the start of another.

www.ingramcontent.com/pod-product-compliance
Lightning Source LLC
La Vergne TN
LVHW032202070526
838202LV00007B/282